Free Will

A Divinely Curious Novel

Diana Kathryn Plopa

All rights reserved. All characters appearing in this work are fictitious. Any resemblance to real persons, living or dead is purely coincidental.

No part of this publication may be reproduced, distributed, or transmitted in any form or by any means, including photocopying, recording, or other electronic or mechanical methods, either now known or unknown, without the written permission of the publisher, except in the case of brief quotations embodied in critical reviews and certain other noncommercial uses permitted by copyright law. For permission requests, write to the publisher, "Attention: Permissions Coordinator", at the address below.

Grey Wolfe Publishing, LLC
PO Box 1088
Birmingham, Michigan 48009
www.GreyWolfePublishing.com

© 2014 Diana Kathryn Plopa
Published by Grey Wolfe Publishing, LLC
www.GreyWolfePublishing.com
All Rights Reserved

ISBN: 978-1628280494
Library of Congress Control Number: 2014951388

Free Will

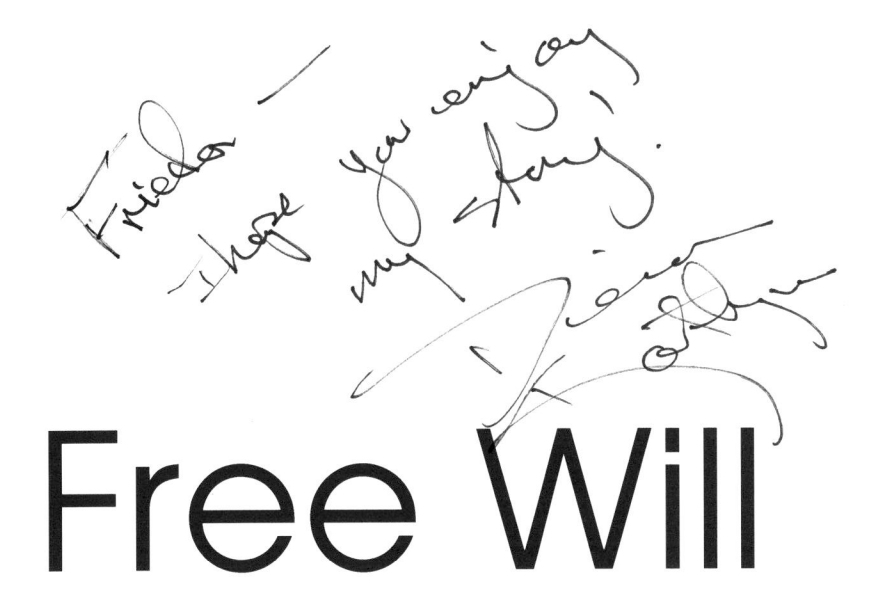

Diana Kathryn Plopa

Dedication:

For my father, Earl W. Wolfe, who believed in a dream and helped me to make it happen.

Thank you, Daddy!

For my husband, David Dylan Plopa, who never questioned my dedication over the four years it took to finally finish this book. He supports my creativity with his love and devotion... even though it hasn't made us a million dollars... yet.

I love you, Dave!

For my son, Zachary Bennjamin Wolfe, your smile, giggle and unwavering belief in me keeps me putting fingers to keyboard.

I love you Zachary... more!

Acknowledgements:

A Huge Howl of Thanks goes out to the Grey Wolfe Publishing Pack. Your kindness and writing support, critique, and beta reading has been invaluable to me.

Your friendship has meant even more... I'd like to say I that I will give you all a free copy of the book... but you're all authors, and you understand the importance of sales and royalty checks...

So, please visit the website at **www.GreyWolfePublishing.com**, and buy a copy for your very own. I'd be happy to inscribe it for you!

~Hugs! Diana Kathryn Plopa

Chapter One
The Two Gates

At five seconds, things were a little foggy. I'm not sure how much time passed by, or exactly how I got there... I wouldn't figure out the details until much later... but I can say that the first fifteen seconds of my life after death were exactly as I imagined they would be.

The corridor where I stood was foggy from my feet to my knees. I couldn't actually see or feel solid ground beneath me, or my feet, for that matter... but somehow, I knew it was there. The sky directly above me held an odd, ethereal light, and the air was dry and soft. There was no sun, no wind, and the space around me was eerily silent. There were two gates: one black and foreboding, one bronze and inviting; just like the storybooks and religious school teachers had foretold. There was a strong comfort surrounding me.

At thirty seconds, logic and comfort took a nosedive.

From out of nowhere, about twenty feet in front of me, appeared a fifty-four-inch flat screen plasma HDTV. As it drifted in place the light around me dimmed, the soft aroma of jasmine lilted somewhere just on the edge of perception, and the screen flickered to life.

The Choice Has Always Been Yours

The opening title appeared in the center of the screen in scarlet biblical calligraphy with an elegant satin silver background.

"An orientation video?" All my presumptions about death had been turned inside out.

****

"Welcome to Purgatory." said the host.

He looked like a pudgy, balding, bowtie clad, nearsighted professor. In fact, he looked just like the man who taught my freshman trigonometry course in college; Professor Tribell. But it couldn't be. "Isn't he still teaching at Wayne State this term?" My thoughts were running amok, and they were doing it out loud. The strange little man droned on.

"We trust your travel from the Earthly realm was uneventful." Before I could catch myself, I nearly screamed an exasperated retort.

"Uneventful? I'd say the demise of my physical body was quite the event. Who is this guy?" I looked around for someone to commiserate with, but there was no one. It was beginning to look like reincarnation was not an option.

"Now that you've shoved off that mortal toil," the host snickered, "You have quite the little adventure before you. But as with everything, you must choose." He seemed to be having much more fun than should be allowed.

The screen then presented two purple check boxes; above the first, in cobalt script, the word "Heaven". Under the second, in gothic silver block lettering, the word "Hell". As the Dr. Tribell doppelganger continued to speak, the images of the two gates superimposed under each check box, and settled gently on his left and right shoulders. A brief flashback of an old cartoon jogged in my memory.

"Before you stand two gates; one offers entrance to Heaven, the other to Hell. You must choose which side deserves you more." I'm sure my face screwed up in a contortion which could only be described as gargoyle-like.

"Which side deserves me? Just how am I supposed to figure that out?" I said with whining frustration. I was a bit wobbly and would have liked a chair or stool, or something to settle my body, or my essence, or whatever they call this thing you get after death. This was not an easy thing for me to process. After all, I'd only been dead for... what was it, maybe a day?

As if in answer to my dizzying brain, the host started talking again. He was sitting behind a desk now, looking even more like my plump trig professor than before. The simultaneous familiarity and oddity of the scene made my stomach do little flip-flops. "You will spend a little time in both Heaven and Hell, on a visitor's pass. You will be given ample time, a full seven days, in each place, to decide where you think you belong. When you finally make a decision, just let us know; and you'll be permanently assigned."

"But what if I know where I belong now?" I said aloud, fully expecting to get an answer.

"No one really knows where they belong, not so close after death anyway, and that is why you must spend this mandatory time as a visitor in each realm before making a final choice. After all, you wouldn't buy a car without a test drive, now would you? Once your choice is made, there is no turning back, no retractions, no do-overs".

For a moment, it felt like the video host had been speaking directly to me—and then I realized that it must have been one of death's FAQs; I couldn't possibly have been the only one to ask that particular out loud. They must have just built it into the program, like that silly little scene at the beginning of Jurassic Park. Of course, it was ridiculous, me talking to the TV. I felt like that first day of boot camp in the Navy all over again—foolish and ignorant. The host went on.

"Although we can't tell you what to expect during your visits, what we can say is that there will be no apocalyptic fight for your Soul, regardless of what you may have read. However, we can't promise you that the residents of either Heaven or Hell won't try to sway your decision by their own means; after all, we can't control everything. We can promise, however, that you won't be harmed in the process."

"Good thing! It'd be pretty difficult to hurt a dead person, don't you think?" I hollered at the screen, and then I screamed one of those primal screams my therapist once told me were... what did he call it? Oh yes, 'healing'. This whole death thing was getting tremendously weirder with each passing nanosecond.

"So, we suggest that you just go with the flow and enjoy your time touring each realm, consider it a vacation... and don't worry about your decision until judgment day, almost a full month away. Just take it slow. Really consider your options. We'll make sure you'll get some regroup time in between each visit and at the end to process your thoughts. Good Luck!"

The screen grew dark and the credits rolled in true Hollywood fashion. I remember thinking that it was amazing how many people it took to put this production together... *lots of dead videographers and grips.* As the final copyright line rolled past, the host chortled somewhere off-camera. He was probably laughing at the same thing I was... *Copyright in the afterlife? Who could possibly steal it?"* The light around me returned to normal. That is, if ethereal can be considered "normal".

As I looked about I noticed that a woman had appeared at my side. She stood only about four feet tall, but was perfectly proportioned in every way. No pitch fork, no pointy ears, and no spiked tail; none that I could see, anyway. I took this as a good sign. "I'm Liza. I'll take you back to your room now," she said. "You'll need proper rest if you're to go on a visit to Heaven in the morning."

I was overcome by a drunken giggle as the little woman took my hand. Absolutely none of my dying process was happening according to Hoyle... Not one of the rules I'd been taught had been followed. It was just all so... not normal. I had to ask... "Why do I get to visit Heaven first? Does everyone visit Heaven first?" I was tired and rambling.

Liza smiled and looked up at me with a strange glint in her eye. "Oh no, my dear. You are visiting Heaven first because it is your right. A priest gave you that last right before you arrived."

Last Rites meant a first stop in Heaven? Do all priests know that? Did they teach that in seminary school? Is that why my Rabbi didn't talk about the possibility of going to hell... maybe he was never taught the bypass code and didn't want to tell his congregation that he was out of the loop. My brain was awash with too many images, too many sounds, too many thoughts. *What time was it, anyway?* I needed sleep.

Chapter Two
The Twain Inn

Soon, the gates were far from view, and Liza escorted me into the amorphous neighborhood of Purgatory. I was beginning to feel more sober now. I was a little more cognizant during the walk through Purgatory's streets. And still, a detailed description would be a waste of printer's ink. Fog, fog, and more fog. The occasional street lamp led the way. And then, more fog. There's simply not a lot going on in Purgatory.

I didn't see another Soul, hear a dog bark, a bird sing, nor smell any aroma that might indicate that life existed as we walked through the vacancy. The whole thing gave me an eerie, acid-churning, creepy feeling in the pit of my stomach. And then I remembered, the hints of life that I was so desperately looking for would never appear. *Oh, yeah, Life doesn't exist, certainly not in Purgatory.* After some time, I couldn't tell you how long; we arrived at Purgatory's Inn.

The Inn was a charming Victorian place; gingerbread lattice work on the trellis over a white picket fence, rose bushes around the edges of a flawlessly manicured lawn, and white wicker rocking chairs and a settee on the covered front porch. I was surprised at how un-Purgatory-like it looked. In all the stories I'd heard, I was led to believe that this was where the dead waited to be judged. I imagined park benches filled with the wretched waiting; those who knew their name wasn't inscribed in the Book of Life; those who knew they had a Sin File and were just waiting for someone to call their number and escort them out. Not in my wildest dreams did I ever conceive that Purgatory might actually be a resort town.

"This looks like a place Mark Twain would have lived in," I said, much louder than I expected.

"Funny you should notice that..." I fixed my eyes on Liza in disbelief. "Actually, Samuel designed the place. Not only is he a great writer, and a fascinating dinner guest, he's got a great eye for architecture. His plan was to make people feel comfortable here, while they were in transition. The Powers That Be decided it was a good idea, and now we've got... The Twain Inn. The view from the back porch is a reproduction of Sam's place in New York. He was a great man, still is, actually. He visits occasionally, and gives lectures on Atheism to the newly dead. Our library is filled with only his books. He really is quite a fascinating man."

I snickered a little to myself. Promotion of neither Heaven nor Hell... in Purgatory. Clemens I had always thought, was a smart man; and this just clinched it for me. He'd found a way to retain his atheism in death. "Well, you've got to give him points for creativity." Liza agreed with a nod and a small smile. As we pushed open the stylish front door and made our way into the foyer, I wondered if I'd ever meet him.

I was immediately comforted by the soft aroma of chocolate chip cookies baking; it made my mouth water for a glass of milk. As we moved further into the foyer, I felt the energy of several pairs of eyes staring at me, but saw no bodies attached to them.   Liza made no attempt to explain anything. She simply took my hand again and led me up the stairs. As we climbed each step higher and higher, I had that "first day of school" anxiety welling up in the pit of my stomach. I thought I might hurl at any moment. We stopped about half-way down the corridor, and Liza pointed out my room on the left.

"Well, here you are number sixteen;" Liza tapped the doorknob, as she was too short to reach the number higher up; and opened the door. "Usually, we like to give our guests the sensation of the familiar when they first visit, and make their space here look and feel more like their old bedroom on Earth, you know, to reduce the panic; but you seem acclimated enough, so I think we can forego all that theatre and just be normal; wouldn't you agree?"

Standing about two paces inside the room, I lifted the pint-sized Liza her by her armpits and brought her to eye level, my voice was fever-pitched. "Normal! Are you kidding me!" I put a slightly frantic Liza down, slouched into a chair near the dresser and pointed out the window at the nothing. "There's nothing normal about this place... any of it. This is nuts!" I stood up again and began pacing the length of the room, with Liza standing in the doorway, bracing for an earthquake.

"Test driving Heaven and Hell; this is supposed to be normal?! No, this is the very last thing that normal looks like. If things were normal around here, I'd be called to appear before the Big Book of Life and someone like, oh, I don't know, GOD maybe, would tell me if I deserved to live out eternity in Heaven. And if I'd been a particularly bad girl, he sends me to a really uncomfortable place called Hell, with no chance for parole or appeal. I was completely prepared for that scenario; all of Humanity is prepared for that. We expected it. It's what you told us was the truth. I've got a leather-bound Book filled with wonderfully challenging prose back in my apartment that says so—it's even been on the New York Times bestseller list ... who would dispute the New York Times... I mean, after all!?!"

I had regained my balance and lost my cool. My forehead was beginning to sweat, my voice was cracking from the strain, my arms were flailing, and the tips of my ears began to heat to what I was sure was a lovely shade of magenta. "And now you tell me that God's on a sabbatical, and we get to choose our eternal destination, salvation or damnation, ourselves? What were all those years of atonement and repentance for... all those Mitzvahs and Sabbath candles... the incalculable hours spent in Sunday School... all those days of fasting and cleansing... what was it all for, if not to show Him our devotion and worthiness... I mean really—all that rigmarole for nothing? It was all pointless? Is that what you're telling me?" I was too far gone to stop now. I had reached the precipice of death's reality and jumped off the ledge, sans parachute.

"You know what I think? I think it's time we write a new Book to make sure Humanity gets the right message this time. Clearly there was a clerical error... or a problem with translation... or something—but whoever wrote it the first time got it wrong. See ... this is what happens when you try to do things by committee over too much time... they got it WRONG! This isn't normal, this is INSANE!"

I'd been in such a froth, I didn't notice the Goon Squad that Liza had summoned. Before I knew it, one had each of my arms and they forced me to my knees. Liza moved toward me with cheetah speed, I felt a sudden pinch in my neck and quickly collapsed as the Goons dropped me onto the bed. Call it magic, call it advanced pharmaceuticals ... whatever it was, it calmed me immediately and I slept placidly for quite a while—dreaming of everything and of the nothing I now knew encapsulated it all.

****

When I awoke, the ambient light of nothingness was beginning to become real. My head was a little fuzzy and my stomach ached with its emptiness. I sat up on the edge of the bed, hung over, and tried to refocus my brain. It was late, maybe. It's hard telling when the sun doesn't shine and there's no moon. The eternal fog of Purgatory was a little more than disorienting. *Had I been here one or two days, or was it three?* It was difficult to tell. *I can see why people don't hang out here for long. They'd all go nuts!* I stumbled to the doorway, still a little groggy from the after effects of my tantrum. I opened the door and made my way down the corridor, meeting Liza at the top of the stairs.

"Feeling better, Miss Raychel?" she cooed.

"Oh, sure," I lied. Looking down the stairwell, my head throbbed from the altitude. "Can we get a little closer to sea level?"

Liza took me by the hand and led me gently down the stairs. We crossed the foyer and half-stumbled into the library. The room was a sight to behold. Liza sat me down on a beautiful mahogany sofa with dark leather upholstery. Nearby, a chaise and two chairs covered in light blue velvet snuggled up next to a lovely coffee table with side tables, atop which were perched stained glass lamps, Tiffany, I supposed. It was like sitting in an antique store ... except for the decidedly out-of-place plasma HDTV tucked into the mahogany bookshelves filled with leather-bound volumes on the far wall.

"Oh boy, if my mother could see me now." My hands held my head, as each heartbeat echoed in my ears and throbbed against my temples. Liza brought me tea and a small plate of what looked like finger sandwiches, and settled in the chair next to me. "Here, this will help your head. Sorry we had to be so rough with you, but you were getting just a little out of control." I stared at Liza through painful slits where I once remembered having eyes.

"Yeah, I got it." I slumped back in the chair, knocking a fringed-edged pillow to the floor and sipped my tea. "I wonder what the family's up to. I wonder if they even miss me. What happens after you die, Liza? I mean, how does the world change—your Earth world change—after you've gone? It's all a great mystery. You know, it's interesting ... when you're alive; you're fascinated with what life will be like when you're dead. And when you're finally dead, you wonder what the life you left behind is like without you. Humanity seems to have terminal fence envy. Always wanting what's on the other side." I was wrapped up in despondent frustration, an effect of the interminable fog that is Purgatory. It was tough to avoid.

"Well, if it's any comfort, they had a very nice send-off for you." Liza offered meekly.

"What... you were at my funeral?" And it was in that moment that Liza realized she'd said too much, too soon, you could see it on her face. But there was no stopping this train wreck now. Liza stirred her tea nervously and tried to keep her tone up-beat.

"Well, no, they don't let me out much. But I saw the video, it looked very nice... lovely flowers, beautiful music and so many friends and family. It looked like a lot of people really loved you..."

I jumped to my feet again, towering over Liza with a near-menacing glare. It felt good to be near-menacing; at least I felt like I was doing something, rather than having it done to me. "Hold it! You saw the VIDEO? How is that possible?" Trying to avoid another Goon Squad summons, Liza calmly walked to the bookshelf and selected a slim case from the collection; my name and photo were on the front cover. My mouth dropped open and I nearly dumped my tea on the floor as I plopped back on the sofa. "A DVD, are you serious?"

"Well, what were you expecting, VHS? We're much more evolved up here than that, you know. I've been pushing for Blu-Ray but they tell me it's just not in the budget." Liza opened the cupboard under the television and inserted the disk. She retrieved the remote and returned to her seat next to me. "Now, I want to warn you, sometimes when people see their death for the first time, it can be a little, well, awkward. Just say the word and I can stop it at any time."

"Awkward, yeah, I could see how that could happen... Wait, people actually watch this more than once?" It was the most surreal moment I'd ever found myself in, and it showed.

As the film opened, there was a nice folksy soundtrack playing behind a dignified presentation of my name and photograph, like something from a high school yearbook. Then, scene one... the intersection I last remembered. Subtitles narrated the story as the screen played out my death in high definition.

> *Raychel had been staring at the red light, thinking of everything and nothing; contemplating her fate. Her job was sometimes stimulating, sometimes boring; but she was good at it. Her social life was without any real excitement, but that wasn't for a lack of trying. She was above average on the intelligence scale, and an avid technology fan; but she had problems meeting people who "got" her. Not long ago, she speculated that her total circle of friends was smaller than Lucifer's Facebook friends in Heaven. Her biggest regret since leaving the military two years ago was also leaving that cute lieutenant behind.*
>
> *It was just as the light changed from red to green that her world came crashing into her—quite literally. The noise was horrific. Everything moved in slow motion, but that didn't keep it from being loud. It was as though the truck had materialized from the bowels of Hell itself. The last sound*

that entered her ears as the hatchback of her SmartCar sandwiched her tiny frame next to the idling engine block was her brother's voice—her little brother Roger, the overzealous car salesman, "Should have bought the Hummer instead." And that was all.

I watched in fascinating horror as Metallic blue paint, gray faux suede seats, plastic, and glass became fused with flesh as my stationary object met with an overwhelming force. My body was almost imperceptible amongst the rubble, landing nearly fifty yards from where I had been.

And she was gone. Her heart stopped beating. Breath did not escape her lungs. Thought did not enter her mind. There was no pain.

As freakishly unnerving it was to watch myself die in color-rich pixels. At least the subtitles were right. There were no thoughts and no pain. I was thankful for that.

Bystanders who had witnessed the tragedy simply stood, mouths agape, in disbelief. Other motorists nearby had been shoved out of the way, and managed to escape fairly unharmed—a few cuts, scrapes, bruises and the truck driver's one broken ankle—but for the most part, unscathed. The singleness of her decimation was uncanny. Before the police and rescue trucks arrived, a priest from the cathedral across the street came running to the scene offering to help in any way he could.

No one in the film uttered a word. They just lowered their heads in solemn disbelief. I watched as the priest walked reverently to the pile of compressed insanity and offered Last Rites to the small bit of my flesh that had managed to peer out from behind mangled tire rubber. "Oh, Last Rites. I get it now." I mumbled aloud.

It was all that could be done. He prayed it would be enough.

There was a fade to black, and then, Act Two: the funeral home. It was an odd scene, yet familiar ... the Rabbi I had grown up with at Temple, the Cantor I'd had a crush on since high school, and my family and friends all milling about with no real direction. Everything seemed normal to me. And then, the camera panned to the casket at the far side of the room. I'd always imagined that mine would be a closed-casket funeral, but evidently my parents had other ideas. Looking at yourself dead is a nauseating thing. The mortician did the best he could, but it was still a bad idea. Car wrecks really don't produce the most favorable results for public displays of the leftovers.

Next, the camera panned to a couple of easels with photos documenting my life from childhood to adulthood... my favorite flowers, blue carnations and white roses in a blanket on the coffin's foot, and surrounded the podium. "Mom over did it again, it's just like her to lose the simple effect of the flowers that I love so much".

"She was probably just overwrought with grief and lost in an emotional upheaval." said Liza. And that sounded just about right.

Once everyone was seated, the camera panned overhead and I got a better view of dead me. My face was a bit mangled... the clothes were all wrong; that hideous suit I wore my first day to Navy registration. I looked at Liza. "You'd think for a final send-off, the family would have dressed me better." From off-camera someplace, I heard my little brother quip to his friends; "Although, if you were going to bury something, that would be the suit to bury it in." My face was covered in far too much makeup—probably the first time the stuff had been on my face, ever—and a hairstyle that looked like the cat had retrieved his catnip from secret hiding places. I was grateful the casket was only half open; I'm guessing that there wasn't enough left to show what was below the waist—

or it was a mess—either way, I was grateful.

The screen faded to black again and gently rose on the next scene. The Rabbi gave his sermon. My mother cried. The Cantor chanted the Kaddish. My mother wept. My father tried to console her but of course, that only made her weep more. My mother loved the dramatic. My younger brother and his girlfriend sat in the third row, seemingly disinterested in the whole thing. Friends and family passed by the casket, paying their respects. I found it odd that people actually spoke things out loud. I was dead; did they really think I'd be listening? But now, while watching the DVD, I was happy they were nuts enough to do it. How else could you know what people thought about you after you'd gone?

Again, fade to black, and then a wide helicopter shot. As the procession weaved around the streets of my neighborhood, toward the cemetery, I found myself enjoying this walk through the familiar. I had a longing to be there again, to walk those streets, hear the sounds of the birds and young children playing. I even missed the obnoxious young boys who hung out at the park playing basketball with their underwear showing. It was quite a contrast from the silence and nothingness of Purgatory. I was beginning to see why someone might want to watch this a couple of times, just to reminisce. When the time came for the internment, I turned a little green.

"Um... Can we skip through this part? Dirt on my dead body... It's a little weird for me..."

"Sure, it's difficult for most people to watch this part. We'll just skip most of this." Liza pushed the fast forward button on the remote and narrated what we were skipping. "There's a lot of crying, too many fruit and nut trays, and a lot of silence." Liza flipped the remote to display the main chapter menu, and moved directly to the last segment of the film; Shiva, Day Seven. Liza was trying to save us both from the un-comfortableness of the entire film; it was long, redundant, and I would imagine, difficult for most newly dead to get through without some kind of breakdown, or alcohol. And for Liza, I guessed that this was a little tedious; *how many of these things did she have to watch?* Actually, I was a little surprised that she wasn't drinking at this point.

   The camera angle hovered overhead... looking down on my family home as if it were a doll house with no roof. My father and a minyan of men were in one room, praying the mourner's Kaddish and others. My little brother was sitting on the back deck, smoking absentmindedly with his girlfriend hovering nearby, talking with other couples I didn't recognize. Every mirror in the house was covered, my grandmother walked around with a ripped shoulder seam on her dress, and there was more food strewn across the kitchen table and countertops than was necessary. *Who eats at funerals, really?* Soft music, Mozart—my mother's favorite, played in the den, where mother sat staring toward a non-existent horizon, sipping black coffee, occasionally being comforted by a well-meaning friend or two.

   Right about the time I was going to reach for the off button, a man walked in and sat next to my mother... gray suit... black tie... bald, a little portly, glasses and a little nerdy looking, yet friendly. He was handing my mother a cup of coffee, engaged in a very intent conversation. I didn't recognize him. The man's body language was quietly aggressive and clearly, my mother was upset.

   "Wait! That's the guy from the orientation video!! I knew I'd seen him before. Hey, can we turn up the volume on this, please?" Suddenly, I felt like I was watching an episode of Survivor; reality at its best.

   Liza nudged the volume up tentatively. If I were in Liza's head, I would think that it wasn't usually a good sign when the dead became interested in their own funerals. Fortunately for me, I wasn't in Liza's head.

"You have to let her go, ma'am. She must have your blessing to move on. It's critical to the preservation of her Soul. There is a better place for her. A place of peace and safety. She'll have everything that she wants, there will be no stress, no pain. You wouldn't keep her from the most important job offer she'd ever been given, now would you? This isn't that much different. Her job is not about living anymore, it's about dying. You must let her choose to go." The man wasn't forceful, just gentle and insistent.

Finally, my mother nodded her head in quiet resolution. She had given up. The man squeezed my mother's hand, got up from his seat, and disappeared out the front door without looking back or saying another word. A gaggle of my mother's closest friends gathered around her as she wept uncontrollably into my infant swaddling blanket from that first day of life. Parents save the strangest things. And in that moment, in the very moment that he walked out the door of my parent's house, he appeared in the doorway of the library. I looked at Liza a little astonished. "Neat trick."

"Hello Edgar. Were you on your way out?" Liza asked pleasantly.

"Yes, I've got two funerals today; one in Newark and another somewhere in the West Indies. No rest for the dead, I suppose. I should be home in time for dinner, though." replied Edgar.

"The West Indies, isn't that unusual for you?" Liza asked, taking another sip of tea.

"Well, yeah, but there's a Tiger's game on this afternoon, and so I told Jason I'd cover for him. Well, got to go. See you later." With a quick little wave, he was gone. Yup, in and out just that fast. I didn't have a chance to catch my breath, let alone get out a question... or sixty.

"Who is that guy?" I asked Liza.

"Oh, that's Edgar. He's one of our ushers." she said.

"Usher?" I asked.

"Sure, you can't expect that all the dead people of the world will be able find their way up here without a little help, now can you? You saw the fog. The agnostics and atheists, they have the hardest time of it, you know. It's so difficult for them to believe that dirt and worms won't actually be the end." Liza was so cavalier... I was stunned.

"Okay, but why was he talking to my mother?" I needed more answers... but started here, since the video was still on pause.

"It's important that we get permission from someone in your family to bring you up. It's one of the oldest rules about being dead. No body snatching. So, Edgar goes out and visits the funerals, invites the dead to come back with him; and then he talks to the family to get their permission and blessings to let them go. He asked your mother because your father was with the minyan, and Edgar, sweet dear, didn't want to interrupt."

"So, that's what was going on. I vaguely remember a conversation with him at the party, but I thought it was for some job interview. My brain was a little fuzzy at the time, you know." I reached for a sandwich, thinking that food would somehow settle me.

"Well, that's to be expected, after all, you were smashed up pretty good," said Liza. "But you heard what Edgar told your mother. Dying really is the last job you'll ever have. Not to mention the fact that, depending on the person and the culture, he often introduces death using that metaphor. It makes it easier to understand. After all, would you have really believed him if he'd said that you were dead and he was inviting you to join him in Purgatory so that you could choose between Heaven and Hell?"

"No, I suppose not." I had to admit, it was a good strategy. I can't imagine a lot of Americans who would turn down "the job of a lifetime". It made me wonder what the strategy was for other cultures. *What does he tell the Muslims? Virgin stories? Or Buddhists? Nirvana tales?* The idea of having that conversation with Edgar fascinated me, and simultaneously frustrated me because I couldn't remember it. And it made me wonder... *was he just a talented voice-over guy, or was he an involved member of the planning commission for this whole thing?*

"So, Edgar said he'd be back for dinner, eh? Any chance I could sit next to him?" Liza shuttered just a little bit and flipped off the DVD player. She could tell by my teenager's voice that this was an encounter I was eager to have. My curiosity was a cat bound and determined to skitter amongst as many rocking chairs as necessary to learn more about my death.

"I'm not sure it's such a good idea. Too much information all at once can cause confusion. But I don't suppose I'll be able to stop you, will I? Countered Liza.

"No, I doubt it." The championship grin I now wore felt very good. Assertiveness had never been my strength, and I was discovering its helpfulness. Too bad I didn't know this before; life would have been very different.

****

I had a couple of hours before dinnertime, so I went back up to my room to try to relax. I took a quick peak out the window, just to make sure there weren't any changes. *Unending fog. Yup. Still dead.*

I looked around my room and found a "Welcome" packet on the desk with a cover letter typed on lovely parchment stationary. On the bottom margin, in green script, flanked by images of ivy, was a single sentence: "The reports of my death have *not* been greatly exaggerated." A smirk crossed my face. *Twain. Of course.*

> "Dear Raychel;
> We are very pleased to welcome you to the Samuel Clemens Mark Twain Purgatory Inn. We hope that your stay will be soothing and relaxing as you prepare to visit Heaven and Hell, and then reflect to make your final choice at month's end. If you need anything, or have any questions, we are always here to help. We know you will find great comfort in your life after death."
> ~Fondly,
> Liza and Edgar

It's a pity I hadn't seen this before my meltdown, I might have saved myself a nasty hangover. Inside the folder were a trifold brochure, a fact sheet, and two over-sized postcards. It appeared to be the after life's PR packet. *This might be helpful...* I sat down at the desk and began to read. The title of the brochure was:

"10 Key Thoughts On Being Dead"

1. Eat, Drink and Be Merry!
Yes, you still get to eat and your nose and taste buds will continue to function as they always have. Bonus Feature: There are no calories in the afterlife. When you eat, you will not gain weight. Your appearance is the Soul Perception of you. So eat to your heart's desire—we believe food should be enjoyed.

2. *You Can Sleep After You're Dead!*
Yes, you will still have the desire and need for sleep. Even though your physical body is no longer a part of you; remember that your Soul Energy still needs replenishing. The best way we know to do that is to take a little time out and sleep. You may notice, however, that since you don't have all those internal organs to power anymore, you may not need as much sleep as you once did. Bonus Feature: You can choose your dream topics before going to sleep and enjoy them as you would a favorite film, with total recall.

3. *Use Your Words!*
No, you're not instantly a mind reader upon death and neither is anyone else. Privacy is one of our strongest mandates in the afterlife, which means that your thoughts are your own. Communication still requires talking, just like it always has. It's the best way we know to keep your privacy secure.

4. *The Clothes Make The Soul!*
Clothing is NOT optional. You no longer have a fleshy body to give you definition; therefore, clothing is necessary to allow others to see who you are in a familiar form. Most Souls, because they have been people for so long, don't understand the essence of naked Soul Energy—so why frustrate them, put on some clothes for goodness sake.

5. *Why, You Haven't Aged A Bit!*
The aging process stops when you die. Your body has returned to the dust from which it came, but your Soul Essence is still growing, changing and evolving. Your naked Soul Energy is too difficult to understand, so we've placed your visual appearance in stasis. Others will see you as you appeared, in good health, just before or at the time of your death. A Special Note: Vanity has no place in the afterlife, so you will find no mirrors. Get used to not seeing what you

look like, it really doesn't matter... you can't do anything to change your appearance anyway, so why waste the effort.

6. Laugh, Cry, Scream!
Yes, you will continue to retain all of your emotions, positive and negative. Your emotions are the Soul Essence of who you are. To allow you to only express happiness dilutes the fullness of your Soul. We want to know all of you, not just the selective "good parts". The use of emotions on a regular basis is one of the batteries that recharges your Soul Energy. Engage your emotions often to maintain maximum acuity after death. Caution: Use your emotions carefully as most Souls are much more sensitive now that they no longer have the distractions of the physical world to fend off the energy of your emotionality.

7. You Can't Go Back!
Visiting Earth to spend time with those you left behind is NOT permitted. This practice causes confusion for everyone involved, both the living and the dead. The living have a hard time coming to terms with the eventuality of death and your visit may prolong their feelings of loss and suffering. Returning to Earth in the essence of your Soul Energy only depletes it, it will not strengthen it. Once your Soul Energy is depleted, you will be forced to wander the streets of Limbo, unable to exercise your Free Will.

8. No Sniffles 'Round Here!
While you may feel a slight brusqueness in acclimation from the sensation of your physical body to an understanding your Soul Energy, illness, disease and physical pain have been completely eliminated—unless you choose to experience them, and we don't know why you would want to do that. These ailments are counterintuitive and downright distracting to the growth of the Soul. If you were sick when you died, you're not anymore!

9. Be Fruitful, But Don't Multiply!
Even though your fleshy body is long gone, you will still have the physical experiences of touch. Because our positive physical experiences are frequently a large contributor to our Soul Essence, you will continue to experience these pleasant sensations after death. Sexual intercourse is considered a divine gift—and yes, it'll still work the way you expect it to. Give it often. Use it wisely. Enjoy it thoroughly. There are no pregnancies in the afterlife. Creating a New Soul is much more complicated than creating a new body. Also, there are no STDs in the afterlife, either; but that doesn't mean you get to be reckless with your activity. Maintain a little decorum, please. Gossip is still Free Will. CAUTION: Sexual trysts are discouraged until after you have selected your eternal address.

10. The Fat Lady Has Sung!
This is all there is. Three realms, Heaven, Purgatory, and Hell. Each realm has only one level, there is nothing more spectacular or more dastardly waiting just around the river bend. This is all we have. If you were expecting Dante's Inferno, keep in mind that's fiction. Accept and move on."

All in all, good tips for the newly dead. It was nice of them to provide the basics. I had a lot more questions but I was sure I could get those answers on my visits to Heaven and Hell. The fact sheet on the Law of Free Will read a little like a disclaimer, and perhaps it was.

Facts For The Newly Dead

Free Will is the purest expression of choice. It was the first and truly, the only gift from the Divine to Humanity. From the moment of your birth until the moment of your death, your destiny has been within your grasp. Every choice you made has been your own—with the exception of those very early moments when you had influence but were not yet evolved enough to make your desires clearly known. Each person you have encountered, each piece of news or literature you have been exposed to, each bit of stage, music, film or television entertainment you have enjoyed has contributed to your view of society and the world. The decisions you made based on these perceptions—and the influences you chose to accept from those around you— these decisions have been yours alone.

There has been no divine intervention. There has been no demonic trickery.
Whenever you made a choice in life, and in fact, even in those moments where you decided not to choose and leave your fate in another's hands and influence, you were engaged 100% in the Law of Free Will.

The Law of Free Will remains valid after death.
Your Soul Essence retains the advantage of the Law of Free Will; with only one caveat: once you choose which will be your eternal address, Heaven or Hell, your choice may never be revoked. Contemplate your decision with careful wisdom.

That last one was a sobering thought. *Eternity is finite. There is an un-revocable end.* I don't know anyone who would have seen that one coming.

Finally, last in the packet were the two over-sized post cards. Each had the traditional color schemes; blue and white for

Heaven, with a stereotypical Angel on the front with wings and a trumpet; red and black for Hell, with the stereotypical Demon with horns and a fiery pitchfork. I read each one in turn, twice.

> "Ah Hell... Could there be any place more perfect? I say, no! Drunken debauchery, Evil intentions, and foul-mouthed Souls... Let's face it, we all have our eccentricities. And if you've got a few, this just might be the place for you. There are a lot of things I could verify and several secrets I could disclose... but why? You'll get to see it all first-hand on your visit to our realm. Remember, we would never buy it if it weren't disguised; so Heaven may not be all that you think it is. Keep your eyes open and your ears perked... Hell just might turn out to be all that and a bag of chips. ~Your Fallen Archangel, Steve."
>
> "Ah Heaven... Could there be any place more perfect? I say, no! Blue skies, congenial neighbors, all your wishes fulfilled... We have the best address in all of eternity, and we can't wait to welcome you home. You'll meet new friends and have opportunities to experience things that only Angels could provide. Travel, leisure and abundant Love, that's what awaits you beyond the pristine gate. Be wary of false prophets and the entertainment program in Hell. Remember, if they have to give it away, it just might not be authentic. Keep your integrity a priority and you just may find that Heaven is the eternity you've been looking for. ~ Your Archangel, Michael."

The idea of carefully placed ads in Purgatory struck me as a little odd. But then, nothing here was what I expected, and I expected there would be a lot more of that to come.

In the top drawer of the bed-side table I found a copy of Gideon's Bible and the Book of the Dead, with a small sticker affixed to the cover of each which read:

A Little Light Reading: Please return to nightstand when finished.

    I decided to pass on the reading and get in a little nap before dinner. There had been a lot to process and my brain—or my Soul Essence—or whatever it was I was using to think with nowadays was pretty wiped out. I cued up a Vivaldi CD and drifted off somewhere in the middle of *Spring*.

Chapter Three
Dinner at The Inn

"Great chicken, Liza." said Edgar as he added another drumstick to his plate. I don't know what you do to it, but it's fantastic, every time." Edgar raised his glass and offered a toast. "To Liza, Queen of Purgatory's kitchen!"

"To Liza!" the table cheered. Liza's cheeks grew a little flushed and she demurely nodded her thanks. It was clear that there was a long history between those two. Their coy glances were about as well hidden as fireworks at a Roman Catholic funeral.

One of the newly dead, George, asked the question that I'm sure Edger gets a lot, and one I was dying to ask, too. "So, what happens if someone who dies won't come with you, you know, back to Purgatory?" George was about forty, wore coke bottle glasses and a pocket protector. He looked like a throwback to the '50s, but Liza assured me he had just arrived a day or so before I had.

"Well, the people who don't choose to go with me willingly, or the ones whose families can't or won't let them go… well, that's where that old concept of reincarnation comes from." George looked at him strangely and glanced around the table for some sign of recognition. We returned his stupefied stares, and Edger, unfazed by our confusion, continued.

"You see, if we don't have permission to bring them back here, the dead are simply recycled to live out another lifetime until they are ready to die or until they find a family that is willing to let them go when their time comes again. The Law of Free Will mandates that those who are really against the idea of dying, are free to make the choice not to die."

Fred's eyes got saucer large. "You mean that if I had refused to go with you, I could have thwarted death and avoided the whole thing?"

"Well sure," said Edger. "But the catch is that reincarnation happens without any transfer of cognitive memory, and your Soul gets recycled into a new body. It's not like you get to stay who you are and live out your days being an immortal."

"Oh, that's no fun;" said Fred, lowering his eyes to his plate.

"No, your essence continues but embodied in another empty casing. You're given the opportunity to live on, but you have to start from scratch, and without the knowledge you had at death. Oh, some of it lingers—that's where de'ja'vu comes from—but most real working knowledge and memory is wiped away."

"I'm not quite sure I understand", said the little old lady across the table from George. She was clearly someone's grandmother, but seemed pretty together for a woman in her eighties. She had dyed her hair blonde and wore comfy jeans, sneakers and a Nantucket Marina sweatshirt.

"Okay, do you know how computers work?" asked Edgar.

"Yes, my grandchildren taught me how to use one a few years ago. I got quite good at creating electronic scrapbooks with all my darling's photos." Her eyes beamed with a pride that I'm sure was rightly earned.

"Fantastic. Okay, imagine a hard drive wipe on your computer. Same concept. Although there may be lingering binary snippets of code, for the most part, everything that was once stored on that particular hard drive is gone, and you start with the thing empty and fresh. That's how Soul recycling works."

"Well that's a bit of a disappointment, now isn't it?" George seemed simultaneously dismayed and relieved that he didn't try to avoid dying.

"Well I should say so. I would be lost without the memories of my darling grandchildren." said Agnes. "No, I've lived a good, long life. Better to leave with my faculties intact. But I do have one question, Edgar; what happens to those reincarnated Souls when they finally choose to die? Which lifetime memories do they retain? What do they get to keep, the first lifetime or the second?"

"That's a great question, Agnes; and yet another of the disappointments of Soul recycling. You see, those who are reincarnated are left with a very confused history. Most can remember individual events, places and snippets of time; but sadly, they have little emotional thread to bind it all together. It's a little like awaking from a dream. You remember the essence or maybe a few key details of the dream, but never the whole thing. It's akin to Alzheimer's for the dead. That's how those Souls must spend their eternity. Never really understanding if they actually lived a life or dreamed it."

"Oh those poor dears." sighed Agnes. "Whatever becomes of them? Do they ever find peace?"

"Again, sadly, not many. For the most part, they wander around the fog of Purgatory, lost in what they think was a life, trying desperately to grab on to a past they are unsure of. It's difficult for those Souls to make a choice between Heaven and Hell because they are so tormented by the limbo effect of trying to sort out so many lifetimes. We try our best to provide a space for them to heal; and some do. But most simply wander endlessly, occasionally trying to slip back to Earth; and that's where one of the mysteries of hauntings come from."

"Hauntings? You mean like ghosts and specter? That's pretty unnerving." Fred was wide-eyed again.

"I wish more mortals understood, things would be so much easier," said Edgar. "It's not really scary ghosts trying to torment those they've left behind. They simply don't know where they belong and so they just end up rambling up one street and down another, in and out of an emotional and physical fog. It's really very sad."

The table grew solemn as we all fell into a moment of silence in honor of those frustrated, lost Souls.

The silence was interrupted by a condescending voice from around the corner. "Oh come on, people! It's not like you all weren't warned."

"What do you mean, 'warned'?" asked George.

She strutted through the door like she owned the place. "Well, you all knew you didn't have much time left. I thought I made it pretty obvious." The woman sat at the one empty chair at the table and began to collect a plate of leftovers. I could tell that Liza was less than impressed with this woman, her table manners, especially. Liza was tolerant, but I got the impression that she would have rather the woman never showed up. The rest of us stared at each other, looking for someone who was in on the joke; but confusion filled the room.

"Ladies and Gentlemen," said Edgar. "May I introduce you to Miss Mortality." Edger, too, tried to be civil; but you could tell that there was some rift between the three of them. And, it was clear Miss Mortality didn't really care.

"Oh please, Edgar. Much too formal. Call me Marji." she said, taking a sip of wine and positioning a clump of mashed potatoes on her fork.

"How nice to see you again, Marji." said Liza, feigning politeness.

"Yeah, whatever." Marji picked up a drumstick and began to gnaw enthusiastically.

"You didn't really answer my question." said George, with a look on his face like he was still hoping that someone would give him a straight answer. None of us had gotten many of those since our arrival and I could tell it was beginning to irritate him. "What do you mean we were 'warned'?"

"Look," said Marji in between mouthfuls of chicken and gulps of wine. "I've visited all of you, at least once, sometimes more than once... depending. I told each of you that your time was coming close to an end and you needed to either change your path to extend your time on Earth, or accept your fate."

"I don't remember you visiting me." said a puzzled Agnes.

"Oh sure you do, that one time when three of your friends died of heart attacks in the same year; and you thought you could still handle life without your blood thinners. Remember, that overnight stay at the hospital and the nurse who said that you really needed to take your medication regularly? Well, that was me." She swallowed another mouthful of potatoes. "But did you pay attention? Of course not." She reached gratuitously across the table for a dinner roll, nearly tumbling the gravy boat. "Everyone thinks they can just ignore Miss Mortality when she comes knocking at their door, and everything will be just fine. Wrong!" Marji was pretty worked up at this point, but still somehow managed to help herself to another heaping spoonful of potatoes and corn.

"I don't get it," said Fred. "I don't remember you coming to visit me. And I'm sure that with a personality like yours, you'd be pretty tough to forget."

"Well... remember that little boat ride you took out about two miles off shore on that dreary day that quickly turned into a storm? Do you remember your fourteen foot aluminum boat capsizing... Do you remember the lovely DNR officer that came to your rescue and reminded you that you really should have checked the weather reports and had a radio with you before you headed out to fish that day? Well, you guessed it, genius, that was me! I know a DNR uniform isn't really all that flattering, but I'd think you'd remember the woman behind the badge."

"Yes," said Fred. "I remember that day; it was a real 'near-death' kind of thing for me. But I still don't understand how you can claim that was you. She had red hair, for criminy's sake." And in that moment, without any effort from her, Marji's beautiful blonde curls instantly turned red. Fred nearly coughed up a lung. Good thing he didn't have those anymore.

"Well, enough of this depressing conversation. Who's up for desert? I've got fudge brownies a' la mode!" Liza was the consummate hostess. Immediately, the table lit up with cheers and raised hands. The conversation worked its way back around Marji and her insolent identity. It was Liza's job to keep the people focused on making choices and get them to move along; and I could see that she really needed them to take that step; and talking to Marji wasn't helping. I got up to help Liza clear the dishes and help bring dessert from the kitchen.

"Nice save, Liza." I congratulated.

"Thanks. Things were just getting out of control in there. With every new group it's the same thing. I know that we're all dead and everything, but geez, do we really need to dwell on it? Can you grab the ice cream out of the freezer?"

Chapter Four
Walk Away From The Light

"Raychel! Wake up!! We've got a serious problem." Liza's voice was near-frantic, almost screaming. It was the middle of the night, and I was lost in a deep sleep, probably the first real night of restorative sleep I'd had since dying, and now Liza was pulling me out of it.

"Oh come on, Liza... really? I was so comfy." I opened my eyes to see Liza groping through the closet for my robe. When our eyes met, I understood that something was really wrong. Calm, cool, collected Liza was vibrating with something that might have actually been fear.

"Hurry up, put this on and come with me." Liza screamed.

"Liza, really. Relax. Whatever it is, it can't be that bad. After all, everyone here is dead." I was trying to wake up and get my bearings, but evidently, there was no time for that. Liza was pulling me by the belt on my robe out into the hallway.

"No, this is bad... usually we can catch this stuff ahead of time... but this was a complete surprise. How could those idiots at Intake have missed this? This is nuts. We really need your help, Raychel. You're the only one who can make this right again; Thank goodness you're still here."

As we reached the top of the stairs, I had to grab the railing to steady myself as Liza began pulling me toward the bottom. It felt like we were on an escalator, trying to outrun the appearing steps. When we reached the bottom, there was a hoard of Souls collected outside of the sitting room door—all of Purgatory must have been there. A bright white light was focused into the room from some invisible spotlight behind the crowd, and there was a lot of serious conversation, crying and screaming, coming from inside.

"What is this all about, Liza? What's going on?" Liza pushed me down into the hall chair, so we could meet, eye-to-eye.

"It's your brother, Raychel. He needs your help." Suddenly, I was wide awake.

"Roger? Why, what's wrong with him?" I implored.

"He's crossing over too soon. There was a party, alcohol, drugs, and stupid choices. Now, your brother's lying in the emergency room, and he's not fighting. Usually we can see these things coming a mile away... but this time, he just got too stupid too fast, and we had no time to prepare. You've got to get him to go back."

I was stunned. Roger was reckless, true, but he was always in control. He never let things get too out of hand—never took his left hand off the wheel, or his right hand off the gear shifter. He can pull a 50mph spin and bring the car to a controlled stop—no rollovers, no injuries, no fatalities. This seemed strangely out of character for him.

"Not Roger... how could this have happened?" Liza squeezed my hand and drew my focus away from the room and back to her eyes.

"We can figure all that out later... right now, you've got to stop this."

"But how? What am I supposed to do?" I was shaking with insecurity.

"You have to talk to him, Raychel. You've got to tell him that it's not time yet. You've got to tell him to go back. You've got to tell him to fight."

"But how?" I had no idea what I was supposed to say. Roger rarely listened to me when I was alive, what made anyone think he would listen to me once I was dead?

"I really don't care how, just do it!" Liza screamed.

I stood up and began walking toward the door. "Make a hole!" yelled Liza with a voice bigger than seemed possible. The crowd parted like the Red Sea, and I walked through the walls of Souls toward my suffering brother. "Don't cross the threshold, Raychel," came Liza's voice from behind me.

When I reached the doorway, I could see Roger standing there, looking back on himself lying on the table. The doctors and nurses were working furiously with all the medical expertise in their vast arsenal. My parents and Roger's girlfriend stood near the door, weeping their pleas to him.

"Please don't go!" they said. "We love you. Please stay with us!"

It was then that Roger caught sight of me. A wide grin came over his face, and he let go a belly laugh that would have rivaled Santa's. "Raychel! How cool! Can you believe this? They're making fools of themselves. Look at them, they're losing their minds. You'd think I was dead or something."

"Roger, you are dead, well almost, and you have to go back. It's not time for you yet. You wouldn't like it here anyway, it's pretty dull. Lots of fog. You've got to go back." The white light from inside the Inn was growing brighter, and Roger was becoming a moth. "Roger, Stop!" My face held fear and anger, Roger saw it, and stopped.

"But I don't get it. You're there, and you look so good, Raychel. Why can't I come with you?" He was six again, and I knew I needed to use that to my advantage.

"Because you still have too much to do. Besides, what will the little bimbette over there do without you? She'd be lost. You can't just leave her all flummoxed like that—it's not nice." Roger took a step closer and somehow, reached out and grabbed my left wrist. He started to pull me toward him.

"Raychel, No! Don't cross the threshold—it's Limbo, once you go there, you can't ever get back, and neither will he if you cross over!! You'll both be stuck. It won't be pretty! Make him let go!!" Liza's voice was frantic now, she grabbed hold of my robe from behind, trying her best to tether me to Purgatory. Liza looked at the others around her. "Don't just stand there idiots—help me!"

A few more hands reached out to anchor me, and just in time, too. I'd nearly lost my balance and now, my left elbow was in Limbo. It felt a little strange, sort of that feeling you get when your foot falls asleep; all tingly and cold.

"But I hate it here, Raychel. Life is just too damned hard." I tried to soothe my little brother as best I could, while trying to maintain my footing in Purgatory. I had the sensation of being tethered to a fifty pound weight while standing on a tightrope.

"Roger, I know you have hard days, but every new day is a chance to make it better. Think of Mom and Dad over there." Roger turned his head to see our parents clinging to each other, weeping helplessly. "It's bad enough that I left them, you can't leave them too—at least not until they've recovered. My death is still too fresh for them, it's still too hard. You have to stay there and help them get stronger. You have to be a man now, Roger." He had a really strong grip on me now, both hands, clinging to my wrist as though it were the only life ring in the middle of the Bearing Sea.

The mayhem around me quickened my pulse and tightened my resolve. There were Souls all around me attached to my arms and legs like the lines from a sailboat moored to a dock during a hurricane. Liza was shouting orders, sounding a lot like a sled dog musher. I felt like I was the main attraction at a taffy pull. The scene would have been comical if the problem hadn't been so serious.

"Roger, you've got to let me go. It's not your time. Mom and Dad need you. The bimbette needs you... She's pregnant, you know. You don't want to leave her now." Serene surprise came over Roger's face. It was a look I never expected to see, but there it was. Could this have been what he was looking for—his purpose? I didn't have time to wax philosophic right that second, so I filed the thought away for later contemplation.

"She's pregnant? Really?" There was the young Roger again, just like that Hanukkah when he got Tonka trucks and Dad let him play in the snow with them all day.

"Yes, and you don't want to leave your child fatherless, do you? Come on, things will work out... just go back and deal with it. You're a strong guy; I know you can do this." At that moment, Roger released his vice grip on my wrist. I landed rear over tea kettle on the Souls behind me, as if the airlock had just been opened on the space shuttle.

Roger began to drift slowly back toward his body. "I love you, Raychel!"

"I love you too, Roger! Go be a great dad!" The bright white light faded, and the sitting room was a simple sitting room once again. I climbed off of the pile of Souls beneath me and staggered to the hall chair as the crowd dispersed.

Funny, I didn't remember a white light when I died... Another thought for later dissection.

"Very well done. But how did you know that his girlfriend was pregnant? I don't even have that information." I saw that Liza was confused, and I mentally patted myself on the back for the achievement.

"I don't," I said with a sly grin. "But if I know my little brother, and I do, the moment he becomes well enough, she will be. It was the only thing I could think of that I knew would get him to let me go. Sometimes, you just have to mess with his brain a little to get him motivated. It's been that way ever since he was a kid."

"That was quick thinking. Let's go get some breakfast and relax for a little bit;" suggested Liza.

"Yes... cocoa, cocoa, cocoa." I murmured. We staggered off to the kitchen; Liza was a little surprised at my ingenuity and was a little overwhelmed by seeing an actual episode of *The Ghost*

Whisperer. I suppose Hollywood is right, you can't make this stuff up.

I dragged myself into the kitchen and poured myself a steaming cup of cocoa. I'd been run through the emotional ringer first thing in the morning, and all without the benefit of chocolate, that's tough. Liza was busying herself getting the ingredients together for cinnamon French toast, with Challah bread, and I plopped myself down at the table, trying to make a little sense out of why it took an avalanche of Souls to save Roger's life.

"So, Liza, what just happened in there? I thought people couldn't cross over to Purgatory until they were ushered over by Edgar?" The warm cocoa felt good going down, although I wasn't sure where it was actually going. That wasn't covered in the Welcome Packet.

"Yes, usually that's true," said Liza as she whipped the egg mixture with a fork. "But there are exceptions to every rule. For instance, in this case, your brother made the choice not to fight; he gave up. That's still a choice, and it still falls under the Law of Free Will. Technically, he still gets to die, if that's what he really wants. But so often, you know, rash decisions like suicide are rarely what the person actually wants. It's a desperation or depression move." She dropped the first slice into the hot pan with a sizzle, making me wish I still had a tummy to growl so I could justify wanting it as badly as I did.

"He doesn't need an Usher to find his way up if he really wants it badly enough," continued Liza. "That's why we have the white light you saw. It's a homing beacon for those who want to die before their scheduled time. If we didn't have that, they'd never get to the Inn and we'd have more Souls wandering around Limbo than we'd know what to do with."

Liza set a plate of French toast and sausage down in front of me, and I began molesting my meal as though I hadn't been fed in decades. In between mouthfuls, I managed to create a few coherent sentences. "You said that usually this doesn't happen, usually you know that people want to change their death date in advance... How?"

"There's a schedule; usually the suicide watch cases are red flagged. We monitor them like we do funerals, just to keep on top of what's going on so we can be prepared to either turn on the beacon and welcome them in or try to convince them to go back. It's an automated monitoring system, but sometimes, the program misses a few. We try to catch them before they get lost in Limbo, but it's not always possible. It was a good thing you were still here, because we wouldn't have been able to recall you if you'd already gone out on your visitor's pass, and then who knows what would have happened." There was a frustration and a sadness in Liza's voice, as if she'd encountered this problem more often than she cared to mention.

"And on top of the defectors, Edgar and his team have a certain number of regular cases they have to reach each day, and bring them back—we've got about a hundred Ushers, they are stationed in Inns like this all over Purgatory—it's a pretty big place, it has to be."

I couldn't help but imagine a diligent, compassionate army of Little People with their Goon and Geek Squads strewn throughout Purgatory, each one with a cross-stitched pillow sitting on the foyer couch that read, "We Will Take No Soul Before It's Time".

"Anyway, we know who is supposed to come back through accident, illness, and other predicted endings. Most of that is prearranged so that we can keep Earth from getting overrun with too many people. Think of it as Humanity conservation."

I had finished my breakfast and was on to a second cup of cocoa. This idea of eating with no negative consequences was really nice. "Yeah, but there's a lot of starving and wasting away of Humanity going on back on Earth, not to mention war... why would you still need to schedule death for regular people like me? Wouldn't man's own stupidity take care of culling the heard?"

"Well, that's a nice thought," said Liza as she stacked our dishes in the dishwasher. "But the reality is that not everyone who is in a war or famine is living in the Detroit metropolitan area. Conservation means everywhere, Raychel, not just in Africa or Afghanistan."

"I suppose that makes sense. But who decides when someone is going to die, and by what means? Is all that figured out ahead of time, too?" It was difficult for me to dismiss the idea that the Hand of Fate controlled the moment of death. After all, it was the central theme in almost every religious story ever told.

"Well, basically, here's how it works. At the time of your birth, the Powers That Be divide people up into categories; geographical location, marital status, employment status, illness, and predicted despondency due to economic conditions; then they pull a lottery for each division and put the names and corresponding Device of Death on a calendar. The concept is really very simple, but in practice, it's a logistical nightmare, and I'm so glad it's not my job to organize it all. I just manage the people coming and going through this particular Inn of Purgatory and give them a place to let their Souls adjust before making that final choice."

I thought hard about this concept while draining my second cup, pouring myself a third, and rejoining Liza at the table. This was turning out to be a long day, and it was only nine o'clock in the morning. "So, the reason no one else was killed in my car accident is because it wasn't on the schedule for them to die on that day and by that method, just me?"

"Yup."

"Well that's just a little disenfranchising. I thought sacred, divine intention was the key player, when really it's just some old guys sitting around a table someplace drawing straws and scribbling your name in a day planner? What a perfectly non-glamorous process. Here I thought death was about destiny—when what it really is—is case management." My exasperation was showing, which is a nifty trick when you consider I didn't have a body to react to the sugar.

"I know... it's difficult to understand. You'd better get ready. You have to be in Heaven in at noon." Liza was nothing if not punctual.

"Fine. But this discussion isn't over." I got up from the table, trudged up the stairs and jumped into a hot shower. The steaming water and sudsy lather was just what I needed to revitalize my fatigued Soul. I'm not quite sure what it was I was washing, but it felt great, just the same.

Chapter Five
Prayer Fulfillment

After my shower, I had some time to think about Roger's suicide attempt, and I was furious! How could anyone—let alone The Powers That Be—allow such a flaw in their system? Sure, I expected clerical errors to happen on Earth; the place would be lost without them; but this was beyond making a simple mistake. I took my anger straight to Liza and Edgar.

"Look, what happened this morning with Roger—that was disastrous. Where's the suggestion box? I have a few choice words I'd like to drop in there."

"We don't really have one." said Liza, glancing tentatively at Edgar. "No one's ever thought to offer suggestions before."

"Okay then, take me back to the Gates. Call someone who's in charge, those Archangels maybe. If I can't talk to God, then I'll just have to settle for dealing with his flunkies instead."

"I don't know if that's such a good idea. We don't normally bother them. They're very busy, you know." Edgar said.

"I don't care how busy they are. This is important! My little brother almost ended up serving out his eternity in Limbo, and all because someone wasn't doing their job. I'm not happy, do you hear me?!" I was back to my fever pitch, arms flailing. Liza tried her best to calm me.

Edgar, in an attempt to save Liza from another of my meltdowns, took my arm and... I'm not sure what method of travel Edgar uses, but it was much faster than the walk I took with Liza. When we got to the Gates, we were met by Michael and Steve.

Michael was a normal enough looking guy, but not at all how Michelangelo had painted Angels. Michael had to have been several hundred years old, or maybe even thousands of years old, aren't all Angels really old? But he only looked to be about sixty. He walked with perfect posture and was well mannered—exactly as I had been told Angels would be. Michael wore a pair of Levi's 501 jeans, a comfy red flannel shirt and Docksiders. He had perfect blue eyes, salt and pepper gray hair and a little five o'clock stubble. His voice sounded like my father's: calm, even and warm. He stood relaxed with his hands in his front pockets, as if watching a pheasant lurching into flight from an overgrown cornfield.

Steve was not at all what I had expected from a Demon. No horns, no red hooded cloak, no cloven feet, no pointy tail, and certainly no fiery pitchfork. Steve appeared to be an average looking, thirty-year old. His voice was a little gravely as though it had been beaten up by too many cigarettes and too much whiskey. His brown hair looked like it was done by someone who didn't like him. His knee-ripped jeans hung about his middle without benefit of a belt which his rotund frame sorely needed; his team jersey had been so over-worn that now, his allegiance had become blurry.

"Look, you two; you've got some serious quality control issues. I mean, who's manning the store, anyway? Were you aware that my brother somehow made his way to The Twain Inn this morning? I'm told it was a 'mistake'. This is the afterlife—there aren't supposed to be any mistakes here, remember? This is where you're supposed to have it all figured out, complete control, that's what The Book said! Just what is the problem?" I was not happy, and I was not hiding it.

"Hey, look;" said Steve, "We don't control what kinds of retarded choices your brother makes. He can be as head-up-his-butt-stupid as he wants to be. That's Free Will, baby."

"That's true." agreed Michael. "As much as we'd appreciate it if people would keep to the schedule, if they choose to deviate from it, it's not a defect in the plan, just willful humans taking their Free Will for granted. We do the best we can to help them go back if they choose too early, as you witnessed with Roger; but really, there's not much we can do to preempt the situation."

"Well, so much for Angelic Omnipotence, eh? You two are a complete disappointment, you know that?" Disappointment was a huge understatement, but the only word I could spit out of my infuriated brain.

"Hey, it's not our fault your brother can't appreciate what he's got." said Steve.

"And besides," said Michael; "We can't be everywhere all at once, you know. We're Angels, not God, we have limitations!"

"Well, this little incident was quite traumatic for both my brother and me. I know I'm dead, I'm stuck with this insanity, but who knows how this will affect him. He didn't know what was happening to him. He could be emotionally and spiritually scarred forever. And how will this little brush with the other side of death affect how he one day raises his children? The ramifications from this one stupid little mistake could have long-reaching effects. Not to mention all the other newly dead Souls who are already incredibly confused by the misinformation that they've been given. They were forced to help fix the problem you allowed to happen. That's not fair to them! If there's any shred of truth to the 'energy of the collective of Souls' as your stupid little pamphlet describes; well then, I would bet that this morning's little foray into the land of poor management has drained a large quantity of your precious resources. Just how do you intend to prevent this from happening again, hmmm?" I was on a wild rant, demanding answers; although I somehow knew they wouldn't come.

"We can't prevent it, Raychel. That's what we're trying to explain to you." Michael spoke in a hushed voice that I'm sure was intended to deflate my inner tube of angst. "This is simply the Law of Free Will operating on all cylinders. We can help people who haven't completely crossed over to find their way back again; but once they make that final choice, the best we can do is explain their newly dead situation and help them make the best of it."

"Yeah, shit happens. So sad, too bad." said Steve.

The fog enveloped the two of them then, and they disappeared into the nothing. I looked at Edger, expecting him to come out in my defense, but he just shrugged his shoulders and said nothing. Confrontation was not his thing. We were greeted at the back door to The Inn by Liza who had a look of hopeful disquiet on her face. "How did it go?"

"Not great." Edgar sulked away as quickly as he could, working hard to avoid whatever I might be throwing at him next. Even though he chose an afterlife as a gentle envoy, I'm sure he didn't sign up for my ire. Admittedly, I wasn't utilizing all I'd learned from Dale Carnegie about winning friends and influencing people on this trip, that was clear, but could you blame me? I mean, dealing with the unknown of death is one thing; having to be completely reprogrammed after death is something else again.

"They're so frustrating! I wish there was some way that I could have known that the afterlife was so horrifically dysfunctional before I got here. It would have made things a little easier to take." I said, collapsing into the hall chair.

"Yes, well ... sorry about that." Although she tried, there really was nothing more that Liza could have said to make this experience any more logical for me. I wasn't so self-absorbed that I could blindly enjoy defying The Book and choose my destiny; and at the same time, I wasn't so feeble as to simply accept things as I found them. I'm sure I was just as frustrating to Liza and Edgar as Steve and Michael were to me. I trudged up the stairs and worked hard at continuing to be pissed off for what felt like an hour, until finally, I gave up and fell asleep.

"Well, it's time that you go off to visit Heaven." sang Liza while opening the window shutters to allow the diffused light of afternoon nothing flood across my eyes. "The shuttle will pick you up just inside the Gate. You'll be going to the Power Center. Here's your contact card. Just give it to the driver; he'll know where to take you." I sat up in bed and Liza handed me a small business card which read:

Department of Natural Resources
Power District, Building Five, Suite 4260
Tuan McCarell; Director

"The DNR; really?" I couldn't imagine what I would be doing with them or why Heaven would even have a DNR... I loved animals and the great outdoors just as much as the next guy, but I didn't think this was how my trip to Heaven would begin. "Four years in the Navy as a communications specialist, and then another seven with a manufacturer of forklifts can't possibly be of benefit to beavers and bears! Oh well, I've come this far, might as well make the best of it. I don't really have a choice, do I? Who knows, it could turn out to be a cushy government gig with easy hours and a nice pension."

Liza snickered and patted me on the back. Fifteen minutes later, after declining lunch, I was standing in front of Heaven's Gate, not sure I really wanted to go in. Who would have thought that there'd be trepidation about going to Heaven? The Gate opened, and I waved to Liza. "Save some of those brownies for me, would you, please?"

"Sure thing. Have fun." Liza smiled broadly as though she were sending off her youngest child to summer camp. The Gate closed silently behind me and the fog of Purgatory secreted her away once again.

I waited only about a second and a half, when a small bus appeared and the friendly driver welcomed me on board with a toothy smile and a perky radio-announcer voice. "Welcome to Heaven's shuttle. We'll take you anywhere you want to go, free rides for all. What's your destination, Miss?"

"Um, I'm going to the Power Center." I said, showing him the card Liza had given me.

"Excellent, that's just a quick little jaunt down the road." he said. "Sit back, relax, and enjoy the ride."

After finding a seat, which wasn't difficult in the completely empty bus, I closed my eyes and tried to seek out that imaginary spot in my head where my equilibrium lived. My search was fruitless. It must have been the altitude. When I felt the motion of the mini-bus stop, I opened my eyes to find myself under the ornate portico of a large office building. "Well, here we are, Miss. Enjoy your visit in Heaven. We hope to see you back again real soon."

"Thank you." I said, gingerly placing my feet for the first time on Heaven's ground.

As the bus pulled away, the glass doors in front of me glided open. A directory on the wall before me listed suite number 4260 as *The Department of Prayer Fulfillment*. "Holy Crap! When they said Department of Natural Resources, they weren't kidding!" I looked around, worried that my little outburst might have attracted unwanted attention. No one seemed to notice. I squinted at the business card in my hand, stared at the wall for a long moment, and then looked back to the business card again. "Well, this looks right; but..."

Just then, a security guard sashayed up alongside me. *Security Guards in Heaven?* I kept my disbelief to myself, not knowing what might offend whom, and how it might affect me.

"May I help you Miss?" Questioned the guard.

"No thank you;" I answered, waving the business card in the air and taking a quick step backward. "I'm all set." I turned quickly down the hall in search of the elevator.

****

The elevator doors opened to the fourth floor, a large sign read: *Department of Natural Resources* and hung directly in front of me. Before stepping into the hallway, I heard Jon Bon Jovi's voice singing "Who says you can't go home". The song triggered a memory of my grandfather and a conversation we had when I was twelve, on the day of my great-grandmother's funeral.

"All babies sleep in Heaven waiting for their perfect parents to be ready, so they can be born. So really, when you think about it that way," my grandfather whispered, leaning in close to me, "Dying isn't anything to be feared; it's simply going home again." In that same moment, it hit me strangely to consider muzak in Heaven's elevators; and then a new thought, *Wait, Heaven has elevators?* I stepped off the elevator and headed left.

After passing offices labeled *The Department of Childish Affairs*, *The ME Generation* and *Animal Husbandry*; I finally found suite 4260. As I read the title etched in bronze on the door, *Prayer Fulfillment Headquarters*, I had a hard time accepting that any of this was real. I paused a moment with my hand on the doorknob. *Could Heaven's greatest distinction really be nothing more impressive than a red-taped bureaucracy? What a letdown that would be.* I tentatively pushed my way through the door to discover the truth.

Inside I found a small reception area with a demure yet excessively pleasant woman sitting behind the desk. "Welcome to Prayer Fulfillment, you must be Raychel, we were told to expect you today. How was your trip? Did you sleep well? Have you had lunch? How nice to have you visit us! I'll buzz Mr. MacCarell and let him know you've arrived." The woman didn't give me a chance to answer any of her questions, which was fine, considering I wasn't exactly sure what I would say. "Mr. MacCarell; Yes, this is Eunice, in reception. Raychel has arrived. Certainly sir, right away."

There was no telephone, and there didn't seem to be an intercom system. *Angelic psychic connectivity perhaps? The weirdness factor is multiplying.* I hoped my uncontrollable mumbling was undetectable by the sweet, gray-haired receptionist. Eunice looked up at me over her glasses; "Please come with me, dear."

Her tone was less condescending and more motherly, and still, I had a hard time not being slightly irritated. *Irritation in Heaven, is that allowed?* I noticed that since I'd become newly dead, the voice in my head was speaking more frequently and much louder than usual.

Eunice led me through a door and past a row of cubicles, each filled with an industrious Soul typing feverishly on computers unlike any I'd ever seen before. I couldn't help but stop and stare at the remarkable technology. Not one face glanced up or noticed my presence. "We get all the neat toys up here," said Eunice, gently nudging my elbow ahead.

We continued on past a glass-walled room filled with about a dozen well-dressed men and women around a large oval table. Most eyes focused on one woman at the head of the room with an electronic white board and laser pointer, presenting what looked like sales figures. Fingers were furiously sliding across tablets and cell phones, and one particularly curious pair of emerald eyes followed me as I walked past. "It's like a marketing meeting on mute, all movement and no noise." Eunice giggled slightly, and I realized that I'd said that out loud. "Sorry." I let go a shy smile.

"Oh, no need, my dear. Everyone is a little surprised at first." Eunice reminded me of my elementary school librarian; a lovely woman with a high nerve-grating quotient.

As our tour continued, we waked past a water cooler with a few people milling about; a cafeteria filled with all the normal activity one might expect; and a young man pushing a chrome mail cart, laden down with small boxes and envelopes of every color and size. It all looked too familiar, and I decided that this must be some sort of hoax, the result of a well-planned practical joke and creatively camouflaged pharmaceuticals during the Halloween party the night before. And then I remembered, Purgatory. *I'm not sure even the best acid trip in the world could have created that.* But it was still a possibility.

Finally, we arrived at a frosted, wood-framed door, the name *Tuan McCarell; Director* etched on the glass in Scottish script. Eunice gently knocked upon the door, and with a slight twist of her wrist, opened it. "Miss Raychel, sir." I felt Eunice's hand upon the small of my back gently easing me across the threshold. The door closed behind me with a gentle click, and Eunice was gone. Across the room stood a slate-blue marble fireplace, with two mahogany leather wing-back chairs positioned nearby. The room was gently lit, though I couldn't find any lamps or ceiling fixtures. To the left hung an enormous window, though from my current vantage point, I couldn't see what it revealed. From my right came the sound of someone politely clearing their throat. I turned to notice Mr. McCarell sitting behind a large but simple pine desk, with a computer and a few pages laid out before him.

"Welcome to Prayer Fulfillment. I trust you had a good night's sleep. You're going to need it." Tuan was an interesting fellow. His broken Scottish accent and the kilt that hung around his waist as he stood to shake my hand, betrayed his authenticity. The fact that his red hair was more orange than red and he had that mischievous glint in his eye, made me consider again the likelihood that this was actually a hoax.

"Those RenFest crazies really outdid themselves this time;" I remarked just under my breath.

"No, Raychel, this is not a ruse. This is for real. I am Tuan McCarell, director of Prayer Fulfillment in Heaven. As has been explained to you, you have a visitor's pass to share the next seven days with us; getting to know Heaven so that you can make a sensible choice about where you'd like to spend your eternity. You have been assigned to this department rather than just turned out in the streets because we find that it is helpful to newcomers to have some hands-on experience with what goes on in Heaven before making their choice. Contrary to popular belief, Heaven is not all sitting around basking in the glow of doing nothing." Tuan puffed out his chest as though someone had just reminded him that his team won the championship; and then he continued. "One of our cornerstones is Community Service, and most of us actually have jobs up here—it's the only way we can live up to Humanity's expectations. And, truth be told, most Souls would be bored silly without something to fill their time. This is the department that most matched your skill set, and frankly, this is the area of Heaven that gets the most inquires. 'How and when do you decide to answer prayers', that sort of thing. We're a very popular department. But let me assure you, Raychel, you are indeed deceased."

I swayed slightly, feeling like I might faint, and found Tuan ushering me into one of the chairs next to the fireplace. The warmth of the fire soothed my... skin... abundant with goose bumps. "Just sit for a moment," he said, handing me a cup of water. "I know it's a lot to take in all at once. So many of us get jolted by the reality of dying—naturally, it's a shock to the system—not to mention the altitude."

I sipped the water, not really aware that I was drinking, and stared off into an unknown horizon, eyes fixed on the flames before me, but unable to focus. "This is not what I expected... not supposed to be this way... jobs in Heaven... computers... this is all wrong..." My voice trailed off into nothing more than a faint whisper. And then out of nowhere, the emotional outburst neither of us had expected arrived.

"Where are the wings!? There are supposed to be wings!!" I was clinging frantically to Tuan's kilt, and I needed an answer. This was the most important thing I could think of at this moment, as was clear by the panicked expression on my face. I looked to Tuan who returned my bewildered gaze with a hearty Scottish belly laugh, as gently, he began liberating himself from my clutches and easing me back into my seat.

"Oh child, we don't have wings in Heaven. Someone invented them long ago during a momentary lapse of reality and an evening of too much poetic license, but they've been long gone for centuries. We get around here the same as you, feet and legs. Wings, indeed! Ha!!"

I sat slumped in the chair as if someone had thrown me there, discarded rags and a worn-out shell. *This couldn't be real, it's insane to accept that it could be real... The Purgatory Orientation Video... The Gates... Michael and Steve... Liza... Free Will.* For someone who prized herself as being fairly analytical, the fact of the matter was, I felt completely out of my element here, and I was having a hard time making sense of anything from the past two days.

"Has it really only been two days?" My question was a weak attempt to try and put some clarity to time and space.

"Actually," replied Tuan; it's been just about ten days. We had to wait to receive your soul until after your family sat Shiva; it's the whole—respect the mourning process—thing. That's very big up here."

If it was possible for me to be any more confused—that statement did it for me. Pushed me off the *Cliff of Simple Confusion;* and right into the *Abyss of Absence of Cognitive Thought.* My head was swirling like toilet bowl water. "So where have I been all this time? I mean my Soul, where has my Soul been while my family and friends were eating kosher desserts and covering mirrors?"

"Purgatory. It's gotten a bad rap over the centuries, but really, it's not a bad place to hang out for a little while. The beds are comfy, and the food's not bad—and never a hotel bill. Not bad, really..." Tuan was almost talking to himself. There was a wayward yearning sound to his words; almost like he would have preferred to have stayed in Purgatory a little while longer... and then he caught himself. "Remember Liza; when she met you at the Gate, she said 'Let me take you back to your room'? You never caught that little past tense thing in there, did you? That's okay, few people ever do. Call it our own special form of jet lag." Tuan moved to the chair opposite me, and sipped a cup of tea that I didn't remember him making.

"Basically, you've been sleeping all this time."

I considered this notion carefully. "So really, when my parents told me they had to put my dog to sleep, they weren't kidding?" The idea of it validated my belief that euthanasia wasn't cruel.

"Yes, that's true. Except the process of moving to Heaven is a little faster for animals, few people sit Shiva for the family dog or cat. Snakes I think, are the only ones who go directly to Hell, but that's more of a legacy thing from way back." Tuan was rambling now, a little on the ADHD side; but that was okay with me. I was still having a bit of difficulty believing it was even partially true.

Me? Dead? And this is Heaven? Not possible.

Tuan gave me a moment. He explained to my blank stare that it was often difficult for people to adjust to the newness of being dead. "It never turns out to be the way that anyone expects—although expectations are funny things, usually motivated by some religious ritual or similar guilt-based teaching. There are an occasional few who are open and accepting, but I've noticed that those were the ones who usually subscribed to a more general spiritual path than those forced into one type of doctrine or another. The Atheists and Agnostics, though, they have the worst time of it. It's difficult to finally admit to a concept like Heaven and Hell; God and the Devil after you've spent your life avoiding it."

I had to admit, he had a good point.

"Well, I suppose we've put this off long enough. No point in prolonging the inevitable. Let me show you around the place, and give you some idea of what you'll be doing here."

Try as I might, I had a hard time managing more than a blank stare in Tuan's direction. I knew I was being rude, but I couldn't help it.

****

Tuan gently eased me to my feet and guided me to the large window on the far side of the room. "This, as you've learned, is the Department of Prayer Fulfillment. What you're looking at down there is the All-Religion Central Clearinghouse. This is where all of Humanity's prayers come in, get sorted and decisions are made about which ones will get attention. Well, they all get attention; just some of them actually get answered while others get filed away."

I looked through the window at the cluster of activity below. This could have been a mail room in any corporate office on Earth. One thing was very obvious—subtlety was not part of the design plan. The old maze of plastic mail tubes clinging to the walls and ceiling had been replaced by hundreds of desks and computer terminals coordinated by color, every color in the rainbow's spectrum, it seemed. Each section had at least a hundred workers intently focused on the screens before them. It was an enormous room! My eyes felt larger than normal, and I couldn't get them to blink. My voice was lost, and my brain a jumble of thoughts and questions. There I stood, mute and paralyzed, lost in cerebral defeat.

"Each group of computers handles a specific religion or philosophy, and the prayers that come in from those believers get sent up here to be sorted and entered into our system." Dozens of denim overall-clad clerks pushing chrome carts delivered small colored envelopes and boxes to each station. "The delivery people bring the prayers up from the Manifest Room, and deliver them here for recording and processing." Each person sitting at a computer station, wearing the a short-sleeved polo shirt of their group's color, opened the delivery and logged its contents into the computer, reading each and then typing with full concentration, but with a surprisingly relaxed speed. When they were done, the delivery was deposited into a trap door beneath their chair.

"You see, we really can't make any decisions about worthiness until we have had an opportunity to perform due diligence on each request, we can't just go granting prayers willy-nilly. We've found that computers cut down on the time involved. Everything used to be date/time stamped by hand, and then filed, but that just got too cumbersome. We were running out of storage space.

"Heaven, running out of space? Didn't think that was possible." My mumble was barely audible; Tuan missed it completely; I was glad.

"This way, we reduce our shelf space and maintain a more effective tracking history for future use. Once the packages are tracked, they are sent to the recycler and the materials are reused for future prayer manifests. You might say, Heaven's gone green."

It was then that I noticed the far right wall, three stories of glass looking out upon the picturesque landscape of Heaven; above the room, a dozen skylights dotted the ceiling allowing natural sunlight to dance about the room, eliminating any glare on the monitors. "Yes, definitely green;" was all I could utter.

On the back wall, directly facing us, hung a plasma screen that filled the entire wall, from wall to wall, from floor to ceiling, three stories tall. It reminded me of the giant screen in Times Square, but I knew this technology was far more advanced. Wouldn't it have to be? There was an olive green and sea blue world map projected on the screen, with hundreds of tiny colored dots, some flickering, and some solid. It was a stunning display of technology that seemed decades, perhaps centuries, before it's time. Tuan noticed the direction of my gaze and went on with his tour.

"That's the Big Board of Angel Activity. That's how we track which Angels are handling which prayer requests and in what part of the world. Each Angel is equipped with a GPS transceiver, and when a prayer assignment has been fulfilled, the Angel can be recalled and given a new assignment. It's important to track the Angels because we wouldn't want to dispatch too many Angels to a concentrated area—it would create media anarchy. Not to mention, we'd hate to lose anyone."

I was stunned at the torrent of activity below me. The operation met my brain with the speed of cold maple syrup dripping over hot waffles. The room was much like Wall Street; but here, people sat and typed rather than stood and hollered. Supervisors dressed in khaki pants, light blue shirts and a baseball style cap of their group's color. They walked among the rows of desks, stopping every so often to check progress or answer a question. There must have been a thousand people in that room. I couldn't hear anything, but I was certain introspective silence was not the prevailing wind.

"Well, that's it; said Tuan. "This is where you'll be working for a while." I was awe-struck. Sure, I had experience with this type of work, but this was beyond any project scope I had ever imagined. "Why don't I take you downstairs and introduce you to your team lead. She'll be happy to show you around and get you settled." At last, I looked away from the spectacle below me and managed a stuttered nod toward Tuan.

****

As we left the office, Tuan offered a quick hello to Eunice as we passed by. I could only smile. My voice was on hiatus. "Have a nice day!" called Eunice behind us, waving until we were out of sight. She really was overly perky, that woman.

We headed out of reception and took a left down the hall. "I hope you don't mind taking the stairs. I'm trying to stick to my exercise program."

When we entered the stairwell, I noticed it immediately—no echo. It was as if we had entered a vacuum. The familiar double clap of feet on tile moving down stairs, the reverberation of my own breathing, it was all gone. And then I realized, there was no echo under the cavernous portico, either. "That's odd." I held the words just out of notice; but of course, Tuan did.

"Oh, that. Yeah, it freaks everyone out at first. There are no echoes in Heaven. The Powers That Be decided they're redundant. We only need to hear things once around here to get it."

Arrogance... In Heaven... Really? Who would have thought. I kept that one to myself; although I wasn't completely convinced that Tuan didn't have some secret conduit into my brain.

When we reached the first floor, Tuan opened the stairwell door as a rush of sound, light and movement assaulted me in ways I couldn't begin to accurately describe. Every hair follicle on the outside of my body and every blood cell on the inside of my body stood at attention, waiting for instructions. The back of my throat was dry and sticky; my eyes began to flood with the protective tears produced from insufficient blinking; my mouth hung agape. Or at least, that's what would have been happening to me, if they hadn't taken away my good ol' reliable body!

Tuan bounced forward a little on his toes, hands clasped together behind his back—almost in self-restraint. "It's pretty nifty, don't you think? Not another place like it in all the known Universe. I've heard that Hell doesn't even have an operation this impressive. But I wouldn't really know, I've never been." I thought I heard a twinge of regret in his voice, but I wasn't sure I wanted to know that story. I had enough to deal with right now.

Tuan motioned toward one of the managers who immediately began making her way to us, full of smiles and attention. "This is Hailee. She'll be your team lead. Follow her closely and ask as many questions as you'd like. She's here to help you through the transition and get you working just as quickly as possible."

Hailee was an unfairly cute person; she reminded me of a wood nymph—brown, shoulder-length curly hair, a light olive complexion, and deep brown, twinkling eyes. She was nearly 5'1", about five inches shorter than me, yet jubilant in her stature. "Hailee, this is Raychel, take good care of her."

"Of course, Tuan. You can count on me." I shot a hesitant glance back at Tuan as Hailee led me by the arm deeper into the room. He had a satisfied smile on his face and was still bouncing on his toes, kilt swaying to and fro.

"He must really love this place." I mumbled.

"Oh, he truly does." said Hailee. *Does everyone here have super hearing?* If it were true, I hoped I could learn that trick quickly, it could prove useful.

"Tuan's been here the longest. Back when we first started out as just a small division; Self-Esteem Enhancement. But Tuan saw a bigger vision and built the department into what it is today. All this," she gestured wide with her arms; "This was all Tuan's idea. He requisitioned the technology and brought it all to life. Now, he's so well respected and valued by The Powers That Be, there's not much he won't be denied." Hailee's voice was filled with infatuation, bordering on worship. Clearly she "more than respected" him and his position here.

"Denial in Heaven, isn't that an oxymoron?" I was beginning to get my voice back, and my sarcasm along with it. It was my way of dealing with things I didn't quite understand, a habit holdover from my days in the Navy. Sink or swim, there is no float; or emotional weakness. Hailee ignored it.

"This will be your station." We had arrived at a tall, square table, much like those found in many bars back home, with an accompanying high straight-back chair, and a cushy leather seat. Table, chair, monitor, keyboard, mouse—everything matched in a steel-turquoise hue. The four positions immediately surrounding me, and in fact, all those within sight, held the same; an industrious turquoise-clad dead person typing furiously at a duplicate workstation.

Not half a moment later, a cart-pushing older man, clearly someone's grandfather, brought me a large collection of envelopes, two small boxes, and a short-sleeved polo shirt; the word 'Agnostic' was embroidered in bold black lettering on the left collar. The silent old man whizzed away with a broad smile before I had a chance to catch his name or thank him.

I took off my blazer, hung it over the back of the chair, and pulled the turquoise shirt on over my white one. It was a little big, but I expected that. The details were too perfect here for it to be too small; and I imagined that it would magically shift down a size when I tried it on the next day, without the other shirt on underneath. The absurd was beginning to appear normal to me, the expectation of it was being planted in my psyche. I wondered if that was the first step to accepting death, *or am I on to step fifteen now?* I couldn't be sure.

"Okay, so here's your job." Hailee took a deep breath and spoke with speed skating fury while the mouse darted from one icon to the next. It was like watching Chip and Dale lead a computer seminar, and Hailee played the part of both rodents.

"You open each envelope or box, call up the name on the database, enter in the request, the location of origin, and the delivery request—that is, the place and person where the prayer is to be fulfilled. Then, once all the information has been entered, put the envelope and boxes down the shoot under your desk. They'll go on to be recycled for use with future prayers. After all of your mail has been entered for the day, call up your activity log— that's this icon, and begin researching the requests. You'll check on the requester's history of prayers, both fulfilled and denied; locations, and frequency of prayers. Compile all this data into a brief, one paragraph summary using the summary feature, here. After you've done that, then write another brief paragraph explaining why you do or don't believe that this prayer should be fulfilled. And this is the tricky part, you have to use common sense, logic, and a little bit of love and compassion when writing these summaries."

I stared at the pile of packages before me. "Just a little compassion? Aren't these people's prayers we're dealing with here? They're deepest, most heart-felt wishes?" I stared at the strange icons peppering the monitor, trying to make sense of it all.

"As I said, it's tricky business. We have a quota to meet, areas that can't be too over-saturated with prayer fulfillment, and we have to make sure we don't step on Miracle Maker's toes. If we start getting in his way, he'll get very bent out of shape. The last time that happened, Germany had a Holocaust. Trust me, it's not a good idea." Hailee genuflected and looked to the skylights. This was serious stuff, and she was serious about it, that much was very clear.

"Once you complete your research and assessment, save it to the database and click the flag next to the entry, here. That will send it to my desk for review, and I'll send it up to Tuan for final approval. He coordinates Angel allocation with the team leads from each of the departments. Then dispatch sends the Angels down to Earth and they take care of business."

I looked around the room at the myriad of computers. "Couldn't this be done faster with, oh, I don't know, magic or fairy dust, maybe?"

"Actually, magic was part of the program at one point, and then the spells got too complicated, and one belief system got in the way of another, and the whole place went into a tailspin. No one was happy unless their specific brand of magic was chosen to be the sole prayer fulfillment implementer. It got really out of control—and that's when Tuan..." Hailee sighed gently as she gazed toward his office window three stories up. There was a look of longing on her face. The idea of unrequited love in Heaven seemed preposterous to me—but clearly, it existed. "Um... Oh, that's when Tuan decided to remove the emotional component of the process and he computerized the whole thing. It was a terrific breakthrough, really. The bickering has been reduced to almost nothing, and we're tons more productive now."

And here I thought Heaven was all about doing a lot of nothing. Who knew productivity was part of the plan?

"Well, I'll leave you to it. Just click the chat button on your desktop if you have a question or need any help. I'll be over in a jiffy! Have fun." Hailee disappeared into the sea of turquoise around us, and I was left alone and bewildered.

"Fun? How could so much pressure be fun?" I felt completely unprepared—but I picked up the first envelope from the stack before me, and dove in. "Sink or Swim, there is no Float!"

The first envelope was from a middle-aged man who was asking to win the lottery so he could pay off his gambling debts. The second was from an elderly woman who was asking that her ailing husband be relieved of his suffering, either through a cure or death, she really didn't care much which. The next held a plea from a young child to bring back her cat, Fluffy, from the horrible encounter with the clothes dryer—she promised that it was an accident. Another held a request for world peace, and still another for an end to global warming, and yet another was very graphic, asking for the brutal, painful and public death of the current President of Iran.

"How am I supposed to get through all this in one day?" I muttered aloud. I looked again at the pile of mail I'd opened, and at the pile yet to reveal its requests. It was an emotional deluge. *How do you fill a sardine can... one fish at a time. I guess I'll just go through it step by step, after all, I'm only here on a visitor's pass.*

Yes, I was talking to myself, but my guess is, I wasn't the first, and wouldn't be the last. I was not a fan of responsibility, especially when it involved affecting other people's lives in some monumental way. I liked being anonymous most of the time; it kept my life simple. Not a lot of fun, but simple. I really was outside my comfort zone here. Hands on attentiveness to someone else's deepest desires—I was not properly equipped. Even so, the day ended quickly for me, although I'd be hard-pressed to tell anyone how late it truly was if they'd asked. It seems Heaven didn't need clocks any more than it needed echoes. In fact, the only way that I knew the day was over was because the room got quiet, and Hailee was again chittering at my side.

Chapter Six
Heaven's Rules

"So, how did your day go? Any problems or questions?" Here she was again, a cheerleader on steroids.

"Well," I sighed; "I don't think I was as productive as I could have been, there's still all these to get through." I gently nudged the small stack of envelopes with my mouse and one fell to the floor.

"Oh don't worry too much about it," said Hailee with that eternal optimist tone in her voice. She picked up the envelope and returned it to the stack. "You'll do fine. It always takes new Souls a day or two to get speedy with this stuff. Not to worry. Hey, I got a note from Tuan this afternoon; you'll be staying with me during your visit. We can be roomies... bunkies... cohabitators... I haven't had a roommate since college; this is going to be fun. I'll show you everything, you'll choose Heaven, and we'll become great friends, I just know it!"

"Swell!" I feigned excitement, mostly because I knew it was exactly what Hailee wanted to hear. What I really wanted was a few hours to myself with the "Welcome to Heaven Guidebook" that didn't exist. My reality had been screwed with, and I was just going to have to make the best of it.

"Hey, are you hungry? It's dinner time, you know." The bustling room was nearly empty, and being so focused on the demolition of people's dreams, I hadn't noticed. "Why don't we go to my place and get a bite to eat?"

The two of us walked toward the door together and stepped out into the precise twilight of early evening. "Oh my..." was my only response.

The expertly manicured lawns, the soft, warm breeze, the twinge of gentle humidity... it was a meteorologist's nightmare—perfect weather—too predictable. Off to my left, I saw a small Japanese garden with a cheerful brook and a pair of Mandarin Ducks. Off to my right I detected the succulent aroma of a barbecue dinner; there was no mistaking the smell of charcoal and mesquite sauce dripping from chicken. From behind, I heard, "On your right!" just before a family of four passed on bicycles. It was like Central Park without all the crime, drugs and disease-laden homeless people. It was idyllic. It was beautiful. It was nauseating. Nothing about this place reminded me of home—or even seemed real.

A few minutes later, we arrived at Hailee's house. Without question, it was flawless. White picket fence, check. Pony in the back yard, check. Blue trim and shutters, check. Kitten on the porch banister, check. Puppy curled up on the front porch swing, double-check. *Oh my gosh, it's the Stepford house!* I let go a small cough to stifle the wretch that tried to leap from my throat.

"What was that?" asked Hailee.

"Oh... I... was just saying how much I loved your house." I lied. The mind-reading thing the brochure mentioned seemed to be true; thank goodness. But I still had to be careful, super hearing was real up here. Nonetheless, I was relieved to find that Free Will still applied to my thoughts.

"Oh, thank you! It's pretty keen, don't you think. I've always wanted a place like this—it's nice to finally realize that dream." Hailee's voice was wistful, it made me wonder what Angel processed her prayer requests... or rather... didn't. *How long has she been up here—who says 'keen' anymore?*

"You must be hungry after such a long day. What can I get you for dinner?" Hailee was peering into the fridge as if it's depths extended into the next room. "You can have anything you want, you know—the sky's the limit... actually, even the sky's not the limit, but you get what I mean. What would you like?"

I imagined Hailee didn't get many dinner guests. *She is far too friendly—or is that just the Angel thing coming out?* It was hard to tell. "Thank you, but I'm really not very hungry," I said. "What I think I need is just a good night's sleep." I knew Hailee's story would be a fascinating one, but I just wasn't up to it, and I got the impression that once she started talking, there was no stopping her. My head was spinning and I felt like I needed to decompress. There would be plenty of time for 'girl talk' tomorrow. Right now, I just wanted sleep.

"Well, of course. That makes perfect sense. How silly of me. Your room's just down the hall here, and there's a bathroom right across from it, just for you, fresh towels and everything. My bedroom's right next to yours. Just knock if you need anything." Hailee's words trailed into the hallway with her as I smiled and clicked the door shut.

Exhaustion had overtaken me, and I'd lost the ability to be polite. My eyes were mere slits as my body hit the bed. I fought hard to keep my wits about me, considering what happened the last time I went to sleep. But it was a struggle. Since my death, my body had been racked with an uncomfortableness that couldn't really be classified as pain – but it was certainly a high-level of irritation. My muscles yearned for relief, the soles of my feet throbbed whenever I walked, and the harassing static that had taken over my brain threated my sanity. I just wanted it all to stop. Praying for death wouldn't work, so I prayed for sleep instead. A few moments later, I curled into the comfort of the fetal position, surrounded by a nest of down pillows, and evaporated into a deep slumber.

After two days working at Prayer Fulfillment, my third morning in heaven brought with it an interesting mix of relaxation and weirdness. I took a tremendously therapeutic hot shower and a put on a fresh change of clothes—I never thought clean underwear would be a luxury—and then joined Hailee on the lanai for breakfast. Sun shone brightly through the garden trellis, accentuating the beauty of the purple passionflower and white hydrangea of early summer. I had been yearning for bacon stuffed waffles while standing in the shower, and I was tickled to find them waiting for me at the table. Maple syrup, orange juice, cocoa, and whipped butter; it was like Hailee had taken my order by osmosis and *poof!* Little did I realize just how true the *poof* really was.

"Good morning, Hailee. Thank you for the wonderful breakfast. But how did you know what I liked?" I started to dive into the sumptuous meal with absolutely no refinement whatsoever. I was starving!

"Oh, that wasn't me. Heaven is a really cool place. You see, if you put enough energy into a thing, it will happen for you. Just think a think hard enough and it will happen." Hailee spoke with a distraction not easily hidden, as she sipped her juice and skimmed the morning newspaper.

Although I couldn't read the paper from my vantage point, I imagined the headlines of the Heavenly Rag; *Angel Lost GPS In Brooklyn—StarCab Guides Him Home*, or *Canonization Pot Luck Tonight—Welcome To Saintville: Mother Theresa*, or maybe even *Chuck Heston's Return To Film In The Original Brothers Grim; Cane & Able*. It made me wonder if journalism in Heaven might be more interesting than Prayer Fulfillment... *was job reassignment an option?*

Hailee absentmindedly rambled on. "My mentor told me it was part of *Heaven's Eternal Reward Policy*. Of course, it doesn't work for everything—your thinks need to be Heaven approved—but if you choose this place for your eternal address, you kinda already know the guidelines."

We cleared the dishes together to the kitchen sink, and put the leftovers in the fridge. "I'm pretty impressed. Heaven is much different than I had imagined... most definitely different than all those religious zealots had painted it to be; but it certainly is nice, there's no getting around that." I stood at the kitchen window, watching the colt kick up its heels as it ran through the paddock. It was a story book scene, one I never thought I'd live to enjoy... and in truth, I hadn't.

"Heaven's not always so great, you know. I mean, yeah, it's beautiful and everything—but it's pretty dull. It's always the same thing day after day; perfect food—exactly when you're hungry; perfect weather—even when it's raining—it's a nice warm rain; and the most restorative sleep I've ever had. And that's it. No spontaneity, no pizazz; and no surprises. But... it's got to be better than the alternative, right? I mean, every day we get to do work that really benefits a dysfunctional Humanity on Earth, and sifting through all those envelopes can be an inviting distraction from the unblinking monotony of perfection."

Who is Hailee trying to convince, herself or me? The jury was still out on that one. *Amazing. Regret in Heaven. Who would have thunk.*

After my experience yesterday with her on the Prayer Fulfillment floor, I never would have thought it possible; but there it was—a bundle of puss-filled regret oozing from every orifice of Little Miss Devotion. I felt sorry for Hailee. Loneliness in Heaven had to be a real let down.

****

A little Harry Connick Jr. music began to linger in from the living room. A sultry, New Orleans jazz tune. "So, what do you want to do today?" The quick distraction of domestic chores was all it took for Hailee to return to her normal chipmunk persona.

"I thought we had to go back to work... prayers don't take holidays, do they?" I asked.

"It's Saturday, silly. We don't work today." Hailee dropped her newspaper into the recycle bin and pulled out an Oreo from the cookie jar.

"Saturday—The Sabbath—isn't that when most people do the bulk of their praying? I would think this is your busiest day." *Heaven is confusing.*

"Well it is, but we have an specially trained crew who work the Sabbath. They've been doing this for centuries, they're really speedy, and they're allowed to make fulfillment decisions without authorization. It needs to be that way, otherwise, the backlog would be immense. There's a special cadre of Sabbath Angels to handle the fulfillment on Earth, too. They're a crack team—really amazing. I wouldn't worry too much about it. So, what would you like to do?" Hailee was blandly confident. It was clear that she'd been around quite a while. Not much seemed to phase her.

"Oh, I don't know... do you have putt-putt?" I was trying to be funny. The notion of a work week in Heaven just seemed ridiculous. Days off in Heaven... let alone work... the whole thing was backward. Hailee didn't get the joke.

"Of course, we've got putt-putt. But wouldn't you rather do something more interesting? Something a little more 'out there'? This is Heaven, after all." She chirped.

The notion of looking outside the box in Heaven struck me strangely. Throughout my life, I'd been taught to think within the confines of religious doctrine when fantasizing about eternity; and now I was being given the opportunity to mold it to my liking. It was odd. Too odd. "Honestly, Hailee, I'm having a problem grappling with the notion that I'm supposed to choose Heaven over Hell—or vice versa. Even the simple thought of having a choice has got my brain turning somersaults. I mean, this isn't something you're ever prepared for. It's not like they teach you this in HomeEc. They don't teach you about funerals, let alone the nuts and bolts of dying. And religious school is no better. They're great at regurgitating the Old Book, but they don't really do anything to get you looking forward toward eternity; at least, not in any real sense of it. How am I supposed to decide?"

"I don't know... Would it help you to talk to someone else who has had to make the choice? Maybe there is a friend or relative up here, someone whose opinion you admire, who you think is smart, or just simply makes good choices? Would that help?" Hailee offered.

The idea of talking to someone else about the notion of Free Will was indeed enticing to me. There were a lot of people who might be able to give me some insight... but who to ask? "Yeah, I think that might help... it might give me a little extra perspective, at least."

"As I understand the rules... you're allowed to meet with at least three people that you already know and as many strangers as you want before making your choice." Hailee recited.

I had fixed my gaze on the colt throwing up its hooves in the paddock and the kitten turning somersaults as it played with a grasshopper, sort of half listening, when the word "rules" made it to my brain. I blinked hard. "Wait just a second, Rules? There are rules?" Intellectually, I knew that there were rules governing Heaven, how could there not be? But in light of the fact that nothing else that I'd experienced since I'd gotten here had been what I'd expected... I just assumed that expecting real rules was wasted energy.

"Well, of course there are rules, silly. This is Heaven, after all." In that moment, Hailee sounded a little like a drunken coed. She looked at me with a ridiculous left-sided cock to her head, reminding me of a puppy who'd just heard a dog whistle for the first time.

"So, what are the rules... I mean, I should probably know them before I get myself into trouble."

"Yes, I suppose that would be a good idea." Hailee poured two glasses of water from the sink, dropped a couple ice cubes into each glass, and moved to the kitchen table. She sat there for a moment until I sat down, too. The look on Hailee's face was that of a student recalling important information before a final exam; a little confused, a little hopeful, and very stressed. Hailee bit her lip.

"Well, there's the rule of Common Sense. That's a pretty big one up here. Don't do anything REALLY stupid, and you should be fine. Do you know about the Darwin Awards?"

The Darwin Awards? Was she serious? "Sure, people so stupid that it got them killed?" I said.

"Yeah, that happens up here sometimes, it's not pretty. There's a memorial in the town square to remember those lost to stupidity. Heaven isn't Indy without walls, you know. You can still crash and burn." She said solemnly.

"Good to know." I made a mental note. *Don't run into the walls.*

"Oh! We can't forget The Big Ten; those go way back. It's all the standard stuff you learned as a kid; the first one, don't kill anyone; in Heaven, that kinda nominates you for a Darwin Award."

"Okay, don't be overly stupid and don't kill people, got it. What's next?"

"When you were mortal, if you had a soft spot for some of those other gods, you know, Zeus and the like; chalk it up to childhood fairy tales and mythological distraction, and let it go. There's only one God up here, and you know who He is." Hailee had a very serious look on her face—like the one you'd find on a four-year-old's face when they discovered losing something down the toilet for the first time—bad plan.

"Well no," I said. "We haven't actually met yet." I said, half-hoping I'd get a response. Hailee continued, near absentmindedly.

"He's really touchy about that one, so don't even press the issue—it'll never work out in your favor. Oh, and he's pretty big on the no idols thing, too. Divas aside, idols really don't have a place up here. Way too much ego to deal with."

I took mental notes as if I were the new kid in an elite boarding school playground. All the details I could get now would certainly make life here easier in the long run, and since there really wasn't a "Heavenly Welcome Guidebook", Hailee was probably my best source of survival information.   "Let go the Ego, got it!"

"Um, don't covet stuff; wives, husbands, other people's special stuff. Coveting is a big no-no up here, too. They figure that they've given you everything your heart's desired, made it super easy to enjoy life, so you really shouldn't want for anything—so simply put, don't indulge in jealousy. It's a big time-suck, and completely non-productive. And rumor has it, He takes it as a personal insult; you know, the whole, "what have you done for me lately", attitude just isn't His favorite."

"Not a Janet Jackson fan, alrighty, then." Again, the joke was lost to the ether.

Hailee rolled her eyes skyward, as if recalling writing on a chalkboard. "Okay, the next one; honor your parents." I thought back to my time at home, and then the military. This one didn't seem too difficult to understand, or to follow; I'd had lots of practice. "Yeah, I'm pretty familiar with that one; no back-talk, right?"

"Yup, that's it. That goes for supervisors like Tuan, too. They put those guys in the same category as parents up here 'cuz in some cases, your parents may not be here yet, or maybe they've made a different choice."

"My parents, choose Hell? How weird would that be?!" My face took on the appearance of a first encounter with horseradish and the thought made my head swim.

"Also, The Head Guy, well, He is pretty secure about his power position here, and really doesn't like that challenged. You know, it's the same old story... be reasonable, do it my way. You've got to remember, he's the original engineer."

Oh, Hailee could make a joke, too. I giggled to reward her. *I was wondering where my Dad came up with that one... now it all made perfect sense! Too bad I had to wait for death to get it, my childhood would have been a lot easier with that little tidbit of info in my back pocket.*

"Well, I suppose that about does it." Hailee got up to put her glass in the sink, and I caught her arm.

"But you said the Top Ten. If I'm remembering my Sunday School days, I don't think you mentioned all of them. What about the others?" Hailee returned to her chair, and smoothed out the wrinkles on the tablecloth in front of her. Clearly, this conversation made her uncomfortable. But I couldn't decide if it was because she had things to hide, or just disliked rules in general.

"Well, the others, you see, um... they're really not major rules... never really huge like the others. Oh, don't get me wrong, they're important too—just not... um... vital." Her face sunk a little, sensing my disappointment. I got the impression she didn't like disappointing people.

"So, don't take the name of the Lord in vain, that's a minor request?"

"Yup, it simply boils down to If you can't say anything nice, bite your tongue." *Another one out of Dad's playbook. How did he know this stuff?*

"Okay, what about observe the Sabbath day and keep it holy; how does that one fit in?" I asked.

There was a small smirk on Hailee's face, as if she were remembering an inside joke. "Oh, that's just there to make sure people don't overwork themselves and die from stress. There have always been a lot of Type A personalities on Earth; that's not a problem up here."

"Okay... What about don't steal and don't commit adultery? What about those?" Curiosity was looming large... nothing was as I expected.

"Well, those sort of fall under the whole don't covet stuff thing. If you don't have jealousy about other people's things, or their loved ones, stealing and adultery sort of become moot, wouldn't you say?" It made sense, in some strange, twistedly logical way.

"And what about that last one, you know, the one about not bearing false witness against your neighbor; how does that one work into Heaven's Rules of Order?"

Again, Hailee let go a sly smile. "Oh, that's the easiest one... don't be a tattletale. No one likes a snitch. Mind your own business, do what's right, and let the chips fall where they may."

I was a little uneasy with the smiling Hailee and what it was she wasn't saying... but I reassured myself that eventually, I'd find out, one way or another. It's so much fun being the new kid in town. *Not.* There were a few moments of silence between us while I tried to memorize everything I'd just been told.

****

"Well, I suppose we'd need to make a list of people you know who have died, and then somehow figure out if they've chosen Heaven or not." Hailee said.

"What?" I was in a distant, emotional stupor.

"Your friends or relatives? We need to figure out who might be around so you can go see them, silly!" Clearly, Hailee was more excited about this little adventure than I was. I felt a great deal like I'd had one too many Long Island Iced Teas.

"Um, okay. How do we do that?"

Hailee thought for a moment, dunking an Oreo in the glass of milk she'd just poured. She really loved her Oreos. Her face was a little scrunched, as she pondered the process. "Well... it should be quite simple. After we decide who to look for, we would need to go to the Registrar of Deeds, and find out who on your list decided to stay. After that, we can easily find their addresses in the yellow pages and..."

"Wait, you've got the yellow pages up here?"

Hailee slid a small smirk between her lips. "Well sure, you really can't be someone until your name's in it, you know." *Ah, so Hailee could be funny, too. That's nice.*

"After that, it's just a matter of knocking on doors and finding out who's home. But we'd better get a move on. It'll take half a day just to get through the Registrar's office, and then once we verify that who we're looking for is up here, who knows how long to go through the yellow pages; even though ours is electronic and cross-indexed, it'll still take some time to find out where they live. Did I mention Heaven's a big place? And then, if they're not home, we'll have to look for them using the GPS locator." Hailee rinsed her glass and tucked it in the dishwasher.

"Wait, GPS?" I looked at Hailee as though she had just sprouted a second set of arms.

"Well sure, you really didn't think Bill Gates invented that too, did you? How else do you think we can find each other up here? We should get started; you've only got six days left."

Six days... it seemed like eternity!

"Okay so, who's on your list?" Hailee's next question hit me with wind-knocking force, square between my shoulders. "Who's dead... and more importantly, who do you think would have chosen Heaven?"

I always thought this was a simple question to answer, until faced with the reality that we are not assigned, but instead, choose. It was a little weird. I sat down at the table, and Hailee grabbed a note pad and pen from the kitchen drawer and joined me; a canary-eating cat grin on her face, ready to record all our exciting Angel Scavenger Hunt clues. "You should probably make a list of six, just in case everyone you're looking for isn't here. That way, if you find all six, then you can narrow your list down to your favorite three." *So, Hailee could be clear-headed and logical too? Who knew?*

"Well, there's my friend Meghan. She died in an evil house fire about ten years ago. She was a good friend, we grew up together. There's that really cute Navy pilot I spent a six month on deployment with, Thaddeus Macintyre. It would be nice to reconnect with him again. We had a good time together..." My voice dimmed as I swam deep through thoughts of romantic nights splashed between horrific days on an aircraft carrier. And still, they were nice memories.

"Um... Raychel... Back to Heaven, please;" nudged Hailee.

"Oh, sorry. There's Uncle Seymour; my Dad had always talked about his older brother like he was God..." Hailee winced and I quickly added, "But he was never completely serious about the comparison—he just really admired Seymour, that's all." I hoped my quick retraction wouldn't get me into trouble with The Powers That Be. Hailee dropped her shoulders and sighed in relief as though I'd caught it just in time. I took a deep, contemplative breath, hoping the lighting wouldn't strike and tried to move on. "Grandma and Grandpa would, of course, be good people to talk to; they always gave me good advice."

"Okay, that's five... who's the last one?" Hailee looked up from her note pad expectantly, as though I was about to give her the final winning name at the Tony Awards.

"Um..." This was tough. I knew a couple other people who had died since my college days, but given the way they partied at school, I was dubious about whether or not they'd actually choose Heaven. I figured that a safe bet would be a good choice, and so I gave Hailee the name, "Mrs. Mulrooney, my tenth grade Philosophy teacher. She always seemed to have all the right answers. I heard that she died a couple of years ago. Let's put her on the list."

"Alrighty, then. That's six people that we can search for at the Register of Deeds. We'd better get a move on, they'll be closing soon, and this is not always a 'bunny-quick' process." Hailee folded up the little piece of paper, stuffed it into her pocket and checked her watch. She grabbed my hand we ran out the door. The Angel Scavenger Hunt was about to begin.

****

A two minute jog down the street brought us to the Tram stop just as the last Soul in line was about to board. "Thank goodness, we made it," wheezed Hailee. We took two seats just inside the door, facing the aisle. Heaven doesn't have cars. Lots of bicycles, lots of people walking about, but no cars, no motorcycles and no scooters; nothing with a combustion engine. The tram lurched into motion and the silence chaffed at my ears like cotton against sandpaper, leaving bits of fluffy white stuff behind to clog my perception.

I didn't fully realize the scope of Heaven's acreage until we started on our trip toward downtown. Horizons seemed to go on forever. Mountains in the extreme distance were so immense they appeared to be only a few feet away; and the lake we passed seemed more ocean than lake. Apartment buildings, townhouses and condominiums were conspicuous by their absence. Houses with generous yards created a patchwork urban utopia. Closer to the city square, the office buildings, shops, markets... they all had open windows! This was a novelty to me. In the past half century, Humanity had shunned windows that opened in order to maintain climate control. There were none of those glass traps here. *How nice.* I thought to myself. *Pristine and perfect, there didn't seem to be a flaw anywhere.* Very quickly though, I understood that Hailee's comment about Heaven's monotony was an understatement.

"Hailee," I said, how long until..."

"Shhhh..." she said, her head bowed in prayer.

I looked around and discovered that everyone's head was bent toward their lap in solemn silence. I felt guilty about not joining them in whatever prayer of thanksgiving it was, and tried to think of something to be grateful for. That's when I noticed that it was technology, rather than reverence, that had kidnapped their voices. A tablet or cell phone lay gently in every lap, fingers tracking quietly across the smooth surfaces. I thought Heaven would be filled with the lively art of friendly conversation; when actually, it was filled with the stoic silence of disinterested Souls sitting next to one another as they waited patiently to reach their destinations. The angelic disposition I had yearned to find in Heaven's residents had gotten lost, or at the very least mismanaged, through the upgrade. It was a real disappointment.

Traveling closer to the square, we passed an enormous plasma screen billboard calling the faithful to worship. A single white dove against a pristine blue sky flew over a post-card perfect ocean scene. "Be Ye Righteous and Attend" was all it said; and yet the message was very clear. The colossal, naturally inviting echo of Frank Lloyd Wright's Taliesin, resting gently just below the sign couldn't have been anything but Heaven's House. There was no getting around the fact that although your imagination wanted to believe that services were held in the rolling fields of the Old Testament under blue skies and warm sunshine; the fact of the matter was, Heaven had a mega-church; and there seemed to be only one.

How strange; back on Earth, there was a house of worship— or a gas station, which was almost the same thing—on nearly every street corner. I was stupefied by the idea of worship in Heaven. *So, the faithful gather up here. That makes sense. But... where... how... and which doctrine?* There was no end to the questions. It made me wonder if this was how new Souls felt for the first time, when arriving on Earth... confused and overwhelmed. When the tram stopped and we climbed off, I looked at Hailee and said; "What was that all about? Why wouldn't you talk to me back there?"

"Oh, I'm sorry, I forgot to tell you; there's a policy of no talking on public transit. The Powers That Be are very sensitive to noise pollution, and they've made it clear that too much talk is simply unnecessary. With tablets and cell phones we can still hold conversations with each other, without thrashing the open air with vulture-like chatter. You'll get yours when you choose Heaven as your eternal address. They're standard issue. By the way, that young man, with the multiple piercings, two seats down from you, he thought you were cute."

"Uh... thanks." I said, as the tram disappeared around the corner.

****

The Registrar's office was large and incredibly imposing. It reminded me of the ancient Coliseum of Rome, only square... massive and meant to stand forever. Unlike the other buildings around town, this one had no windows. It was an information fortress, guarding carefully against any leaks. There was a uniformed, sumo wrestler-sized guard, smelling faintly of smokehouse charcoal, standing silent sentry at the front door. He gave us a gentle, Don Corleone smile and a look that reminded us we were being watched as we passed by.

Inside, the cavernous space was illuminated and warmed by sunlight cascading through the vaulted glass ceiling hanging ten stories overhead. Fifteen feet in, a wrought iron double staircase met at the mezzanine. At that level, and all around me as well, were rows of bookshelves, not unlike Earth's Library of Congress, tall and robust, filled with volumes of every size and binding material. Occasionally, there were arranged a small grouping of chairs flanked by low tables and Tiffany lamps. As my eyes tracked to the ceiling, I could see four or five such floors winding around the perimeter, beautiful iron railings holding its contents safe from the plunge to the foyer below. Above those, more floors with glass walls looking down to the marble floor under my feet.

Probably offices, study rooms and meeting spaces. I imagined. In the center of the space was a hub with several computer kiosks stretching out like branches from a mighty oak tree.

"In case you were wondering," said Hailee. "This is Heaven's Tree of Life. Everyone who lives in Heaven is in the database; their name, photo, address, date of arrival, and a brief bio. There's also a historical file for everyone from their time on Earth. Some call it a "Sin File"—but you have to get special permission from The Powers That Be to access that information."

I was stunned. *Humanity in the afterlife has been digitized. It isn't a book, it's a mainframe.* I wondered how that might change the blessing at Passover... "May you be digitized in the kiosk of Heaven." It just didn't roll off the tongue as gently as the old "May you be inscribed in the Book of Life". There was a certain romance in tradition. Before each kiosk stood two tall chairs, similar to those at Prayer Fulfillment, and each had a screen that danced with Heaven's logo, the Dove of Peace. As we approached one of the kiosks, I noticed a small red Apple insignia on the lower right corner of the terminal.

"Apple?" I said, looking confused at Hailee.

"Yeah, pretty cool, eh? Steve hasn't been with us very long, but it's amazing what you can build with tenacity." She pulled out the chair and typed her login information. I sat down next to her and watched her go to work. Hailee pulled the slip of paper with the names we'd listed from her pocket and typed the first into the terminal. At her tap of the enter key, a robotic whirring could be heard in the distance, and a few minutes later, an SD computer card was delicately placed in Hailee's hand by a grapefruit-sized hovering luminescent sphere and its two tiny robotic arms.

"Thank you." Hailee said, taking the tiny chip from the robot's little fingers. It hovered there, humming a little song, as Hailee tucked the chip into her tablet and downloaded the data. She returned the chip to the sphere, and it disappeared from the direction it had come. One by one, Hailee typed in the names, downloaded the data from each chip, and handed them back to the sphere. When they were all downloaded, Hailee said, "Thank you, again. Have a nice day." And as if it had understood, the little whirring thing pulsated magenta then blue, chirped, and hovered on its way. *Heaven's technology really is quite fascinating.*

"Okay," said Hailee. "I've got all the GPS coordinates for the people on your list. The only one who isn't in Heaven turns out, is

Meghan. Seems she made another choice."

"I wouldn't have expected that one." I said hesitantly.

"Well, people do some unexpected things sometimes. But the good news is, Uncle Seymour and Mrs. Mulrooney are pretty close by. Who would you like to visit first?" Hailee asked. I figured that family would probably be a better first choice.

"Let's look up Seymour." I said to Hailee.

"Okay;" she said, looking at her watch. "The next tram will arrive in two minutes." We headed out the door to wait.

****

The short tram ride to Uncle Seymour's place was uneventful. I tried to keep to the no noise pollution thing, and did my best to remember all the questions I had for another time when Hailee and I could talk freely. The only problem was, memory doesn't work the same way in Heaven as it does on Earth. The same triggers don't work. Almost nothing is familiar... the sights, the smells, the sounds. It's a little difficult to get used to... a little difficult to form new associations and brain files to keep them all in. Even the brain doesn't work the same way up here. It was only day two, and I was pretty frustrated.

Seymour had a nice little house. Not unlike my grandparent's place. It was a moderate, three-bedroom, red brick with white trim and a two-car garage in the side-yard, which I'm sure didn't house a car. Hailee and I walked up to the front door and she rang the bell... an actual bell, not a button. It was a bronze ship's bell, the kind we had for years on the side of our house when I was growing up. My mother used to ring it to call us in from playing with our friends at dinnertime. But Hailee's ring brought no one to the door. Hailee looked at me with worry on her face. I know she didn't want to disappoint me.

"Let's look around back;" she said, feigning chipmunk optimism.

Seymour nearly slammed into us as we rounded the corner. "Sorry. I was out back tending to the garden," he said. "Took me a couple of minutes to get off the ground." He was a tall man, nearly six-foot-four with brown hair, blue eyes, and a carpenter's build. He was slim and muscular all at the same time. Immediately, I saw the family resemblance. He and my father could never deny they shared DNA. His hands were huge but gentle. My hand was swallowed up in his, as he shook it, and Hailee made the introductions.

"Seymour, hello. I'm Hailee, and this is Raychel, your brother's daughter." There was a relieved excitement in Hailee's voice. She was happy she'd fulfilled her promise and found me someone I knew. I'm sure she felt she'd gotten me one step closer to convincing me to stay in Heaven. "She's in town on a visitor's pass."

"Well, Raychel, the last time I saw you, you were no bigger than a bug. Look at the wonderful woman you've grown into. How long have you been in town?" Seymour's voice was genuine and comforted me like the French horns in Tchcovsky's Peter and The Wolf. His smile was infectious, and I couldn't help but smile back.

"This is just day two, I think. But so far, I'm having a good time. It's not at all what I expected, though." I replied.

"Yeah, that's not going away anytime soon. My advice? Let go of normal; it doesn't exist up here." Seymour chuckled.

"Oh, Seymour, you know that's not true;" chirped Hailee, giving him a little jab in the arm.

"Okay, it's not true;" said Seymour, nodding his head up and down, while silently mouthing, "Yes it is".

I broke out in a giggle that could not be stifled. Even after this brief encounter, I could see that Seymour was everything that my father had described. I was looking forward to getting to know him better.

"Well, I'll leave you two to visit for a little while. Seymour, can you help Raychel catch the tram back to my place when she ready to come home? I'm in the Prayer Fulfillment District." I could see that Hailee was a little uneasy, almost like sending her youngest daughter off to preschool for the first time. It was sweet and annoying at the same time.

"Sure, I'll make sure she gets back safe and sound;" said Seymour, flashing a smirk to me that said he thought it might be more fun to get lost.

"Okay, and... take it easy on her. She hasn't been dead that long, you know," warned Hailee.

"Not a problem, Hailee. I'll take good care of her. After all, she's family." He said, wrapping a large, entertainingly protective arm around my shoulder.

"Thank you." Hailee walked away, and we watched her board the tram a few yards off.

"What a ninny that one is. Where'd you find her?" Seymour asked, a playful tone in his voice.

"It wasn't by choice. She was assigned to me." I replied.

"Oh, I'm sorry." Seymour's sarcasm was a welcome change from the chipmunk cheering squad. "So, not to be nosy, but how'd you get here, anyway?"

I animated the accident with my hands. "Me in my Smart Car... fertilizer truck... squish." I thought the short version would be easier. Besides, I wasn't sure he wanted to hear the whole, long story; and I wasn't sure I wanted to tell it.

"Tough break, kid. But, hey, it's nice to finally meet you! How's the family?" Seymour led us toward the swing on the front porch and we sat down to talk. The gentle sway of the swing and Seymour's friendly, easy-going disposition made it easy for me to imagine that we'd known each other forever.

"Oh, the family's fine. Roger tried to crossover the other night, too early. He's not real bright. I got him to go back, but it wasn't easy. Don't ever want to live through something like that again. It was just a little weird. Mom and Dad are the same. Mom's still an emotional over-achiever and Dad is still holding down the fort. Grandma and Grandpa passed a few years ago... "

"Yeah," said Seymour. "They live down by the lake. I see them every once in a while. We try to have dinner together occasionally."

"That's cool. I'd love to see them again," I said. "But I don't know if I'll have time on this trip. Things have been pretty hectic since I got here."

Seymour shook his head and looked out across the front yard. "Yeah, I tried to petition The Powers That Be to extend the visitation to fourteen days a few years back, but they're pretty stubborn. All caught up in rules and traditions. I think it's a bunch of malarkey, but what can you do?"

"Say, I'm meeting a bunch of my friends for lunch, would you like to tag along?" asked Seymour.

"Sure, that sounds great." I said.

We walked a few blocks to a nice little outdoor cafe. Seymour's friends were all there, and they greeted him with a fraternity brother's welcome.

"Friends, I'd like you to meet my niece, Raychel. Raychel, this is Robert; he was a rocket scientist for NASA on the Apollo project. Sam here was a brick layer for a general contractor. This is Anthony, he used to be a Priest for the Holy Catholic Church." Seymour put great emphasis on the priest's title, as though it was a terrific teasing point. The priest shared a shy smile while the others jabbed at his shoulders or patted his back. "George here used to be a cardiac surgeon; and this is Jon, a great, but unknown politician of America's debilitating Great Depression."

"Hey, lay off, that was not my fault!" rebuked Jon.

Jon stood and held a chair out for me. "Thank you, Jon. And if it's any consolation, I don't blame you." I said with a sympathetic smile.

Jon returned the smile and addressed the table sarcastically, "Why thank you Raychel, it's nice to know that some people around here get it." At that, the friends broke out into uproarious laughter.

A waitress appeared and took our orders of sandwiches, soup, chicken fingers and cheese sticks. It was comforting to me to see that the restaurant foods that I had adored on Earth were still available in Heaven. I had been worried that they would only serve healthy, "good for me" foods. I just wasn't the Organic, Vegan, Gluten-Free type.

"So fellas," said Seymour, as he began pouring the wine. "Raychel here is new to Heaven, on day two of her seven-day. She's a little overwhelmed. What's say we give her the inside scoop?"

"Well, I guess we should start with the Good Samaritan Law, then shouldn't we?" said George.

"Yeah, leave it to the doctor to start there;" chided Sam, rolling his eyes. "Boring!"

"Hey, it's important stuff. Practically everything runs on it up here;" returned George. He looked at me with that "everything's going to be fine" distant gaze that every doctor in the world has mastered, and began to explain. "Okay, here's the thing. You have to remember that this is Heaven, a little like what you were taught..."

"Very little, from what I've seen so far." I mumbled

"Okay, true... but the most important thing is that the Good Samaritan Law is real up here, and it's serious stuff. You could be deported for ignoring it."

"Yes, that's true," chimed in Father Anthony. "I knew a guy who..."

"We'll get to your stories later, Tony," said Seymour. "Let's just give Raychel the basics for now."

"Anyway," George continued; "If you see someone in need, no matter the time of day or the situation or degree of peril, it is your contractual obligation to help them to the best of your ability, using whatever resources you have available at the time."

"Wait a second, 'Contractual Obligation'? What does that mean?" I asked.

"Oh," Interjected Sam, cheese stick hanging from his mouth like a Cuban cigar; "When you finally decide that Heaven is where you want to stay forever, they make you sign this contract that says that if you deviate from any of the Rules or Expectations of Angelic Behavior..."

"They've got a whole book on it." interrupted Robert

"...The Powers That Be reserve the right to have you deported." finished Jon, raising his glass and taking a sip to punctuate his remark.

"Fortunately, there's not a lot of occasions where someone is in need." continued George, reaching for another chicken finger. "You pretty much get everything you need and want up here, and there are very few obstacles or opportunities to get hurt. Not a lot of the unknown; very little risk."

"That sounds pretty reasonable, but what's this deportation thing all about?" I had always been a little shy of consequences that I couldn't see coming, and so this was a technicality I wanted to get straight.

"Deportation is when they shun you for a month, and if you still misbehave..." Robert put emphasis on the word 'misbehave' and made little quote marks with his fingers in the air... "They deport you back to Limbo where you're stuck wandering aimlessly for all eternity. From what I've been told, it really sucks."

"What's shunning?" I asked, taking another bite of my sandwich. "It sounds a little Amish."

"Actually, that's where The Powers The Be got the idea. Shunning is when they ignore you and don't fulfill any of your prayer requests for an entire month. For all intents and purposes, you're on your own." said Jon

"Oh, and no one else is allowed to talk to you or spend time with you, either. You're pretty much ostracized unless it's a perilous situation where the Good Samaritan Law would trump the Shunning Policy." Robert said, matter-of-factly. "There's an email sent out every day with the names of the Souls on the shunning list. Violating the Shunning Policy means that your name appears on the list the next day."

I took a sip of wine for courage and stability. "Wow, Big Brother really is watching you up here, eh?" I exclaimed.

"You have NO idea!" said Seymour, as he drank down the last of his soup.

"So what really keeps Heaven running? I mean if people are all just kind of doing their own thing—perpetual retirement—how does the place stay afloat. It's so pristine. I know The Powers That Be are amazing and everything... but my logical brain tells me that there's got to be more to it than that. I've been assigned to help out over at Prayer Fulfillment—and I thought that was eliminated up here... the concept of working, I mean. I can't imagine anyone actually collects a paycheck up here—what good would it be?" I noticed I was rambling, but I couldn't help it. There was so much to know, and I thought that as long as this cadre of Uncle Seymour's friends were willing to give me the "inside scoop", I might as well dig for as much information as I could get.

"Community Service;" said Father Anthony flatly.

"Really? That's it?" I was astonished that it could be that simple.

"Yes," Father Anthony continued. "There is a reasonable and customary expectation to serve in Heaven."

"It's all in the book they give you when you sign up." said Sam.

"After all, Humanity can't be served if Heaven is filled with Souls who are not dedicated to service." As Father Anthony prattled on, it sounded as though this was one of his favorite sermons, and he took great pleasure every time he got to deliver it to a new audience. The rest of the table, surely, had heard it all before, but they let him continue without interruption, probably out of reverence or friendship, or some combination of both.

"Sure, fun and relaxation is part of the reward of Heaven; but Heavenly Souls have a responsibility to keep Heaven as a viable and desirable eternity choice by all of Humanity. We need to keep the place working, and in good condition, otherwise, no one would want to come here. The Powers That Be can't be expected to do it all, my child." I had to admit, Father Anthony had a great delivery.

"Look at it this way", said Robert. "Heaven's goal is to increase Soul numbers in order to relieve the burden of "Prayer Fulfillment" to Humanity. If too many Souls choose Hell, Heaven's infrastructure will collapse and Humanity won't get the spiritual support they need and expect. However, if not enough Souls choose Hell, quality control of service in Heaven can't be maintained. Heaven's focus needs to be on those who choose to serve; too many idle Souls simply don't get the job done."

"It's all about quotas." said Seymour. "They have to keep the numbers balanced or else the whole infrastructure of Heaven and Hell collapses; Limbo grows to be overcrowded and Earth has to deal with the lack of synchronization. You see, if Limbo gets too crowded, the process of creation hiccups, and the result is spiritual anarchy. It's all about the quotas."

"There really is a lot more science and math involved up here than traditional spirituality..." started Robert. The others around the table shot him looks that told me he was about to reveal too much to someone on a visitor's pass. Robert acquiesced. "But that's a discussion for another day."

My curiosity was appropriately piqued. I made a mental note to ask Seymour about it later.

"The simple draw of Hell is that there is no requirement to service," said Sam, as he fingered the stem of his wine glass and leaned back in his chair. "It's the concept of the eternal vacation with zero responsibilities. It's a nice place to live, if you're into that sort of thing. But for me... and I might guess for everyone at this table... being helpful and being of service in one capacity or another is why we chose Heaven. It simply feels good, sort of gives us purpose. I mean, if you can't find anything positive to do with your eternity, what's the point?"

The friends around the table raised their glasses and nodded in agreement.

Chapter Seven
Mass

    Sunday morning had arrived. It would have been easy to miss, except for droning voice coming from Hailee's tablet... "Sabbath Mass" it chimed in a voice that sounded a little like a cross between the automated Siri voice of Earth and the whispering Angel's voice we had all imagined growing up in Sunday School.

    Hailee came bounding out on to the lanai as if it was Christmas morning and she had boxed to unwrap. "So, are you ready for Mass?" It was early—just shortly after sunrise—and I was still trying to get my bearings with a cup of cocoa. The birds sang, the cat mewed softly in a corner, and the puppy rolled about on the lawn with a tennis ball. My head throbbed with the pounding of disassociation and frustration. My brain and body still hadn't become accustomed to the spiritual plane.

    "I guess. Say, Hailee, when does the hangover wear off? This is getting irritating." I grumbled.

    "Oh, that. Sorry, but that won't go away until you make a choice."

"You've got to be kidding! Three weeks of this nonsense?"

"Yeah..." she said timidly. "Until you make a choice, your body won't associate. It takes a conscious choice from you to establish the ethereal umbilical and have that grounding feeling again. But, once you make a choice... you'll feel right as rain—I promise! I'm sure Mass will take your mind off all that uncomfortableness. Shall we?"

"Sure thing; lead on."

As we began walking down the sidewalk toward the trolley stop—I kid you not, it was a red trolley, just like the one in Mister Roger's neighborhood, only full-size—I was surprised by how remarkably quiet everything was. There were birds in the skies, and it seemed they were the only soundtrack to be found in Heaven. Other than the occasional friendly bark or mew as we passed by their homes, no other sounds polluted the air. No airplanes, no helicopters, and no traffic, save for the occasional bicycle bell. It was simultaneously nice and eerie. Coming from Earth, a place bombarded with every noise imaginable—even at night, conspicuous by its absence—this near-silence was unnerving.

As we walked, we passed a small lake—perhaps just five or ten acres in diameter—with a surface like glass. Every once in a while, I'd see a small ripple as a fish jumped to catch a passing insect; but beyond that, the water was also strangely silent. The Twilight Zone feel of the place was beginning to make me feel a little paranoid. "Hailee, doesn't the silence bother you?"

"Oh, no." whispered Hailee in a most revenant voice. It's so soothing to be without all that noise pollution, don't you agree?" I nodded, not really agreeing, but allowing the topic to drop. Hailee didn't seem to care, either way.

When we stepped onto the trolley, we were greeted with the silent smiles of the multitudes, each extending a distant warmth that was simultaneously insincere and exuberant. *Odd, how those two emotions don't appear to be mutually exclusive in Heaven.* During the trolley ride to the center of town, and the tabernacle that awaited, I thought about the historical significance of Mass and I contemplated what might be the same or different about it in Heaven, as opposed to my memories of it on Earth.

****

Mass is, and always has been about preaching. You know, the incessant one-sided conversations about what you do, why you do it and why you shouldn't... and most importantly, what will happen to you later if you do—or don't. Back on Earth, the preacher's job was to drill into you all the rules you already knew; reminding you weekly of your failings and the fact that you'll most likely never be good enough to deserve paradise. Consistently, it was a method used to keep Humanity's self-esteem at "manageable levels". This way, no one ego got so large as to conceive of accomplishing the unthinkable. So the remarkable remained unthinkable—except by a few very special people who had figured it out.

On Earth, Mass through the years had always been a kind of "crowd control". When the service began, what I discovered is that it's not that much different in Heaven. As I sat there listening to the rhetoric being spewed in my direction from the man at the podium, projected larger than angelic life on the multiple screens hanging from the rafters, it occurred to me that The Powers That Be really don't want a bunch of Souls running around thinking that they can change the rules. And they certainly don't want anyone thinking that perhaps they can make improvements. Heaven must also be maintained within "manageable limits". Otherwise, dead people might get the impression that they're omnipotent... which I have a sneaky suspicion they are... and begin really mucking up the works. Being in the Navy taught me that there must be a certain level of conformity for any society to work, and I suspect that Heaven is not exempt from that Universal Law. *There are parameters for everything up here—if there weren't, it would be chaos, not paradise.*

So, the Souls of Heaven attend Mass every Sunday to hear the doctrine again and be reminded that without the watchful custody of The Powers That Be, they would be no different than the lost Souls wandering around the fog of Purgatory—never really sure what being an active participant of a comfortable eternity might be like, or the peace it could bring them. Mass in Heaven holds many gentle reminders of how important it is to maintain the status quo. It's what some might call *redundant to the nth degree*—but you won't catch anyone up here complaining. *Complaining could get you into trouble; and I don't think anyone wants to be in that much trouble.*

So, here's what I learned at my first Mass in Heaven:

Gentle Reminder Number One: "Silence in public places reminds us of the gift we have been given of a peaceful eternity." A control of opinion in public places (and even at home) makes sure that no one is unduly offended, and everyone can continue to live in harmony. "Positive thought beget positive actions and keep anarchy at bay." That was the most resilient mantra I kept hearing throughout the morning. According to the preacher in charge, keeping to The Top Ten is the best way to show The Powers That Be that you are grateful for having your daily wishes and "asks" fulfilled. So basically, it boiled down to this: just like with my father when I was a little kid, it's a good practice not to push the envelope by making a lot of unnecessary noise.

Gentle Reminder Number Two: "You have been given everything you need; there is no reason to expect anything more." I could see how this little bit of doctrine might be difficult for many ambitious people like entrepreneurs to accept. After living their entire lives always wanting and working for more, being told that their eternity now has limits, is hard for some. Nope, my guess is you won't find many of the Walt Disney, Dave Thomas, Ray Kroc, Henry Ford or Robert Kennedy types up here. I could be wrong, but I doubt it. This one little thing seems far too limiting for those Souls who were well versed in experimenting with limitless living. Although this theory doesn't explain the overwhelming influence of Steve Jobs... that's an enigma I don't think I'll ever resolve.

Gentle Reminder Number Three: "Free Will is real, but not without its constraints." The gentleman sitting next to me offered in a shy whisper, "this thought alone is the reason why many choose Hell. At least in Hell, you're encouraged to try to build the better mouse trap—even though you may never succeed—you are at least told to keep trying, if that's what you want to do. It's that continuance of Hope—a thing that many thought was a staple of Heaven, and turns out not to be true—that draws some to Hell. In Heaven, you're told to not even try—simply because it's not necessary." His face was grave with the resentment of a man who probably would have made a different choice, had he been given all the information at the onset.

So this was the "don't upset the apple cart" mantra. It seems to me that trying continuously is exactly how the uber-successful got that way. Stifling them now, after a full life of reaching, is counter to the core of their personalities. I could completely understand why some would bail. "Be careful," my new friend warned me; "Some who chose Heaven and continued to try ended up disappearing. No one really knows where they went.

Some suspect the fog of Purgatory; some suspect that their Souls were recycled against their will. We'll never know for sure." His shift from shy introvert to ominous Marshall frightened me just a little. *Fear in Heaven... huh.* From what I had heard at my first exposure to Heaven's Mass, fear was a part of daily life up here. It didn't seem right.

So, after my first Mass in Heaven, this is my take-away: for the most part, those who choose Heaven live with the limitations placed on them and learn to temper their ambitions. Their reward for following the rules is nearly unlimited request fulfillment and nauseatingly perfect weather every day. *Would it be worth it?* I knew I needed more information and a little more time in Heaven—and an equally informative trip to Hell—to make my choice.

Oh, one other thing I discovered, attending Mass with your fellow angelic neighbors focuses a great deal of energy on how good everyone's got it and how their choice to remain in Heaven was the right one. There's a lot of ceremony and celebration about how great it is to be a Heavenly Soul and spend an eternity free of complaint and worry. This was reinforced in song, theatre and the obligatory "community handshake" during the service.

After two hours of continuous nice and the reminders of how we've all got it so good, I was more than ready to cash it in. *Yup, my father was right, too much of a good thing can become annoying very quickly.*

****

When the pomp and circumstance of Mass had concluded, Hailee and I were making our way down from the nosebleed seats in the rafters. As we reached the foyer, I overheard a small gaggle of what sounded like new arrivals talking. "You know," said a red-haired man in his early thirties, "although it's been promised to us for centuries, Souls never actually get to talk with God or His Son, let alone sit at their right hand. Can you believe that?"

"You're kidding," said the rotund man walking next to him. "That doesn't seem fair, after all that time we've spent waiting? What a rip-off."

"I've read about this in the Guide to Heaven. The story is that they are both far too busy maintaining all the comforts of Heaven and Earth; and they simply don't have the time to meet with just any run of the mill average Soul who wants an audience." Retorted a woman whom one might have mistaken for Hermine Granger three decades past her Hogworts days. "Just one more thing that doesn't match The Book. Men and their stories—I bet if women had written it, they would have gotten it right!" She chided her companions, half under her breath. Her friends shot her worrisome looks and led her quickly from the building. Fear manifested once again.

As the throng moved further along the passageway toward the exit, a kindly man of middle age handed me a trifold brochure. I thanked him and ebbed along with the rest of the tide. I turned it over in my hands and glanced briefly at the back cover; "For anyone who has questions, there are several Preachers and Emissaries who will be happy to make themselves available after Mass." I had to admit that it was a nice offer; but as the clique ahead of us had clearly noted, it's not quite the same thing as speaking with the Creator and his Son. I found myself being a bit annoyed by the fact that this expectation had been blatantly ignored; but a few steps later, I was resolved. *I might as well get over it. I have lived my entire life never being able to talk with them one-on-one; not having that opportunity now that I'm dead isn't really an indignity.*

"Well, that was quite the experience." I mumbled.

"Yes, it's quite inspiring, isn't it?" Hailee cheered.

"Well, if that's what you need to call it... Look, would it be okay with you if I hung back a little bit and looked around?" I asked.

"Um, I suppose so. I can take you on a tour, and then we can catch lunch at the little cafe near the house before we go back home. How does that sound?"

"Actually Hailee, I was thinking that I'd like to do a little research on my own. Think about it; I can't possibly be expected to know for sure if this is where I want to stay if I don't spend a little time reflect on it independently, right?"

Hailee was hesitant, glancing to her feet then back at me, then back to her feet again. I could tell that she was reticent about leaving me on my own. It was almost as if she thought she might get into trouble if she didn't fulfill her responsibility to be a dutiful chaperone for my entire trip. But I really needed to ditch her. I had to figure out a few things on my own, and I knew that she would censor my experience if I let her tag along. I was sure that wouldn't help me make a clear choice.

"Well... are you sure you can find your way back home all right?" Hailee reverted back to her worrisome parent face.

"I'm sure I can. And if I need help, I'll just stop and ask directions. Everyone is so nice up here, I'm sure I can find my way." She was still hesitant, but finally relented and shrugged her shoulders, walking toward the Trolley stop; glancing back to make sure I was still unscathed. It was as if she had expected me to turn into a pillar of salt simply because I chose not to go with her. *I feel sorry for her. Her incredibly poor self-esteem and need to "do the right thing" really runs her. I'm glad that the Navy training I endured has beaten that stuff out of me.*

As I made my way back into the Great Hall, swimming against the deluge, I finally found myself before the bimah. The head preacher was still there, shaking hands with the dwindling crowd; his minions had disbursed almost immediately after our decent to ground level. Not an over-abundance of Souls hung back, but when you consider that the Hall probably held as many as a large football stadium back on Earth, still a good many Souls were in line.

As I waited, I constantly shifted my place in line toward the end. My strategy was to be the last one, and perhaps because I was last, have more time to ask my questions, as no one else would be drawing the preacher's attention at that point. Trying to be patient, as I waited, I peered about the great space. Hailee and I had sat in one of the upper balconies, and the view from down here was much different. I noticed a few flat screen Teleprompters setup facing the preachers' podium, still giving them a good view of the crowd, as well as the doctrine. There were speakers and microphones and music stands still standing in the area where the choir had sat and sung. And as I looked out at the thousands of seats, I could plainly see the collection of cameras, each with a different vantage that, during Mass, projected their images—in what I'm sure was in no way random—on the giant Jumbotron that hung directly above the bimah. This was the reincarnation of every rock concert I'd ever been to back on Earth—except the freedom was gone.

****

"I'm new here in Heaven, and I was wondering if you could answer a few questions for me?" I shook the preacher's hand and tried to act as mild and meek as possible.

"Why of course, my dear. That's exactly what I'm here for. I'm Brother Abraham. How about you walk with me back to the dressing room, and we can talk along the way?"

"That sounds fine; thank you."

"So, what's on your mind?' Abraham was a kindly gentleman, somewhere around seventy years old, it appeared; although I'm sure he was centuries older. Standing at about six foot two, his hair was more salt than pepper, and he wore a tasteful five o'clock shadow. A little bit George Clooney and a little bit my grandfather; he put me at ease immediately.

"Well, I've heard rumors..." I began.

"There have always been, and always shall be rumors, child. But you shouldn't put much stock in them." he admonished gently.

"I realize that, sir; that's why I've come to you. I'm only here visiting, and I feel like I need to get some answers from an expert, before I can make my choice. You understand, don't you?"

"Of course. How can I help? And please, call me Abraham." His smile was broad, not unlike a used-car salesman who knew the surety of the sale was in his back pocket.

"Well Abraham, I've been told that Free Will is alive and well, living in the afterlife without regret." I ventured.

"Yes, that's true." He said.

"Yet, there seem to be some limitations to that Free Will. For instance, I've been told by my chaperone that Sunday Mass is mandatory. Those Souls who refuse to attend are 'put on notice'. If they miss three consecutive Mass Sundays, they are sent to an 'Angel Re-Education Camp', I think she called it. My chaperone, never having been there, couldn't give me many details about this program, and I was hoping that you could. You see, a big part of the way I was raised, and my time in the military, taught me to understand the consequences of my choices... so, I need more information in order to gain that understanding, so I can be sure to make the right choices."

"Absolutely. That makes perfect sense, and it's what we expect of our Souls here in Heaven. The Angel Re-Education Camp, or ARC as we've come to refer to it, is on the outskirts of Heaven where, during an intense seven-day program, the misguided Souls are reminded that they made their choice, invoked their power of Free Will and agreed to play by the rules. The methods used at the Camp aren't cruel. But just between you and me, they are oppressively annoying; and most don't repeat the mistake; just so they can avoid the program." He gave me a sideways grin that warned me not to push too hard on this topic. "Some extremely rebellious Souls are sent to ARC for repeat visits; but after three, they tend to disappear."

"Where do they go?" My eyes were doe wide, and I'm sure my curiosity reflected in them brightly.

"Even I don't know that, my child. It's best not to ask the questions to which we may not want answers. Suffice to say that they are no longer in Heaven, and they are no longer infecting other Souls with their negative attitudes and laxidasical ways. It's important that we keep our wits about us, you know. We have so much to be grateful for... best that we focus on that and not dwell on the other side of things. There's a reason why Dorothy and her companions followed the Yellow Brick Road; it's because straying from the path would take them into the dark forest where they may be lost forever. Stay on the path—remain true—and all will be well." I could tell that he'd been at this game for a long time. Brother Abraham knew his stuff... that, or he was so motivated by his own fear of deviation from the program that he worked hard to keep his nose clean. It was hard telling which was the truth.

"But there is another rumor of a small faction of around ten thousand Souls who have discovered the secrets to omnipotence and are organizing a revolution. What of that?" I tried not to sound too rebellious—who knew who or what may have been listening... but hiding my derision was not easy.

"Oh my child," chortled Abraham; "that rumor has been around since the time of the Crusades... so no one is sure if it's actually happening or not. But, every once in a while there is a subversive event that makes you think it might actually be possible... about as possible as a witch eating small children for breakfast." His bravado again made me wonder if his sarcasm was real or simply a cover for his embarrassment in discovering that another visitor saw through the veil. *If more of us thought this way, asked these questions, his job would certainly be in peril.*

From what Hailee told me, there is a very rigorous selection process for Souls who want to become Heaven's Preachers. One might think that those who were Priests and Preachers on Earth would naturally be the obvious choice for this role in Heaven, as well. Evidently, it doesn't work that way. Oddly enough, a vast majority of those who preached on Earth either chose an eternity in Hell, or couldn't pass the standardized testing. If they do pass the test, they are sent to ARC for three months before they are given time in the pulpit. Hailee told me that this is not only to help perform a much needed service to re-educate straying Souls, but also to make sure that they have embraced the doctrine well enough so that they can not only teach it, but follow it blindly, without reservation or hesitation.

If wayward Souls were disappeared... I could only imagine what ambiguity might befall a preacher who had created doubt in, and then lost, a member of his flock. The rhetoric continued to flow liberally for the next thirty minutes, until I gently took my leave of Brother Abraham, and had him convinced that his words had taken root in my mind... lifting the copious fear that flushed upon his face.

I slowly made my way along Heaven's streets, back to Hailee; opting against the Trolley ride that would have gotten me there sooner. I had a lot to think about.

Chapter Eight
Thaddeus McIntyre

As I walked along the frustratingly quiet streets—things were never this silent on Earth—I passed several little park benches that lined the sidewalks of the perfectly manicured boulevard, void of potholes and teenagers screaming gang epithets. About halfway back to Hailee's place, I decided to take a moment... rest— although I don't remember being tired—and consider all I'd seen and heard. Mass in Heaven was the epitome of organized religion... it made sense, on some level, I'm sure; just not one I could fathom at that moment.

I was staring at what should have been my sneakers, but for some reason I couldn't see them, when a voice interrupted my trance. "Don't worry, your feet will be there again when you feel like you want to walk. It's odd, but trust me, it works." The voice was strangely familiar. I looked up to discover that the face was indeed one I recognized.

"Thaddeus? Thaddeus Macintyre? What are you doing here?" It was amazing. He looked exactly like he did the last day I saw him... that last day we said good-bye after that weekend of Liberty just before he was to be shipped out on the Nimitz, bound for the Aegean Sea. I remember being envious of his new post. Three months in Greece didn't sound all that bad to me, especially since I was turning in my Cracker Jacks for that dull job at the forklift company. *It figures, just as I decide to quit, our boat gets sent to one of the most beautiful and romantic places on Earth. Blue skies and seas, and perfectly white buildings.* I had always believed that Greece was heaven on Earth—yeah, I know, I was wrong. But it was nice to have that vision of a place mortals could visit that could be so close to the embodiment of wonderment. Thaddeus left for Greece and I left for forklifts. I was astounded to see him here.

"Well, I thought at least that part would be obvious. I'm dead." Thaddeus chuckled. He wasn't wearing his uniform, but a soft, white, cotton T-shirt, a comfy pair of blue jeans, a beige camel hair blazer and docksiders with no socks. *At least his family got him. No crazy outdated really horrific suit for him.* As he starred at me from his six-foot-four perch above my head, I was rejoicing at the fact that I had visited the Salvation Army store while in Heaven. The white cotton T-shirt and the ankle-length cotton sun dress that now hung from my essence was much less atrocious than the polyester thing my mother buried me in.

"I knew that!" I said, standing on tip toes I couldn't see to give him a hug. "What I meant was, how is it possible that we're here together, at the same time?"

"I died, found out I have to go through this strange visitation process; and so here I am. How long have you been here?"

"I know, isn't this nuts! This is day four for me. How about you?"

"Just got here, day one in Heaven... or is it day three? Time is a wacky thing up here. I've done my seven in Hell already, and a layover in Purgatory. Now I'm here. Have you done Hell yet?" He sat down on the bench beside me.

I was still trying to wrap my brain around how it was possible that I would meet someone of my own generation, let alone someone I knew. Thaddeus and I had been friends... a little more than friends, actually... but I'm not sure I should get into those details. Suffice to say that we knew each other very well. We were stationed at Norfolk together. I was in logistics, he was in communications. We had a lot of interaction, and got to know each other quite well. At first, we just shared cocoa, and then dinner, and then, well... Thaddeus cleared his throat.

"Nope... just Heaven so far..." I was still trying to figure out what I was supposed to do when the one that got away reappeared before me and, potentially, could be here forever.

"So, you've got a few more days here, then." Thaddeus ventured.

"Um, yeah. But my welcome packet said we weren't supposed to..."

"Oh, no, I wasn't thinking that at all... well okay, I was, but really... I thought, maybe, if you were interested, we might go hang out someplace tomorrow, if you're not busy." It was cute to see Thaddeus acting as if it were the first time we'd met. I must admit though, he could have said the exact same thing about me, too.

"Oh, yeah. No, I'm not busy, just this job thing... but I am being shadowed by an incredibly perky, over-protective chaperone. I'm not sure if she'll let me... I'll have to see if I can get away. In fact, um, would you like to walk with me; if I don't get back soon, she's going to call out the Calvary." I was being a blubbering idiot.

"Sure, which way?" Thaddeus stood and offered his hand.

"Oh, it's just a little while down this street, pretty easy to find, actually. It's a little red brick place, sandwiched between two white stucco places. You can't miss it. Red brick, blue shutters, white picket fence, puppy on the porch, pony in the back yard. Just between you and me, it's a little..."

"Nauseating?" Thaddeus asked. We laughed together.

A few minutes later, we arrived at the gate to Hailee's house. She was standing on the front porch with a look of complete and utter terror on her face. It was as if she was convinced I had been kidnapped and left for dead somewhere on the way back from Mass. You could see she was both relieved and worried that I had arrived in the company of a strange man.

"Is that her?" Thaddeus said with disquieting trepidation.

"Yes, that would be Hailee." I mumbled.

"Don't look now, but she's coming this way." He took a step backward.

"Swell." The lack of enthusiasm on my part was not missed.

"Why hello Raychel. I'm glad you made it back home. I was beginning to worry. Who's your friend?"

"Hailee, this is my friend Thaddeus. Thaddeus, this is Hailee; she's helping me through my days in Heaven." I smiled at Hailee, hoping that she would repress her death stare, or whatever it was she did to scare people away. *I know she has a technique, why else doesn't she seem to have any friends?* I could tell she wasn't happy with me. The rules clearly stated I was only supposed to speak with residents, not visitors. In Hailee's mind, I was a rebel. "Thaddeus is a friend from my living days. We..."

"Now Raychel, you know the rules. Let's not discuss it. Why don't you say good-bye to your friend and come inside for dinner. I made lasagna." She gave me the same disappointed look my mother gave me when I was thirteen and got suspended from school because I skipped math class on the day of a test. That night at dinner, I got one of my mother's redundant life lessons that I worked very hard at to ignore. I was sure the same would come from Hailee once Thaddeus left; it was to be expected... Hailee was tasked with the same job of protecting me from myself.

"It's not a big deal, Hailee," I said as she eagerly encouraged me to enter the house. "He just walked me home from Mass—you know, so I wouldn't get lost."

"That's okay, Raychel. I'll go. It was nice to meet you Hailee... See you around, Raychel." Thaddeus winked, allowing the escape of that mischievous imp just behind his eyes, and I knew there was an extraction plan in his head for the next day. With Hailee, the Cerberus of Heaven, standing near the threshold of freedom, the elude and evade maneuvers promised to be as equally entertaining as the first time we went AWOL and no one knew about it. *Okay, granted; it was only for three hours... but still.*

Thaddeus leaned down and gave me a kiss on the cheek, which prompted a disgruntled huff to discharge from the back of Hailee's throat. "Bye, Raychel. It was nice seeing you again." He flashed that "don't worry, I'll take care of everything" smile; and I enjoyed the vivid replay of every moment of our Earthly time together.

"What a fool I was..." I mumbled to myself.

"What's that?" Hailee said.

"Oh nothing, let's have dinner." I walked in the house, leaving Hailee scrutinizing Thaddeus as he disappeared into Heaven's nausea.

****

Hailee didn't let me out of her sight for the remainder of the evening. It was sweet to have this little puppy-like Angel follow me around everywhere, yet I found it to be a bit hypocritical. Heaven was turning out to be a lot less trusting than I had expected. *Who could have imagined that "big brother" thrived in this supposedly altruistic environment?*

After a while, Hailee's shadow became easier to ignore, I was so busy focusing my thoughts on Thaddeus and everything I could remember about him. Our time together when we were alive was wondrous. We worked together in the Navy, which had its challenges, but we also spent a lot of time on Liberty together. *The Navy sure had that one labeled correctly.* After spending eight or ten hours every day—and sometimes twenty-four hours for several days in a row—answering to the calls of someone who had more stars on their shoulders than I had ribs in my chest, it was nice to enjoy a little liberty from the oppression of it all.

Thaddeus was tall, comforting, intelligent and funny. He brought me flowers on occasion and sometimes even made me feel like I was the only one... I'm sure I wasn't, but it was a nice thought. He made me feel important and special—not that I really was, but again, it was a nice thought. In fact, I can't recall one argument, one small disagreement or one moment of angst between us. It was nice; and in a world that was seemingly always on one negative edge or another, nice was... nice.

After a tasty dinner punctuated by grunts of disgust between phrases of the redundant after life lecture Hailee worked so hard to deliver; I helped to clear the dishes; excused myself politely, and went to bed. It had been a long day, and I had lots to think about, without the interruption of Hailee's good intentions.

I haven't really talked about it until now, but sleep in Heaven is an interesting experience. Dreaming and Being somehow meld into a single act of Living; and it's difficult, even when you finally wake up, to be sure what is real and what was imagination. A deep sleep enveloped me that night. Usually sleep came with a relief that attended to my phantom aching muscles and wobbly head. Instead, that night sleep came to me with a peacefulness I'd not known since Earth—and rarely, even there. I remember looking out the bedroom window at the canopy of trees that shaded Hailee's house, watching each leaf dance lightly in the breeze to a song no one heard. I remembered my time with Thaddeus and thought about how nice it would be to see him again... *how nice it would be to hold him again...* Though I knew all of that was forbidden to visitors—I still cherished the idea of it. Darkness surrounded me, as the sun crept its last rays behind the distance horizon.

The last of my conscience thoughts that night, as I looked at the sun's hazy orange-red streaks against Heaven's perfectly blue sky, made me wonder... *is Heaven still within Earth's atmosphere? How else could it have a horizon, or a sun to fall behind it?*

I don't remember anything else of that night—except dreaming of my time on Earth with Thaddeus—until just before dawn, when there was a gentle tapping upon the window. No other noises, just the tap... taptaptap... tap of Morse code upon the bedroom window. When I opened my eyes and saw Thaddeus standing just beyond the glass pane, I was surprised, and happy. Stealthily, so as not to make a noise that might alert Hailee, I went to the window and gently pushed up the sash.

"Do you want to come out and play?" he asked in a small snicker-whisper. It was like we were thirteen, escaping from my parent's house to enjoy an early morning adventure.

"Of course! Let me change." I whispered back.

"You know that doesn't matter up here."

"Perhaps, but it does to me; I'll only be a minute." Thaddeus stifled a laugh while I steeled away to the closet and replaced my pajamas with a t-shirt and jeans. I handed my sneakers out to him and followed; the left half of my body, and then the right, just like over the obstacle course in Basic Training so many years ago. *I suppose old habits never die. Sergeant Youst would be proud.* We sneaked passed the sleeping puppy on the front porch, who, surprisingly, never even flipped an ear in interest; and made our way down the street toward... I wasn't sure where. It didn't really matter though; because my hand was once again inside of Thaddeus'. It just felt right.

We walked a while in silence, partially enjoying Heaven's early morning, and also working hard at not drawing too much attention to ourselves. Two visitors, escaping for a walk in the twilight together—I was sure this was a moment of extreme defiance against The Powers That Be... but I didn't much care. I wasn't sure when I would have this opportunity again, and I wasn't planning on letting it slip away—*no matter what the rules mandated.*

"How were you able to get out, away from your chaperone, to come get me?" I asked, curious that Heaven didn't have better guards at the gate.

"You were dreaming about me." he said, with a sly wink.

"Yeah, so... that's never worked before." I said, remembering all the nights I imagined the two of us together long-term.

"Sure, not on Earth. But in Heaven, dreams are the same

thing as asking—and you know what asking is, right..."

"Oh, yeah, prayers." I said, with a knowing smile, as I recalled my conversations with Hailee over breakfast.

"Exactly; they have a tough time ignoring that sort of thing up here."

"I remember; Hailee told me 'every question within reason gets answered'. I guess seeing you again wasn't outside reasonable limits."

"Someone must have thought so; otherwise, I wouldn't have been able to be with you this morning." Thaddeus said with his finest Cheshire grin.

"Well, how nice that something in Heaven actually lives up to the expectation. I had always expected that Heaven would make me happy, and now it has." Thaddeus squeezed my hand and we continued to walk along the perfectly groomed streets to the katydid and bullfrog serenades from the pond just a foot or so beyond the sidewalk. The dawn air was perfect; it was about seventy-two degrees with a gentle breeze, and no mosquitoes; despite the narrow pond that seemed to expand in length and follow where we walked.

Soon, we came upon a sign post. The arrow to the left indicated the path toward Heaven's Zoo. The arrow straight ahead pointed out the Library, Aquatic Center, and Playlot. The arrow to the right showed the way toward Downtown Heaven. It struck me strangely that Heaven actually had an infrastructure for its population. "Which way?" Thaddeus asked.

"Well, you know my penchant for animals..." I said, recalling that he had the same soft spot in his heart, too.

"Then the Zoo it is." he said; and remembering my preference for people to walk on my right side, he dropped my left hand, maneuvered himself around, and took up my right hand once again.

It was hard not to smile, so I didn't try. "I wonder if the lions and the lambs will actually be lying together?" I said, only half-curious to have my question answered. I was with Thaddeus again, little else mattered.

Chapter Nine
The Menagerie

    The trip to Heaven's Zoo was more like a visit to a wildlife sanctuary than a zoo. There were no bars, and the lion did actually lie down with the lamb; they were kind of cute all curled up together. As we made our way along the footpath, we encountered a lovely young lady—about seventeen, I guessed; her name was Jocelyn; she was one of the animal attendants. She was pruning the landscaping just outside the lion's den.

    "The animals all seem to get along here... there doesn't seem to be that predator/prey thing going on, and more importantly, they're not attacking me. How is that possible?" I looked up at Thaddeus, noticing the same perplexed look on his face that had crossed over mine.

    "It's the natural order of things. The animals never really wanted to live with all that aggression, you know." Jocelyn put her pruning shears aside and led us further down the path. To our left, there was a Bengal tiger snuggled up next to a white tailed deer. It was quite a sight.

"You see, Humanity created two issues for the animals that The Powers That Be hadn't anticipated. The first was that Man, with his ego fully inflated, and thought that he held dominion over the animals. Most of us have blamed Adam and Eve over the centuries. We learned it from those who compiled the Book. They had to draw attention away from the whole 'getting kicked out of the Garden' thing, so they chose to punish the animals. Not real creative, if you ask me. Sure, some of the animals were meant as food for Man, like the deer, but again, that was the natural order of things. And the animals were fine with it. But once Man began to force the animals to work the land without compensation and perform in absurd entertainment venues like the Gladiator arenas—well, the animals became very unhappy."

We moved away from the tigers and nearer to the elephants and hyenas. "The stronger, larger animals were frustrated and began to strike out against Man and against the smaller creatures who were beside them in the Circle. It was the only way the animals knew to stay wild, just as The Powers The Be had intended. In the beginning, it was "take only what you need", but Man got greedy and power hungry. Again, it was that Ego thing getting in the way. After that, the entire balance was upset. It put everyone on edge. And the truth is, the animals never wanted it that way. So in Heaven, we leave them alone and let them live as it had always been intended—free and wild." Jocelyn bent over to pet a couple of prairie dogs as they skittered by. They chortled their thanks for the affection.

"That makes sense. But what about the domestic animals—dogs, cats, livestock. I've seen some still living in Heaven the way they did on Earth, with people, and apparently happy about it. Why is that?" asked Thaddeus. After the explanation Jocelyn had just given us, having pets in Heaven seemed almost boorish.

"There are still some animals who prefer the domestic life, just like there are some people who prefer to be 'stay at home parents'. After centuries of partnering with people, some animals like dogs, cats, horses and guinea pigs enjoy being with people. Some find great comfort in the companionship people offer. But like with everything, it's a choice. Animals aren't forced to live an afterlife they don't want. The rule is, they have the choice to live with people; and they can always say 'no' or move out whenever they want."

"How does that work? I mean, on Earth, even the Humane Societies and Animal Shelters had a difficult time of making sure that animals were well treated. I can't imagine that people lose all of that bile just because they die. How do The Powers That Be make sure the animals won't be abused or neglected?" Thaddeus, back in his living days, gave a great deal of his time to local animal shelters as an adoption volunteer. His nurturing heart made him the perfect Foster Care team lead. Although because of his service to the Navy, he couldn't commit as an animal foster parent himself, he was passionately committed to making sure that dogs and cats had a safe home to live in until they could be adopted. As I think back on that time, I wonder... if we'd had children together... he would have been an extraordinary father.

Frequently, he would tell me at work how frustrating his weekends were, when an animal they had placed was returned because the people couldn't behave themselves. I felt the same frustration; which is why I had always contended that he was a stronger person than me. Week after week, he returned to this work; I wasn't strong enough to remain closer than arm's length—I had always wanted to brutally punish the people that forced such atrocities on the animals. Thaddeus held his ire, and continued to fight the good fight—for the animals.

Jocelyn, already an astounding wealth of information, gave us a greater moment of understanding that day, when she explained what she called the Soul Finder Center, located at the base of The Rainbow Bridge. "You see, she began, 'domestic' animals are allowed complete freedom in Heaven. They are given the option to stay with humans during their time here. Sometimes, it's the one they shared life with on Earth. Those bonds are often times very strong between both parties, and the animals choose to continue the friendship and companionship with the person they shared life with on Earth. Others are not interested. For some, they were mistreated by Man, and don't want to have anything to do with them ever again. But they may still enjoy human companionship, so they find new homes."

I was fascinated about this idea that dogs and cats finally got to choose. It made the thought of our dog going over the "Rainbow Bridge" a little easier to take. *If I chose Heaven, would Muffy and I ever be reunited?*

Jocelyn continued to explain as we walked past giraffes, hippos, cheetahs and alligators enjoying the same lake and grasslands. "There is a small cottage at the base of The Rainbow Bridge, staffed with specialists. Consider it a 'dating' service that domestic animals use to find new homes. Think of Earth's "Pet Finder", but in reverse. Animals visit the adoption center in search of people or families that are interested in sharing their Heavenly home with an animal. With the help of an Animal Husbandry Interpreter, they are matched up with several candidates and then eventually choose where they would like to live. However, it is always understood that the animal has Free Will to come and go as it pleases; and that includes traveling between Heaven and Hell to visit whom they please, when they please. It's a special compensation the domestic animals are afforded because of all the injustices they had to suffer by being 'pets' to mankind for so long. If you think about it, it really is quite a humiliating way to live." Jocelyn bowed her head in a moment of reverence—or apology. "Anyway, the humans are to understand that they are merely friends, no longer owners, to these creatures. Those who cannot accept that simple rule are not permitted to put in an application to become adopted by an animal, no matter which realm they've chosen as their eternal address."

"Ah," said Thaddeus; "That's why it's a bridge and not a gateway. Bridges go both ways."

"Exactly." said Jocelyn.

As we continued on our way, we passed a gaggle of geese with their goslings nestled around; a pack of wolves with more than two dozen pups running under and around their parent's feet; and at a nearby beach, a nest of baby turtles were breaking out of their shells and making the journey to the water, their proud parents looking on from the waves. It was a gentle, wonderful sight. No one was eating anyone else, and they all seemed happy... and then my ego kicked into high gear. "Wait a second. I read someplace that breeding was outlawed. But the animals get to do it?" The question just leapt from my throat. I didn't mean for it to sound indignant, but it did. I immediately felt ashamed.

"On Earth, the animals were in constant breeding mode simply to keep Man from hunting them out of existence. Here, there's no threat of that. So, the animals have gone back to breeding only when the mood strikes them—which, again, is a more natural state of being. Because prey animals are no longer prey, there isn't a need to have more babies than they can care for. The mortality rate isn't a factor. It makes sense that they would be granted certain freedoms that Man is not." Jocelyn said, matching my irritation in her voice. "They have much better control over their instincts and they don't have silly legacy issues. They breed simply, easily, without all the emotional baggage that people bring into the equation. People aren't allowed to breed in Heaven because they have zero control. Animals, on the other hand, make much more intelligent choices. They breed purely to be nurturing and kind, not to one-up each other with their offspring."

"I'm sorry; this is all so new to me, I've only been here a short while. I'm just trying to understand. Tranquility among the animal kingdom has turned out to be quite accurate. It's nice to know that some of the ideals that we were taught and believed in as children are more than just appeasing rhetoric."

"No harm, no foul. I was where you are once—I get it. The truth is, Humans are no longer in charge of the animals, and that's a point some new residents find difficult to accept." Jocelyn continued. "They do, in time, but sometimes they need to go through rehab programs to really get it. After all, like with any addiction, once they discover that they aren't 'all powerful', it takes a little bit of retraining to get them to learn a new approach to Being."

Jocelyn had just plucked a chord of reason that I never thought I'd hear played. Animals really were the higher functioning Souls. It was nice that they were finally given the opportunity to live the simple life they deserved. I liked that the animals were given a choice. It was a right that was taken from them, and finally, justly, it was given back. I felt sad for all the animals left on Earth who wouldn't get to experience that freedom until death.

Earth is less perfection and more prison than my teachers and parents had wanted me to believe. Very frustrating.

****

As we walked along the various paths, Jocelyn stayed with us, giving us more information about each habitat we encountered, and explaining the true nature of the Universe's animals. It was simultaneously invigorating and challenging to have the lessons taught to me as a small child now countered with a new understanding. I could see that Thaddeus, too, was experiencing a questioning of his beliefs, and that this wasn't any easier for him than it was for me. And yet, the process was fun for us both. Like an elementary school field trip; this certainly was the most unique date we'd ever been on together!

As we reached the Mythical Gardens, Jocelyn helped us to understand even more. "The creatures and animals of mythology were taken from the Earth long ago because Man couldn't or wouldn't treat them with the respect they deserved. Animals like the Unicorn, Pegasus, Dragon, Centaur, Pan and others were far too delicate to be treated so poorly." She looked gently at the beautiful creatures in the vast valley and fields before us. I could tell that even at her young age of seventeen—and who could really verify that she was indeed that young, age seems timeless in Heaven—she held her dream job. Caring for these creatures, I was certain, was what she had lived her life waiting to do. I was happy to see that her Soul had been rewarded.

"The myths arose from the early Men who encountered them in the first years of Human history; maintained in the oral stories that one generation passed down to the next. In the beginning, the stories were factual. They described a world were these majestic creatures lived freely and without fear. The stories told new generations what these beautiful creatures looked like, and how they interacted with Man. A peacefulness permeated society then, and everything was okay." We moved from the unicorns and centaurs to the dragons and Cold Drakes. "But over time, the stories became muddled and overdramatized. Soon, these animals were being hunted as trophies rather than revered as the special creatures they had intended to be. It was clear that Humanity was not mature enough to manage getting along with these animals, and so The Powers That Be removed them from the Earth, and brought them to live in Heaven, where they could be safe and comfortable, without fear of harm or prejudice."

"That would explain a lot of our literature, and how the mythology of the ages changed so frequently. Without the animals still on Earth to verify any of it, the stories changed constantly.

One gigantic game of 'Whisper Telephone' over the years." Added Thaddeus, a look of quiet contemplation across his face.

"Exactly," said Jocelyn. "In the beginning, the possibility of humans mating with animals was attempted. The Powers That Be didn't want to prejudice one species against another simply because of appearance or anatomy. So they allowed the practice. In some situations, it worked out very well. In others, it was disastrous."

"Oh, well, that would explain the Greek myths of Zeus, Hera, and the others." I said, an invisible relay finally connecting in my head.

"Yes; the cross-breeding intensified the feelings of fear among humans who were already struggling hard with debilitating emotion. It was difficult for Humanity to keep their fear in check; and that frequently led to violent actions of anger to somehow feel superior over their fear. Unfortunately, the Centaurs and Satyrs received the brunt of this horrific Human lack of control. Many were slaughtered in the name of fear. It's sad, but true. They were a peaceful, loving community that was nearly annihilated because a small group of Humans didn't understand them, and felt that somehow their differences would hurt Humanity rather than enrich it. The Powers That Be acted quickly to save the last remaining, and brought them to Heaven to join the rest of their community. In this space, they live freely; some choosing to keep to themselves, and others choosing to form friendships with Humans. But they are given special land in Heaven, set aside especially for them; outsiders must be invited in by the clan; there is no other entry."

"That's a phenomenal thing," I said, looking at Thaddeus with amazement. He returned my gaze, equally entranced. "At last, there is a place of peacefulness for these creatures—where they won't be maligned or bullied anymore, where they are allowed to decide who and what gets close to them."

"It's the way it's been since they were brought here centuries ago; because, even though Free Will allows people to choose to stay in Heaven, that doesn't necessary mean that they have reformed their prejudices. The boundaries are there to keep tensions minimal. And for the most part, it works. Once in a while, we have some new arrivals who just can't let go of their old anger, even after going through the rehabilitation program. They are sent back to Purgatory for a while to rethink their choice. Some reform and return, others choose Hell."

"What about the dinosaurs," asked Thaddeus. Science tells us they were real, and lived on the Earth. I've seen the bones at the Chicago Field Museum. What happened to them?"

"Oh them," Jocelyn said with a nonchalance that surprised me. "They have their own habitat in Hell. They need a lot of room, you know; they're quite big; and they prefer the climate down there; they're partial to volcanoes for some reason." The cavalier tone of Jocelyn's answer surprised me. *Who would have thought that something as monumental as verification that Dinosaurs lived on Earth... and moreover, that they had a choice about where they spent their eternity... would be handled with such calm?*

I said it that morning, while walking with Thaddeus toward the Zoo, and I felt it again in that moment, watching the Centaurs play with their young; *it's nice that Heaven had exceeded my expectations in some ways.* I was beginning to see how this choice of an eternal address was not as simple as it seemed. It wasn't simply Good vs Evil. There was a lot more to consider. It made me curious, again, about what my trip to Hell would show me.

Chapter Ten
A Last Supper With Hailee

"This has been a spectacular day, but I think I should be getting back to Hailee's place. She's probably going out of her tree looking for me. She's a little high strung that way. What's next for you; I mean, you've already done your time in Hell. What's next?"

"I'm not entirely sure. I've never done this before." Thaddeus smiled. *I just love that smile!* "They just told me that my chaperone would take me back to meet my guide back to Purgatory, and I'd get further instructions then. You know, when you think about it, Heaven's a little like the Navy—it's all 'need to know'." We shared a small laugh, easing the discomfort of our parting ways. Thaddeus took my hands in his, and looked at me like I held some great secret behind my eyes. It was a little unnerving, but nice, too. All the attention made me blush just a little bit.

"Well, I've got one last supper with Hailee tonight, and then I guess it's back to Purgatory and my visit to Hell. It's hard to believe I've only been here for seven days. If feels like an eternity. I'm so glad we reconnected, Thaddeus; you made my last day in Heaven perfect. Thank you." With that, he leaned down to kiss me, but at that very moment, a bicyclist sped past, breaking the narrow space between us.

"I should get going. I hope I see you again sometime." I was doubtful that time would ever come. Eternity is a long time, and Heaven and Hell are vast spaces... and I still didn't know his choice—nor he mine. *How would we ever be able to find each other again?*

****

I walked the few blocks back to Hailee's house, ready for the deluge of lectures I was sure would fall upon me. But when I walked through the door, I was pleasantly surprised. "Hailee, I'm back." I called from the front foyer.

"I'm in the lanai, Raychel. Come join me for tea." Hailee sounded calm, content and dare I say, happy. Not at all what I expected. I walked out to join her for tea. When I walked through the door, she greeted me with a great big smile, and a cup of fresh-brewed cocoa. "I know you prefer cocoa to tea... but it's not really something you do, is it, have cocoa with someone? So I suppose we'll just call it 'having tea' even though you're not." She was babbling just a little bit—back to her normal self.

"I'm sorry I spent the whole day away... but Thaddeus..."

"I understand, Raychel. There are some things that we must do in life, as in death; if The Powers That Be saw fit to make it happen, then it was meant to be, and who am I to argue or complain? Did you have a good time?" She put down the book she was reading, *Cannery Row* by John Steinbeck, and looked at me intently. All her attention was on me, and she seemed eager to vicariously relive my day.

"I did, thank you. Thaddeus took me to the Zoo. We met a wonderful girl there..."

"Jocelyn. Yes, she's delightful, isn't she? Been here nearly as long as me. She really loves those animals." Hailee sounded almost envious of her job in Heaven; though you would never hear her admit it. She felt honored to be in Prayer Fulfillment that was clear by her dedication to the job.

"Yes, well we had a fabulous time seeing all the animals and mythical creatures. I had no idea of the history of such things. Neither did Thaddeus. We were grateful to have learned so much. But I must admit, it does make my decision more complicated; I mean, I haven't visited Hell yet, so who knows what I'll find there; but the idea of sharing space in harmony forever with people and animals is incredibly appealing."

Hailee's face turned contemplative. I could see that she held something inside but was reluctant to share it. "But enough of that; this is my last night in Heaven, and I'm looking forward to spending it with you. What shall we have for dinner?" Hailee's eyes lit up at the thought that I was choosing to be with her instead of with Thaddeus or Seymour. I thought it the least I could do, considering that she had gone out of her way to befriend me, show me around, and open her home to me. And, I sincerely liked Hailee. She was just a little... dated... was all. Not something I was used to... But I'm glad I met her.

"Well, it's fairly late," she said, a little begrudgingly. "How about we just stay in, have dinner and chat? How does that sound to you?"

"That sounds good to me." I said with enthusiasm. "What shall we have?"

"The sky's the limit. What are your favorites?" Hailee looked like we were about to embark on a grand culinary adventure. We were from completely different decades. It was a mystery to her what my favorite foods might be; and somehow, this was exciting to her. I can't understand it, but there you go.

"Well, I just love cheese and chocolate fondue. They've always been my favorites because not only are they two of the world's most perfect foods, but they're also so much fun to eat. What do you say?" I was hopeful that Hailee would be excited by my choice; or at least fake it well.

"That sounds divine! I haven't had fondue in ages; this will be fun." I couldn't tell if she was sincere, or faking it, but either way, her reaction was nice. She got up and I followed her into the kitchen. She magically pulled two electric fondue pots from the lower cupboard, and began to peer into the refrigerator. "So, we'll need cheese... and chocolate..." Without looking up at me, both landed from her hands onto the counter. "What shall we have to dip?" At this, she extracted herself from the fridge and looked at me for guidance.

Not to lose the momentum, I responded with as much spontaneity as I could possibly muster; and it was becoming more sincere as I ticked the items off my mental list. "Well, for the cheese, we'll need carrots, broccoli, bread, ham, chicken, and cauliflower." Hailee ducked back into the fridge and began tossing items over the door in my general direction, saying 'check' with each volley. I managed to catch each on arrival and place it on the table just in time to receive the next.

"And for the chocolate?" Hailee asked.

"Whatever fruit you might like..." Hailee produced strawberries, bananas, and cherries. "And of course, we'll need marshmallows..." Hailee bolted to the upper cupboards on the opposite side of the kitchen and tossed a bag to me, which landed deftly on the table with the rest of the ingredients. "... graham crackers, brownie bites, and oh... Oreo cookies!" I had to mention the Oreos... they were Hailee's favorites.

"Ooooh, this is going to be fun! What shall we have to drink with this feast?" She squealed.

"That's completely up to you. I'm not sure what the drinking rules are up here... You choose." I said.

"Are you kidding me? This place practically invented wine! Remember the whole Jesus wedding thing; water to wine? I think alcohol is fairly acceptable up here; at least I've never known anyone who had repercussions for imbibing every now and again; especially on special occasions—which this most certainly is! Do you want white, or red?" Hailee asked, moving to the pantry door.

"Well in that case, let's have white with the cheese and brandy with the chocolate." I figured that if I was going to get carte blanche here, I was going to take advantage of it.

"You do know how to throw a party, don't you?!" Hailee said, handing me both bottles to add to the table. "What's say we move this party outdoors? After all, it seems silly to miss your last great sunset in Heaven, wouldn't you say?"

We collected all of the food and wine, put them on a tray, and carried them, along with the two fondue pots, out to the lanai. The puppy followed us eagerly, hoping for a morsel of food that he was sure to get—this was Heaven after all; and the pony hung near the patio stones, patiently awaiting his carrot quota. It was a picture-perfect scene; two new friends, cheese, chocolate, a puppy, a pony and the most perfect sunset man has ever witnessed. Add to that, a little wine and brandy, and the night became instantly memorable. The cynical side of me contemplated the fact that this was the last ditch effort at manipulation through bribery—but I pushed that thought to the back of my head. I really wanted to enjoy this time being present with Hailee. *I owe her that much.*

We had a fabulous time, talking about everything and nothing, dipping, and drinking. The pots of cheese and chocolate seemed to be constantly replenishing, signaling that the evening didn't really ever have to end. However, by the third pot of both, and two bottles of wine; on the second bottle of brandy, we decided that we were done eating. The two of us settled back onto the lanai chaise cushions, and nursed our brandy while gazing out at the night sky. It looked like the Aurora Borealis out there; which at the time, made sense to me. *If those fabulous Northern Lights hadn't been created here, then where? Certainly not Hell.*

****

Finally, the puppy was curled up at our feet, with a plump tummy, and the pony contentedly grazing in the paddock, I asked Hailee the question that had been teasing me since my arrival... "Hailee, why did you choose Heaven?"

She smiled demurely and said, "You know I'm not really supposed to talk about that with you—I'm not supposed to taint your choice, you know..."

"I know that—I mean, I know the rules. But this seems like a fairly understanding place. Surely, The Powers That Be would forgive you just this once. I'm a sailor in the United States Navy, Hailee. I've been trained to understand the reasons and the repercussions. I need more than just seven days of raw experience. I need expert advice. Why did you choose Heaven; and just as importantly, why should I choose Heaven?"

Hailee contemplated her brandy glass for a long moment and stroked the puppy's soft fur with her bare foot, having removed her shoes and socks long ago. "Heaven's a good place, you know. Good things are happening here..."

"No one disputes that, Hailee. I just need to know why you chose here, and not that other place." I tried to gently, but forcefully get her to relinquish the secret, and she was avoiding the issue devotedly. You would have thought I was trying to get her to divulge the true hiding place of the Holy Grail. Finally, she relented.

"Well... It was the end of World War One... that was a terrible time, you know..."

"So I've heard, I wasn't there, of course; but I'm sure it was terrible." I said with as much comfort as I could muster.

"Anyway, I was working at an orphanage for children who had lost their parents in the war. Understand, we didn't have women serving on the front lines, but you'd be devastated to learn, as I did, just how many mothers could not continue to care for their children after their husbands didn't come home from battle. It was awful. I don't blame them, mind you; how could I? I had no understanding of what those women were going through... but it still seemed a choice that could have been avoided somehow. All those sweet little kids... first they lost their fathers, and then they were abandoned by their mothers... it's a wonder more of them didn't turn out to be serial killers or rapists."

I listened carefully as Hailee painted a picture that I knew no museum would ever hang. This was a part of American history that would never find its way into our schoolbooks, let alone into our churches or synagogues. The military hadn't even acknowledged the truth. In my four years of service in the Navy, and the countless hours I spent in class learning the history and military stratagem of that horrid war, this one detail had been conveniently omitted.

"So, every night, as I tucked these poor children into bed, I would listen to their prayers. They prayed and prayed... to be reunited with their mothers who had left them; they prayed for a new family who would love them forever; and they prayed for an end to their sadness. It was heartbreaking." Hailee wiped the tears now streaming down her cheeks with the sleeve of her sweater.

"Anyway, when I died and visited Heaven; I was like you, a new Soul, looking for a place to fit in. When I spent some time with my chaperone in Prayer Fulfillment... well, I just knew it was the place I was supposed to be. Somehow, I needed to help those children, and the ones that came afterward. The only way I could see to do that was to fulfill a few prayers... just help out in some small way to bring a little bit of happiness and maybe a little bit of peace to their lives." Hailee sighed deeply. "And, after my seven days in Hell, the choice was a simple one for me. I've been here ever since, trying in some small way to make the lives of a few people down on Earth a little easier, a little happier."

"Oh, Hailee, I'm so very sorry." It was all I could say; and it was tremendously inadequate; but there was nothing else.

Chapter Eleven
Heaven's HIP Survey

I spent my last day on the Clearinghouse Floor accumulating prayer requests from all over the globe. Some were serious, like those from the Sudan, asking for water, food, life. There was one from someplace in South America; a young family asking that the coffee crop this year would be enough to sustain them through the lean times through winter. Some were outrageous, like those from a New Jersey housewife who'd been cheated on... she wanted her husband to contract a never-ending urinary tract infection.

A man in the American Bible Belt was asking for the secret recipe to a weapon that only kills people with anger and hatred in their heart, not realizing that would mean the weapon would be used against him. When I sent up the summary on that one, I suggested that we send him a single word—irony—to appear in the whipped cream of his double espresso latte.

There was one very cute prayer request from a seven year old Irish boy who was asking for another famine to strike, simply because he loved potatoes that much; and still another from the American displaced McDonalds executive in England who prayed for a way to make the drive-thru process more effective by asking

Parliament to change the rules of the road to right-side driving. It was a typical day in the prayer world.

I was just wrapping up when I received a message from Tuan requesting that I stop by his office after my shift. When Hailee skipped up to my desk, apparently completely recovered from our night of serious conversation, I asked her about it. It was strange that I hadn't heard from Tuan since day one, and now, this apparently urgent message.

"Oh, I wouldn't worry about it. It's just your exit interview." Hailee said with her patented Heavenly hum-drum.

"An exit interview, from Heaven, really?" *Each day, another weird thing to add to the list.*

"Well sure. They need to see how you see things so they can see ways to make things better. Angels are all about improvement, you know. It won't take you long. I'll see you back at my place, and we'll have dinner. You still remember how to get there, right?"

"Sure, just follow the yellow brick road?"

Hailee gave me her best chipmunk grin and a little snicker, which was really almost a snort. "I sure hope you stay. You're fun." And she bounced away.

I took the elevator up to Tuan's place. It seemed silly to me to take the stairs. I know Tuan said he was watching his weight, but I think that was crazy talk. There is no weight to lose up here. And maybe, that was the case for Humanity, too. The weight loss industry was simply the world's greatest head fake; because in the end, they knew it didn't matter. And still, there was so much money to be made on the vanity of Humanity that they simply couldn't pass it up. I suspected the cosmetic industry was a boat in the same ocean.

When I got off the elevator and opened the door to Prayer Fulfillment Reception, I was once again greeted by the pugnaciously perky Eunice. She drew her finger to her lips, librarian style, and silently invited me to come closer to her desk. "Welcome back, Miss Raychel." She said with an exuberant whisper.

"Thank you, Eunice. Tuan sent me a message to come see him. It sounded important. Will you please let him know I'm here?" I whispered back, not quite sure why.

"Oh, that won't be necessary; I'll take care of everything. I'm sorry about the mix-up. That message is automatically sent on everyone's last visit day, and it's signed by Tuan, which makes people understandably nervous. I've been asking the IT department to fix the glitch, but they've been so busy. And yet, you would think that after two centuries of asking, they'd make the time." A sigh of exasperation escaped Eunice's lips. "But, on to the matter at hand. We need you to complete this survey for HIP; Heaven's Improvement Program. It would help us to make sure we're doing all that's expected of Angels. The best litmus test is to ask those who are newly dead what they think. You know, Humanity has very different expectations about Heaven than the rest of us."

"Um, sure." Eunice handed me a sheet of bright blue 5"x7" cardstock with questions typed on it and the ScanTron form. Yes, it really was a ScanTron; that same familiar green and white 8"x6" form with the rows of letters and circles. As I stood there, staring at the papers, I noticed the pungent aroma of number two pencils and mimeograph ink from my elementary school days; and the heart racing stress of the standardized MEAP testing moments of my middle school years. I felt the prickle of a thousand tiny needles against my palms as I tried to steady myself with Uncle Seymour's words.

"Remember young lady, they may be able to intimidate you with tests and worry you with personality profiles, but remember, they can't take away your choice. The Law of Free Will is your... Death Right!" I'm sure what he actually said was Birth Right; but the way I heard it in my head just then made more sense.

Eunice pushed her finger to her lips again and pointed to the far corner of the room where three neat rows of chairs with little tiny desks were arranged. Four other Souls were sitting there, studying their papers, scratching their heads, and delicately filling in each little circle on their ScanTron with great concern. The scene reminded me of the day after my sixteenth birthday when I found myself sitting in one of those chairs with the little desk, taking my written exam for my driver's license. The pressure was on. If I failed that test, I would never be independently mobile. And on this day, my seventh day in Heaven... *I wonder how immobile I will become, now that the only thing left on the line is my Soul.*

I took my place in the far left chair in the third row and began to scrutinize the exam before me. There were just five questions, and not really questions at that, more like statements. The instructions at the top of the card read; "Please reply to each statement with the choice that is most accurate. Please be sure to fill in the circles completely, and use only a number two pencil. There is no time limit for this survey. Please take as much time as you need. When you are finished, please return the form, this card and your pencil to the proctor. Thank you for helping us make Heaven a little more perfect."

Question One: Community Service is a positive attribute of a Soul.

Question Two: Giving advice that will nurture a Soul toward a more Heavenly existence is always appropriate, even when unsolicited.

Question Three: Staying in Heaven, no matter what it takes, and regardless of whether or not a good friend or relative is excommunicated, is of utmost importance.

Question Four: Idle hands are an opportunity for Soul degradation.

Question Five: Doing what's Rite is more important than doing what's Right.

At this point, I looked up from my desk to notice that every one of the Souls who had been there taking their tests when I came in, were still there. It had only been ten minutes, they had arrived before me, and there were only five questions, certainly one or two of them should have been finished by now. But there they were focused—driven one might say—with making sure to get the answers right. I colored in my remaining two "C" circles with speedy precision and returned the implements of torture that Eunice had so excitedly given me. Eunice pressed a square green button on her desk and the door opened with that impudent Star Trek "swoosh". I took my cue and trotted down the hallway.

****

When the time finally arrived for me to end my stay in Heaven, Liza appeared at Hailee's door and rang the bell once—just once. Hailee opened the door and greeted her with a melancholic mood; though to her credit, she worked hard to hide it. "I've come to collect Miss Raychel." Hailee feigned a smile and invited Liza in.

"Please join us for tea on the lanai, Liza."

"Thank you, Hailee, but we really must be going; we are on a schedule, you know."

"Oh, but I've just put dinner in the oven... it's broasted chicken, one of your favorites, as I recall. Surely you have a moment or two to come in and visit. We get to see you so rarely; and..." Hailee's words were overly polite and near desperation. It was clear that she hated good-byes.

"Thank you for the kind invitation; but I'm sorry, Hailee—we really must be going. You understand as well as anyone that timing at this stage is a critical thing." Liza's voice was stern, yet kind. As I stood listening from just around the corner, Liza reminded me of the fourth grade teacher who nudged me gently, but forcefully through my studies.

"Of course," said Hailee meekly, and she slowly backed from the door with posture of a beaten kitten. I took that as my cue to round the corner.

"Raychel, you remember Liza; she'll be escorting you back to Purgatory as you prepare for your visit to Hell." Hailee was all business now, although I heard a small sneer escape as she uttered the word "Hell". She'd spent the past week trying to convince me that Heaven was all that I would ever need. She really didn't understand why some of the others she'd met had not chosen to stay. It was a conversation we'd had a couple of times, and it still boggled her brain. Yet today, it was hard to detect if the sneer was because she didn't like the idea of me going to Hell, or if she simply didn't like the idea of me going, period.

"Yes, of course; good to see you again, Liza." I could feel the tension building with each second that we lingered in the foyer. "Hailee; I had a wonderful time working with you. I really learned a lot. Thank you for your kindness and hospitality. I have had a nice time here with you, your home is lovely." I hugged her in a way that I hoped would express my sincerity.

Hailee could only offer a weak smile in return; and at that, Liza took me by the elbow and led me to the sidewalk. Hailee was stuck in her moment of sorrow, and simply waved as we made our way toward Heaven's Gate. It was difficult to see Hailee so despondent. *Sadness in Heaven... I didn't think that was allowed.* If I had one major take-away from my week in Heaven, it would be that Heaven's PR efforts are sorely lacking... there's been a rash of false advertising... *someone should sit the Pope down and give him a marketing lesson.*

On our walk back to Purgatory, things started out quiet enough, but I was sure that Liza knew I was struggling with something; so I tried to explain. "So... you probably already know... but..."

"Thaddeus, is it?" said Liza.

"Yeah, I figured you knew already. Is there anything you don't know?"

"No, not much. What's on your mind?"

"Well, how long has he been here, what's his story... he wouldn't talk about it, of course." I was clearly frustrated with this lack of full disclosure.

"Well, you know, he's really not supposed to, and neither am I, for that matter. All I can say is that if The Powers That Be have an expectation that the two of you will find each other again, you will. There is no predicting the Will or the Way; so I wouldn't try." Liza let forth a smirk and a small giggle; and nothing more. I didn't question her wisdom to leave it alone. So far, she hadn't steered me wrong, and I didn't expect that she would now.

Reconnecting with Thaddeus would indeed be a wonderful thing... but I also understood, and not just from the *Welcome*

Packet discovered on my desk that first day in Purgatory, but from my conversation with Uncle Seymour and his friends, too, that this is not something that we could conspire. It was made clear to me that The Powers That Be frown upon the influence of known Souls when it comes to such a serious thing as one's final choice. I accepted this; but that didn't mean I had to like it. I was just relieved that we were able to see each other again before I had to endure whatever Hell had in store. And, I had to admit, it was a comforting thought that Thaddeus had gone to Hell and back, and didn't seem all that worse for the wear.

While walking back through the eternal fog, a last thought occurred to me: *a comforting smile from one you once loved is a nice "last memory" before being flung into a pit of fire, pain and despair.*

Chapter Twelve
Edgar's Gift

As I walked back toward the Inn from the Heaven's gate, the fog looming effervescent purple, I felt exhausted for the first time since I my death. I don't mean tired exhausted, my body had been aching for days and I was becoming accustomed to it. No, I was intellectually exhausted. Spent—like my brain had been scooped out of my skull with a spork. Thinking... about anything... was an incredible struggle. I was astounded at just how much work and how overwhelmingly draining it was to spend seven days in paradise. Liza opened the door and invited me in, again.

"You look like hell." she said.

"Thanks, but I wouldn't know. I haven't been there yet." I said with a smirk. Liza guided me in the door and to the kitchen. She poured me a cup of cocoa, and after a few sips, I began to feel almost human again. I know that the effect of refined sugar wasn't the thing, but the simple belief that it was, did the trick.

"Okay, we're safe to talk now. So, how was your trip? Was Heaven everything you thought it would be?" Liza looked at me like she already knew the answer, and was craving a story.

"You know, it was odd. I thought it was going to be a lot..."

"Cleaner?" Liza offered.

"No... more..."

"Brighter?" Liza ventured, again.

"No, it was plenty clean and bright... I just wasn't expecting the oppressive silence. It was so quiet. And the weather was so perfect, it was nauseating. Ugh! At this point, I'm hoping that Hell is a little more interesting, because I'm just not sure if I could live with all that nauseating nice forever." I drained my cup, and poured myself another. "You know the thing I really don't get?"

"What's that?" said Liza, curiosity clearly painted across her face.

"There are so many rules. My gosh, I never imagined that Heaven would be so restrictive. I really thought that Heaven was a place of happiness, freedom and complete autonomy. Turns out, that's just not how it works. It's so odd." I started to walk toward the stairs and the relative comfort of my room, mumbling as I went.

"Sleep well!" Liza called out just as I reached the third step. I barely heard her... or maybe more accurately, I heard her but her words didn't quite register. I continued to trudge up the stairs and found my room right where I left it.

"At least something is reliable here." I walked in, set down my cocoa cup on the desk, and collapsed on the bed. I don't remember falling asleep. And I don't know how long I slept. But when I awoke, I felt almost human again. I was starting to wish that I could just stay in Purgatory, things seemed easier here—more on an even keel. I didn't have any expectations, so there weren't any emotional violations. Yet one thing was still nagging at me...

Thaddeus. I wondered what had happened to him. I decided to ask Liza. I wasn't sure I would get an answer, but it was worth a try. I found her in the kitchen, mixing up a batch of Toll House cookies.

"New arrivals tonight, eh?" I asked.

"Yeah, you know, got to make 'em feel welcome. How was your nap?" Liza asked as she tucked the pans of cookies into the oven.

"It was good. But, Liza, I've got a question... Is there any way that we could bend the rules just a little bit? I really need to find out what happened to Thaddeus. It's important." I pleaded with all my might, hoping that my desperation would fall on compassionate ears.

"Well... I'm not supposed to..."

"Please, Liza..." I cajoled.

"Oh, alright. Follow me into the library." Liza clicked the oven to "auto pilot" and led me to the library. Once there, she pulled a tablet from the shelf, and called up a few URLs. We sat on the couch together and reviewed the return. The Masthead on the article read "All Hands Magazine". I immediately recognized it as one of the rags put out by the Navy, kind of like their answer to the Army's "Stars and Stripes".

Liza summarized the article for me. "It appears that not long before your encounter with the fertilizer truck, Thaddeus had been caught in an uprising while stationed in Athens and perished in the crossfire. The story has it listed as a 'friendly fire' accident."

"That's pretty hard to imagine." I said. "There had been political uprisings for months in that area. The economy had suffered tremendously and the natives were beyond restless. It seems to me that the Navy wouldn't have made that big a mistake."

"It says here," Liza continued; "that a contingent of the fleet had been posted just outside the Athens harbor on a peace keeping mission—but the locals were not interested in being peaceful. According to this story in "All Hands", I get the impression that they were just supposed to be there to monitor the waterways and nothing more... so I'm not sure how fire, friendly or not, would have been a factor."

"Yeah, I'm sure that's how it's written, but I know how other countries respond to our presence, peace-mission or not. The Nimitz's mere presence was instigation enough... it shouted distrust of the locals... and that's how it happened. No doubt. One thing led to another," I said; "and things got out of control. It only takes one uneasy zealot to create a full-scale battle."

"It goes on to say that thirteen sailors lost their lives that day; it seems that Thaddeus was one of them." Liza finished.

"Thank you, Liza. I really appreciate your help. Somehow it helps to know that he was killed while performing his duty. It's so much better than a headline that reads "man shot by jealous husband". I chuckled.

"You're welcome; but remember, you didn't find out from me." Liza gave me a stern look. I knew that if it were to get out that she had shared this information with me two things could happen: at least, she'd be inundated with requests from other newly dead Souls to discover what had happened to people they knew; and at worst, The Powers That Be would punish her severely—and who knows what that might look like.

"I promise, mums the word." I said, dragging an invisible zipper across my lips.

After a shower, I made my way back down stairs, and ran into Edgar in the foyer. "Raychel, how nice to see you again. How are things going?"

"It could be a lot worse, I guess." I gave Edgar a weak smile.

"Hey, are you up for a field trip? I'm going to the outskirts of Purgatory, to check on a few things... you might have a good time. Want to come along??"

"Are there any snakes there?" I asked.

"Snakes? Nope. The exact opposite, actually. Come one, let's grab some brunch, and then I'll take you on a new adventure. I promise, you'll have a good time."

After a satisfying brunch of French toast and bacon with Liza and a few of the other new Souls, Edgar and I headed off in what might have been an easterly direction—we were walking toward a brighter part of the fog—so I can only assume it was east. After some time of walking in the nothing, I looked over at Edgar, wondering how he was navigating. "So where are we going? And how is it that you know the way? I don't see any street signs, you aren't holding a compass, and you don't seem to be following a carrier pigeon."

"To tell you the truth, I'm not quite sure how I make my way around out here. I've never really questioned it. It's just something I was always able to do; ever since that first funeral where I chaperoned someone back. After that, it was just something I always knew." Edgar's nonchalance matched Jocelyn's on what I thought was a pretty nifty point. *Why is the wonderment lost on them?*

"So, where are we going?" I asked again.

"Oh no, that's a surprise." Edgar said with a smile of gentle deceit on his face. He looked like a child who was about to open the biggest present on the last day of Hanukkah.

"Are you kidding? I really don't need any more surprises at this point. I think I've had my fill." The idea of more contradictions made me a little crazy. It was hard enough processing all I'd seen and felt so far; I wasn't sure just how much more my spirit could handle.

"Well, you'd better get used to it. You haven't even been to Hell yet—they specialize in surprises down there." Edgar said with a cautionary giggle.

A few steps later, I couldn't tell you how many, we arrived at a building I'd never seen before. Actually, it never occurred to me that there might be other buildings in Purgatory. Thinking back, I know that Liza had mentioned that the Twain Inn was one of many, but until this moment, it hadn't really registered.

****

It was a large white building, not quite plaster of Paris, but it looked similar—not quite marble, because it was pure white, with no variations, but it might have been some kind of marble I'm not familiar with; after all, there's a lot in Purgatory that isn't familiar. Edgar pulled open the large glass door, and invited me in with a most gentlemanly bow. *I'm sure Edgar and Hailee were born in the same decade.* Once inside, I was astounded at the size of the place. It was cavernous, with vaulted ceilings that seemed to spill into the foggy sky, and the depth to the room was astounding... it had no horizon... simply didn't end. There were several comfy couches arranged around small, round coffee tables, just right for casual or secluded conversations. No one occupied these seats today. The room was perfectly still with only the sound of gentle Gregorian chanting echoing off the walls, whispering through the space.

As we walked along in silence, I noticed doors with frosted glass, trimmed in bronze fittings on either side of the vast foyer... none of them marked... secrets or confidences; it was unclear which was true. I was so completely distracted by the sights around me that I didn't hear Edgar at first. "Raychel, I think you know this gentleman." he said, in a near imperceptible whisper. I'm not sure how many times he had said it before this time, when he finally touched my arm.

"Thaddeus! What are you doing here?" I nearly screamed with glee... there was a perceptible echo that I could not stifle; it was a bit embarrassing.

"Mr. Thaddeus is also conflicted about his choice, and I thought it would be nice for the two of you to spend some time together in a unique space... just to... get a different perspective for a little while. Maybe it will assist you both." Edgar was almost giddy. I was sure that he was breaking at least a dozen rules—maybe more—but he didn't seem to be bothered by this fact.

"So where are we, Edgar?" asked Thaddeus, as he took my hand.

"This is the Nursery. The place where new Souls are created and nurtured before they are sent to Earth. This place is usually off-limits to visitors; but I think what you find here will help you to comprehend the concept of Free Will a with a greater depth of understanding."

Edgar led us to what may have been the middle of the foyer—the place was so vast, it was hard to tell exactly where the middle was—and stopped in front of one of the frosted doors. "This," he said, "is where life begins. Beyond this door is where

Soul Energy is created for the very first time. You might want to put on these glasses, just to be safe. And please, don't touch anything when we go inside. The space needs to remain untouched by outside forces. Purity at this stage is an absolute necessity." He handed us each a pair of yellow-tinted glasses, and we tentatively stepped inside.

"Each child," Edgar began; "is a combination of the physical DNA and the energetic Soul Imprints from his or her parents. Each component has been stored here from the moment of their creation—just as was yours—until it is needed. These are joined together to make up the new infant's personality, physicality, morality and mortality. How that combination of data grows into a unique person is a combination of nurture and nature; education and environment; and of course, that child's ownership of the Law of Free Will."

There weren't any scientists in white suits facilitating this process, as you might imagine would happen on Earth. This process was completely performed through pure osmosis. Inside small, glass spheres, about the size of an average human womb, combinations of liquid and light were mixing together, glowing with a radiance that would make you question the limitations of the spectrum of the rainbows seen on Earth. The spheres hovered about the room, dancing in a pulsing motion that brought each close to the others, though they never connected. The floated around, above, under and over one another... several stories up, and back down again, forever in a soft, pulsating rotation. We didn't need to move out of the way. We were avoided. It was as if they sensed our presence and changed navigation when necessary.

I reached out to touch one with a fingertip, but Edgar quickly caught my arm and pulled it back to me. "You don't want to do that. I know that the impulse is difficult to ignore, we are curious by nature; it's one of the greatest gifts The Powers That Be gave us; but you mustn't. The damage could be irreparable—to both you and the New Soul. The energy controls here must be precise; otherwise the mixtures of the energy and physical solutions will become unbalanced, instigating a chain reaction and the young ones would not survive."

Thaddeus and I shared a look of horror, as if we had just pushed the red button that would evaporate the world. Sensing our discomfort, Edgar led us back into the foyer.

"Wow, that was pretty incredible," said Thaddeus. "What happens next? I mean, how does that... what would you call it..."

"Pre-Fetal energy." Said Edgar.

"Yes... well, how do you get that to Earth and how does it transform into children?" I couldn't tell if Thaddeus was more fascinated or repulsed. I was certainly fascinated. Who would have imagined that this is actually how life begins—as pure energy with a little bit of DNA fluid folded in for flavor?

"Well, at the time of conception, the energy infusion process is instigated with a very small amount of the mixture you just saw." said Edgar as we began to walk to a door across the hallway. He opened it and invited us inside. There, we saw several slightly larger versions of the spheres with variants of blue and pink clouds swirling inside. "As the Pre-Fetal energy becomes more stable, the remainder of it is condensed and transferred here to wait for infusion. They incubate here for a while, until The Powers That Be are certain of two things: Are the parents ready; and are the children willing?"

"Willing?" I said. "Do they have consciousness at this stage?" My fascination was in full control, and myriad of questions were swirling around inside me.

"Oh, of course;" said a gentle voice from the back of the room. It was the first time I'd seen an Angel in the traditional form—glowing energy... I think my grandmother called it an aura... with wings. She... He... It... was indeed beautiful. "Once the energy is fused with the DNA fluids, consciousness is established. Although New Souls express their Free Will very differently now than after they take physical form on Earth... they still have it."

"This is Sari. She's one of our New Soul caretakers." introduced Edgar.

"But I thought Angels..." started Thaddeus.

"...Didn't have wings." I finished.

"That's true," said Sari. Angels don't. "However, Cherubim do. We've been around since the world began. We only interact with New Souls; and we only connect with them again after creation if their Free Will brings them home. Hence, the wings." She said, glancing over her shoulder. "Expedited aery transportation is best facilitated with wings." Sari was authentically solemn in her response. We knew it was truth, but it was still difficult to comprehend.

"So, does that mean that The Powers That Be are Pro-Life and Pro-Choice?" I asked.

"You mean, does life actually begin at conception? Yes;" said Sari.

"All the building blocks of a living entity are there the moment sperm fuses with egg. That's the easy part, actually. Physical organisms are remarkably good at reproduction. Unchaperoned cell division was one of the best parts of the design plan. But the New Soul is not implanted into that tiny being until the first cry of introduction." Edgar explained.

"In fact," said Sari; "that's exactly why they cry. Think about it, if you didn't have a Soul for nine months and then suddenly got one, you'd be so overwhelmed, overjoyed and probably over-confused—you'd cry too."

"Souls aren't implanted until the moment of introduction precisely because if there is a physical problem that causes a still born, The Powers That Be don't want to waste any of that prime Soul energy." Edgar continued. "It's difficult to create, and easy to mess up—that's why they wait until the very last moment possible. Thank you, Sari." She nodded and floated two stories above us, returning to her nurturing of the spheres.

"What about still-borns? Why does it happen?" Asked Thaddeus, as we waved goodbye to Sari, and went back out into the foyer.

"That is a situation where, for some reason... no one understands why because they don't publish their methodologies... The Powers That Be determine that a child should not be born; in such a case, the New Soul is not imprinted and there is never a moment of introduction. The child has no Soul, and therefore cannot survive outside of the ethereal plane."

"What about preemies?" I asked. "How is it that they are born so early, before their physical bodies, in some cases, are not ready to live outside of the womb without help?" The more time Thaddeus and I spend walking the halls and looking through the doorways of each nurturing chamber, the more questions seemed to arise.

"Sad to say, those are mostly simple clerical errors. In the case of a premature birth, someone in the Soul Implantation and Imprint Department, also known as SIID, got the delivery date and time wrong, and someone on the team implants the New Soul too early. The child, confused by still being in the womb... probably more than a little angry about it, too... screams and fights to get out. And so, they are born. In some cases, these New Souls can handle all that modern Earthly medicine will throw at them, and in other cases they are simply not up for the ordeal, and choose to leave Earth, returning home."

"What happens to the New Soul of a child who dies shortly after birth? Why does that happen? I would think that once a New Soul is implanted and introduced, they'd be good forever... or at least until the moment of their natural death." Thaddeus, I could tell, was having just as many emotional conflicts with this information as I was; he was relying on simplifying things with logic. I was sure logic wouldn't apply well here.

"Sometimes, the early death of a child is because the parents didn't take proper care of themselves; or perhaps they put themselves in a poor living environment that brought on an early physical death for the child. In those cases, there's not much that can be done. As you have both learned by now, the Soul requires physical energy in order to sustain itself outside of the ethereal plane. However, some early childhood deaths—including Sudden Infant Death Syndrome, I might add—are simply because it was the child's choice not to stay. There are some Souls who figure it out pretty quickly, and if they decide that, for whatever reason, a life amongst the throngs of Humanity isn't for them, they can—just like adults—choose to leave. Perhaps the child just isn't emotionally strong enough to face all that mortality has to bring; or perhaps they have a physical challenge that they don't think they can overcome; or it could be some other, more superficial reason. But the reason doesn't matter... not really. The Law of Free Will applies to all Souls, no matter the age or level of intuition or cognition that they may carry. If they choose to leave Earth, the Law of Free Will mandates that request must be granted.

"As for what happens to that youngster's Soul when they die; there are several options. Some choose to stay in Heaven with a relative and live forever as a child, never moving past that stage—I'm sure you've noticed couples with babies up here; well that's where they come from. Others choose to spend time in Purgatory's Nursery until they are ready to be born again, at which time they voluntarily allow their Soul to be recycled. In that process, their original Soul is fused with the Soul of a new child about to be born to a new family; or in some rare cases, the original family. And that's why there are some parents who, when looking at their infant for the first time swear that they have been on Earth before, and claim that the child has an innate wisdom about them. That's because Soul material doesn't forget. It carries with it all of the imprints it has ever received. New Souls who have never spent any real time on Earth tend to retain more of that memory than, say, and adult who chooses not to return with me at the time of their death. The New Soul's energy is far more pure, which makes the memory connection stronger."

"Do child Souls ever choose to spend eternity in Hell?" I couldn't stifle the question. Not having been there yet, I rationalized that if adults chose to go there, children might, too.

"Almost never. In fact, since I've been here, I've never heard of it happening. In most cases, they are simply too immature to understand all that existing in Hell entails. Most just need to get their basic needs met, and they immediately find that in Heaven, and so, they stop asking for other alternatives."

We spent the rest of the day in the Nursery... or at least, what felt like a whole day. There were more nurturing chambers, more Cherubim floating about, taking care of the New Souls... and some of the most soothing music I've ever heard. It was peaceful... it was what peaceful was supposed to be. It was warm, inviting, quiet, and soothing. I didn't want to leave. But of course, a visit to Hell was still before me.

Thaddeus and I said our goodbyes, again, at the Nursery's front door. A woman, who I had never seen before, came to meet him and walk him back to his Inn. I wasn't sure if I'd ever see him again, and it made me a little sad. Of all the people I had encountered in my time on Earth, his Soul was the one I felt closest to... wanted to be with... more than any other. I felt it a tragedy that not only had our lives together been interrupted by death—but that our deaths together had been interrupted by policy. *How could one move through eternity without a Soul Mate?* The question haunted me as Edgar and I made our way back to Twain's Inn.

"Thank you for a most enjoyable day, Edgar. I truly have never felt so at peace." I hugged him hard; hoping that his energy felt the sincerity of mine.

"You're most welcome, Miss Raychel. I do hope our time together helps you to an easier decision." He smiled warmly and bowed as he walked back out the front door, presumably to collect yet another newly deceased Soul. I walked up the stairs, not the least bit hungry, or interested in seeing anyone else—even Liza. I just wanted to hold on to the memory of Thaddeus and this warm peacefulness for as long as possible... But how long could that be... Hell was waiting for me in the morning.

Chapter Thirteen
The Boat Ride to Hell

Liza led me from Twain's Inn, through the fog of Purgatory, to just outside Hell's Gate. "Well, this is as far as I go. Enjoy your trip to Hell. I'm sure it will be great fun for you." There was a twinkle in her eye and a gentle smirk on her lips; and she walked back into the fog.

I had a strange feeling in the pit of my stomach. It's the same feeling you get after an enema... a little knotted, a little gassy, and the most uncomfortable sensation that you just might leak unspeakable things at an inopportune moment. The hazy purple sky held no clouds, but flocks of bats wheeled and dove, skimming the river's surface. Although I couldn't actually see them, I was sure insects were quite abundant—and probably regenerating just after digestion. After all, if I were on the creative team, that's how I would have designed it.

As the Gate opened, there was no ominous, horror movie creek, as I had expected. Instead, it sounded more like Sasquatch's stomach growling... a low, gravely rumble. I turned to say good-bye to Liza but as usual, she had vanished too quickly. That woman has SEAL stealth.

Jared Hoyle met me just inside; a slender fellow, couldn't have been more than seventeen years old, dressed in shabby, torn jeans, sneakers and an over-sized black hoodie with a blood-red pentagram on the chest. His look was completed with multiple face piercings, shoulder-length brown hair, a short-cropped goatee and jet black eyes. He had two horizontal scars, one on each wrist that gave the impression of a difficult adolescence. Imagine a stereotypical 21st Century video gaming teenager, and that would be Jared.

"I'm Jared, welcome to the Department of Homeland Security". He said it with an air of authority that didn't meet his stature—he was trying too hard.

"You've got to be kidding!" The idea that Homeland Security was a department created by the underworld, struck me as somehow politically, poetically, perfect.

"Nope, Homeland Security, that's us." Relaxed, now Jared sounded like the teenager he appeared to be—his true age was well camouflaged by his overly pimpled face.

"Okay, I'll bite, why Homeland Security?" I vaulted the question with a sneer and a wink that I wouldn't have tempted on an ordinary teenager. But then, this Soul and this moment were far from ordinary.

"Well, because it's our job to make sure that the riff-raff stay out." This backward explanation caught me by surprise; although it shouldn't have; nothing turns out to be as you had expected once you're dead.

"Don't you mean stays in?" I ventured.

"Nope, everyone who's here is supposed to be here, they want to be here, we have no problem filling space. It's the others that we have to watch out for, you know, the Lookie Loos who chose poorly; they're all so curious to see if they know anyone who has come down here since they first toured the place. Sometimes the rubber-necking can get downright distracting. The Gate gets clogged and we have to call out the Basilisk just to keep operations moving. We've got things to do down here you know; we're busy, we don't have time for all this paparazzi stuff. It's not like people get a second chance to decide; we've got rules, you know—it's all in the orientation—but some people just don't pay attention." Jared wagged his head in solemn frustration. I could tell that this problem of Gate crashing was a real annoyance for him, but it made absolutely no sense to me; people trying to get into Hell once they've chosen Heaven? It was just weird.

I drew the zipper on my windbreaker. "Strange, it's a little chilly. I wasn't expecting that..." There's always about a ten degree temperature variant between being on the water and on the land, I knew that from my sailing days back home. I just wasn't expecting to notice it in Hell. Rather, I thought it would be an opposite variant. "... You know, what with the whole, 'hotter than Hell' thing..."

Jared's face contorted into a frustrated scowl accentuated by the amber reflection of the Harvest Moon off the rippling water. It looked like his skin was actually crawling. I get now where that phrase came from. It was rather creepy. "It's amazing how a little bit of fear and several centuries of well-placed marketing dogma can really ruin a place, you know?" Jared had a fondness for Hell that was unmistakable. *Cue the 'Twilight Zone' music.* I tried hard to remember that 'normal' is a misnomer after you die.

We walked down the dock together, and as we approached, I began to make out the outline of a carriage lantern, tethered to a pylon, swaying in the almost imperceptible breeze. I saw the hands before I saw the boat. Maybe it was just paranormal light dancing off the water; but the movement under the boat looked almost like a pair of giant's hands, lifting the boat up and out of the water with each wave, closer and closer toward the dock. It was a scene reminiscent of my little brother, playing with his toy boats in the creek. After making this connection, the barge to Hell wasn't nearly as frightening as the elders of my childhood made it out to be. I mumbled, "Is it possible that everything about death is misconstrued and misrepresented... just people making stuff up?"

"What's that?" asked Jared.

"Oh, nothing." I feigned.

At last, when the barge edged up to the dock, close enough for us to board, the hands seemed to disappear, and the barge laid gently upon the barely undulating tide. I thought of mentioning this to Jared, but after another minute or two, thought better of it. *It's probably not a good idea to point out the obvious so soon after getting to Hell. Offending the natives might not help my cause.* The boat was a simple ferry, a semi-flat bottomed vessel with no seats. Evidently, the discomfort of standing while on your journey into Hell is part of the package.

"How many to board?" The Ferry Captain had a typical sea-dog appearance about him; navy blue pea coat buttoned up to his neck, gray hair peeking out from under his wool cap and a salt and pepper beard with a pipe protruding from his lips. He could have been somebody's grandfather—and probably was—there was nothing pirate about this guy, just a soft and gentle sailor.

"There will just be the two of us today, Eril; Thanks." said Jared, nonchalantly.

"Do you have your fare?" asked Eril.

Tentatively, I pulled out the two bronze coins that Liza had given me. "Will these be enough?" I asked timidly.

"Surely, they'll do. Climb aboard." Eril offered his hand as I moved from the dock.

Jared and I stepped on board the barge and braced for the shove off. Another set of hands, or perhaps the same ones, lifted us off the beach and gently shoved off into the blank nowhere ahead. As the ferry glided across the water's surface, Captain Eril began his welcome speech.

"So, welcome to Hell. This is the ferry ride you've heard so much about in myth, legend and song. I know it may not be as glamorous as all those stories made it out to be, but there's no accounting for accuracy in legends, you know. One person starts to talk about a thing and another adds their two cents in, and before you know it you've got a full-blown fantasy on your hands. It's ridiculous."

Jared, who undoubtedly had heard this tirade thousands of times, rolled his eyes and let out a disgusted sigh. "No need to go on about it, Eril, She's got her Guidebook." And in that moment, Jared produced a copy of *Fodor's Hell* and thrust it into my hands. It was a welcome but perplexing surprise. "Understand, this isn't because we're nice," whispered Jared, "We're simply lazy. Want to know something? Look it up."

The land around me was a dichotomy of vision. Needleless pine trees lined the bank to the right, appearing much like stalactites in an open air cave. They resembled old men... sentries, guarding the banks and keeping a watchful eye on anyone who would pass by, with spiny branches at the ready to scoop up anyone who might try to escape—or if Jared was to be believed—infiltrate the Gate. The opposite bank looked like a jungle; large lush trees and moss flowing like waterfalls from their branches. It was strange to see what appeared to be two separate eco systems sharing the same space—but this was Hell, and at this point, anything was possible.

"Oh, right. Sorry." As Eril started to give his tour, I flipped through the Guidebook, following along. "Anyway, to your left you'll find Blackadder Knoll. It's a cozy little place. They breed the snakes and lizards there. And on your right, you'll see Eccup Scree. It's a kitschy little tourist trap but you might have fun there. Lots of mediaeval torture devices and guillotine try-outs." He paused for a moment, giving me time to turn the pages and catch up. "As you look to the sky, you might notice a few stars. This is an illusion. In actuality, those dim lights you see above you are the street lamps from Heaven shining their impudent air of superiority down on us. It's really quite annoying. Before the street lamps, the pitch dark sky was perfect in its simplicity. And then they went and did that, spoiling it for everyone. Heaven's night lights—really bothersome. They're afraid of everything up there—most especially the darkness. It's absurd."

Another set of hands, several of them in fact, began to pass us from fingers to palm as we moved along the water. They seemed rather peaceful. I couldn't tell if there were any arms or bodies attached to those hands, and they looked gentle and caring. Yet as nice as they seemed, I wasn't sure stepping out of the boat would be such a good idea. *I'll need to look that one up later.* I was sure it was an entertaining story.

"Okay, we get it, Eril—can we just get on with it, please?" I wanted to hear the stories, but Jared had little patience.

"Right. Anyway, if you look to the left now, you'll see Mt. Vesuvius. And before you ask, yes, this is the actual, functioning volcano you've heard so much about. There are regular eruptions, and your Guidebook has a schedule, if you're interested. Just beyond the mountain is where you'll find Dinosaur Cove. Watch where you step, they have massive droppings!" Eril chuckled as if he'd never told that particular joke before. "If you're the adventurous type, you can rent a board and surf the lava flows, I've heard it's quite fun." I looked to Jared for confirmation. He waggled his hand in that 'not so much' way that told me that a lava surf might not be so important this trip.

"On the right," continued Eril, "you'll notice the arctic tundra. I'm sure you've heard the phrase, 'when Hell freezes over'; well, it actually did once—and just because people kept asking it to, it's continued to stay that way. I've heard rumors of a band of Yeti living there, but I don't like the cold much, so I wouldn't know first-hand. You can rent a parka at the Welcome Center if you're interested in checking it out for yourself; and I'm sure there are a couple of pages in the Guidebook that go into more detail."

"You mean stuff just happens down here whenever people say it will, like pay-per-view?" I was astonished.

"Yeah, we run a lot on popular demand around here." said Jared. "But not like in Heaven where everything a dead person wants is pretty much given to you, but more like Humanity's majority rule. If enough living people ask for it or curse it—you can pretty much bet it'll happen down here eventually. This arctic place is still here because so many mortals keep asking for it. Wait until you see the flying pigs, and pink elephants; they're a gas!" Jared giggled like he was seven at the image his mind had concocted of these bizarre animals. After quickly flipping to that page in the Guidebook, I giggled too.

"If you'd like more information about the sightseeing stops of Hell," continued Eril, slightly miffed at being interrupted, "look it up in your Guidebook, or go to the Welcome Center and they'll be able to give you directions. There really is quite a bit to see and do down here. I know you're only here for a short time, but try to take it all in, you won't be disappointed. Well, here we are."

"Oh good, we're home." Jared was relieved to have finally arrived. He leaned in close to me, nearly whispering so Captain Eril couldn't hear. "Just between you and me, I hate making that trip.

I've never been a big fan of water travel and Eril just isn't as much fun as he used to be."

"I heard that, you impudent sod!" hollered Eril.

"Just kidding, Eril. You know how much I love you." But I could tell Jared didn't really love Eril or the water. He was just avoiding the argument that would certainly detain him from reaching solid ground.

As the ferry came within about twenty-five feet of the bank on the far side of the lagoon, Jared took a B-1 vitamin bottle from his pocket, popped one in his mouth, and then offered one to me. "Here, take one. It's not that we're interested in your health so much," commented Jared; "The truth is, we're about misery here, not torture."

I wasn't quite sure what he meant, but swallowed the little white pill anyway. *Down the rabbit hole, Alice.*

"B-1 is great for mosquitoes," Jared muttered as he re-pocketed the tiny bottle and got ready to disembark.

As Eril threw the line to the dock hand, I wasn't surprised to find that Hell was not at all what I had expected. The dark skies and ominous harvest moon gave way to a shoreline of lush olive green and brown, teaming with reptilian wildlife. Murders of crows, flocks of albatross, and other haranguing birds filled the skies. The scene was more tropical rain forest than burnt out slum; with a little bit of Alfred Hitchcock thrown in for good measure.

The boat was again, gently landed on shore and we were greeted by a steel drum band, a small choir of reggae rockers singing—I couldn't tell what song—and hula dancers. It was an interesting, eclectic welcoming committee. It was kind of a cross between an international entertainment delegation and an acid trip gone bad. At first, it felt as though I wasn't in Hell at all, but rather on the set of a poorly conceived film. But once they placed the lay of poison ivy around my neck, I knew I was in Hell. The vitamin B-1 tablet Jared had given me didn't work on this weed, and the itching was instant and intense. I immediately threw it to the ground, stomping on it angrily. Jared laughed at me, my arms flailing as I tried desperately to scratch the area on the back of my neck that I couldn't quite reach, cursing and screaming for Calamine lotion.

"I thought you weren't about torture down here, Jared!" I accused.

"We're not," he chortled; "but you can't begrudge us a little fun, now can you?"

"Not funny!" I screamed.

"Actually," called Eril from the boat, "It kind of is." The hands lifted the snickering sea captain and his boat off into the blackness of the water's anonymity.

The itching was beginning to subside a little, but it was still bothersome. As we walked up the embankment, I noticed that there were three outhouses with a little wooden sign near each one that read 'Farting Encouraged. Heckling Discouraged.' "Well, that's nice", I said to Jared as we passed by; "After years of being chastised by my little brother, friends and cousins—finally—I have permission to fart. There's a small bit of comfort in that."

Jared smiled that wry teenage grin that suited him. "So glad we could help. Come on, it's this way."

****

The trees were tall, forming thick canopies, and each had strangling ivy climbing up the trunk. The roots were mangled and mostly above-ground... *Hell's power cords.* And it fit.

There were patches of mushrooms and other fungus infiltrating the limited open spaces between the roots. Thick moss covered most of the land between the trees, where one might expect grass. It would have been a perfectly nice place, except for the snakes, bats and constant rain. Just a mild drizzle, mind you; but rain just the same, trickling constantly from above. No thunder or lighting to punctuate the darkness and make it interesting or bring about the eventual end of the storm... not even darkness. Just never-ending, oppressing, near-debilitating gloom. It was a consistent sixty-five degrees and the sky was murky gray, hiding what might be the sun, if the rain would ever stop—which of course, it wouldn't.

The earth moved with the contented hops and squirms of hundreds of frogs, toads and salamanders. Because of the continuous rain, there was a steady supply of nasty mosquitoes and those little black flying gnats that no one likes. I was thankful for the B-1. "Thankfulness in Hell... this being dead thing is nuts." Jared shot me a look, but said nothing. I probably shouldn't have said that one out loud.

I'm certain that the amphibians thought the waves of bugs a bountiful feast. The grasshoppers were in full supply, which pleased the crows. The mice and rats seemed to run in great packs, avoiding Souls as they paraded conveniently in front of the patiently gaping jaws of constrictors and pythons. Rats were a delicacy for the alligators and crocodiles that meandered their way along the tributaries and estuaries throughout Hell. According to the Guidebook, they usually filled their gullets with piranha, and so the occasional fat rat was a nice change of pace.

I was taken aback by the large amount of water in Hell. After all the artwork and poetic descriptions of a burned out, dry desert, charred remnants of life; watching things move, and seeing this much water really surprised me. I never would have thought that all the medieval artists and poets could have gotten it wrong. Or maybe there was still more to see? I'd have to look it up in the Guidebook when I got the chance.

As we walked along, every so often, I would catch a glimpse of a few hyenas as they scrounged for leftover carrion along the riverbank. Alligators, it turned out, were sloppy eaters. "Why don't the animals seem interested in us? Is this like Busch Gardens back on Earth; if you feed them well enough then they aren't interested in people?" I was trying to make sense out of this place by defining its logic... an exercise in futility.

"Nothing that nice," Jared said. "I told you, we're not about torture here, just misery. Over the centuries, we've found that in most cases, simply having these creatures close at hand and actively involved in the food chain is enough to unnerve almost anyone. We really don't need to go much farther than that. The emotional impact seems to do the job quite nicely."

"I'd agree with that. In fact, I've been a little "unnerved" since arriving, and the relentless nagging of it is intriguing and unsettling, simultaneously."

Jared just snickered. "Yeah, we get a lot of that down here."

Rather than mirroring to me the stories of the perils of the Hell I'd learned as a child, Jared took me on the "fifty-cent" tour, enthusiastically showing me the sights. That old saying about the streets of Hell being paved with good intentions... it couldn't be further from the truth. Fact is, they were paved with cork. Sustainable, durable, recyclable, inexpensive, and as Jared pointed out as he rocked back and forth from heel to toe, "They give off a sensational squishing sound when you walk on them through the rain." He was right, the squishing sounds were everywhere.

Cars didn't exist in Hell, just mass transit. The Guidebook excused this due to the lack of parking space. The cork held up well to all those Souls trouncing about, and it was easier on the feet, too. It was puzzling, but then I remembered the subtext down here. Hell was about misery more than torture. Walking nearly everywhere took a lot of time and required more effort—but as the Guidebook reminded, it didn't have to be completely uncomfortable.

We circled around the "red light district" where whores hooked for the John's who would never pay; and Johns found whores who teased but never satisfied. We walked through the east wing of the rehab center where getting clean from drugs or alcohol meant an eternity filled with schizophrenia.

"Well, that doesn't seem quite fair," I quipped.

"Remember, this is Hell, baby," Jared said in his best rock star voice, clicking his pistol fingers at me.

We took a quick visit to the Hall of Hellish Justice where aging filibusters spent their days talking off-topic, never getting to the crux of the matter or bothering to vote. But several, I could see, were gleefully engaged in taking bribes and crafting persuasive speeches of denial. "Ah, the senior center of political life." I quipped. "It reminds me of home."

We also braved a brief tram ride through a film studio's back lot where producers couldn't make payroll, directors were grossly ignored, writers were perpetually on strike, and actors never saw a red carpet or held a gleaming statuette. But the paparazzi were abundant and abundantly annoying, with no bodyguards or velvet ropes to keep them at bay. "I guess this really proves that dead or alive, they love their work!" Jared and I shared a laugh as our tram left the lot.

We got off the tram and walked the six blocks into Downtown Hell. Along the way, I saw the tenement slum housing I had envisioned as a typical Hellish neighborhood. Old people sitting on front stoops, yelling at teenagers fighting in the streets; drug deals going on in alley ways; and a very busy tattoo and piercing parlor. *Finally, a little of the Hell I was expecting. But it still feels like something's wrong with this picture.* And then I realized... *Ah, no dead bodies and no cops!* As I considered the scene before me, I realized, it really was a criminal's utopia.

When we approached the city square, Jared nearly imploded with rapture as he pointed out his favorite Hellish monument. "And this, of course, is The Tree of Life!"

"You mean *the* Tree of Life, the one..."

"Yup, the one that made Eve famous. We've had it here for centuries, from the very beginning of Hell, in fact." Jared circled around the tree as if he was seeing it for the very first time, scrutinizing it from every angle. There was a neat, three-foot tall cast iron fence marking off a six foot square yard, perfectly manicured, around The Tree. There was no gate. There was no rain. "I think that it's a terrific symbol of all we can ever hope to achieve. There's a nice shrine built to Eve not far from here, perhaps I'll take you there later, after you've had a little time to settle in. Oh, and every month we have The Festival of Eve! Maybe if you feel like it, you can come and join in the fun; it really is quite spectacular!"

From a branch about mid-way up The Tree, there hung a single, very red, very large apple. It's wasn't the original, of course, that one had been eaten long ago; but Jared assured me that this was an exact duplicate. "The Powers That Be decided that The Tree was insignificant without the Apple, so they made another one. I wouldn't suggest eating it, though."

"No, I suppose not, I remember what happened the last time someone did that." Visions of an angry father thrusting his children out into the big, bad world as punishment for their disobedience and defiance came rushing to me.

"Actually, that's not the reason. It's said that if you eat *this* apple, the exact opposite will happen to you. From intelligent to imbecile in one simple bite. How's that for irony?" Jared had an odd look on his face, like he'd just told the funniest joke ever, and had forgotten the punch line.

"Not exactly the same thing, then, is it?" I didn't quite understand, except that irony seemed to be important in the afterlife. It was another one of those things that would take some time to figure out. Never, in my life, my living life, did I imagine that my brain would be working so hard once it was dead!

"Well I suppose not," said Jared with a contemplative look toward his sneakers. "But down here, the atmosphere or the barometer, or something changes its properties... so it flips the effect. And if you bite into it, they return you to Purgatory, pronto, C.O.D. to wander around lost in Limbo. I mean, it makes sense, really; how could they keep you if you suddenly became ignorant 'bout the choice you made 'bout being here in the first place? They'd sort of have to give you up, wouldn't they... just to keep things even, you know?"

"Um, sure." I wasn't sure Jared's logic made any sense, but I was willing to go along with it for the time being, at least until I could spend a little bit more time with my Guidebook, learning how Hell worked. Past experience with both Heaven and Purgatory had taught me that this is not an eternity of "full disclosure". There are some things, most things, in fact, that you must discover on your own.

The rain was relentless, irritating and bothersome. I had been touring Hell for nearly three hours, and I was soaked to the bone. A dull ache was starting to settle in on my muscles and a chill seeped into my blood. I was beginning to see why this really was Hell. Even people who enjoyed a good strong heat wave, and could endure one for a long time—like those weirdoes in Arizona, New Mexico and Texas—even they would be perpetually annoyed about the weather down here.

I guess that's kind of the point Jared was trying to make about Hell. Not endless, brutal torture; but instead, continual annoyance that is impossible to escape. I'd heard friends use this metaphor when discussing their toddlers, and now I understood completely why Hell was not the stereotypical raging inferno. A few people might actually enjoy that scene. This, no one would enjoy one hundred percent of the time. At least, no one who was stereotypically sane.

"Well, we'd better get you to your flat. You look a little tired." offered Jared.

"Yeah, that would be great." I was exhausted, and all that wonderful pain-free living I finally achieved my last night in Heaven was now nothing more than a distant memory. Every crevice of my non-body creaked with irritation. *Sleep would be a nice escape.*

We walked about a block down the main market square, took a left at the first corner, and Jared deposited me on the stoop of a two-story walk up.

Number fourteen, J Street.

"Well, this is it. You're home away from home for the next

week. You're on the second floor. I'd give you a key, but it's kind of not necessary. Everyone here pretty much keeps to themselves. We put you in the lessor crime neighborhood to make acclimation a little easier for you, and besides, security in Hell is sort of an oxymoron."

"Thanks. What time do I have to be ready for work tomorrow morning?" I asked in a dazed near-slumber.

"Work? Oh, we don't have any of that down here." said Jared with a confident tone. It's not like Heaven you know. Idle hands are the Devil's playthings. M would rather that you just have fun and figure it out as you go along. Zero stress."

"Nice, I think. Who's M?" I asked, slowly regaining my intrigue.

"Mephistopheles, he pretty much runs the place." Jared was about to turn and walk away when he stopped a moment and gave me a boyish grin. "Hey, you said you were going to be here for seven days, right? Well, if you're not busy, the Festival of Eve is on Friday, how about we meet up for a buffalo leg or something?" I felt like I was being asked to the senior prom all over again.

"Um, sure, that'd be nice, Jared." Jared's silent smile was the sweetest thing I think I'd ever seen, and certainly not expected in Hell. *I'm happy that I made his day.* As I watched him prance down the street back toward town, *It must be odd to be a perpetual teenager, always hitting on the older women of Hell.* And then it occurred to me that he probably enjoyed playing around with that role. I'm sure his youthful appearance got him a lot of things that his actual age would certainly squash. "How old is he, anyway?" I wondered aloud.

Turning the knob on the door, and pushing it open revealed a staircase directly ahead and another door to my right. There was also a hook on the wall to my left holding a yellow rain slicker with my name on the wall above it. It was a nice gesture. *Hell—nice? Very strange.*

As I began to mount the slender staircase, each step creaked as it bore my weight. Some things, it seemed, stayed true to imagination. My guess was that it was their way of providing something tangible about Hell for you to hold on to; kind of like Heaven and all the nauseatingly nice weather. I mean after all, nearly everything about Hell was nothing that I was expecting. Once in a while, something "normal" had to happen, otherwise, I think the place would be filled with schizophrenic ax murderers, a redundant and boring oddity in Hell.

The flat was sparsely furnished, though the large collection of candles of varying heights and thickness brought a gentle glow to the place. There was a heady aroma of jasmine that soothed the air. *Softness in Hell, isn't that blasphemous?* A bar-height table and two stools stood alone in the kitchen. A desk and chair were placed discreetly in front of the window that overlooked the alley and the trash dumpster. In the middle of the living room on a low pedestal stood my casket, the one that I'd been buried in. The one I saw on my funeral video in Purgatory. *How very strange.*

Two chairs flanked the ends and two more edged the opposite wall with a small table between them. The furniture was arranged almost in a conversational setting, with the casket as the focal point, and a flat screen TV that hung just over the mantle of a fairly large black granite fireplace. A fire poker and a stack of firewood stood at the ready. The bathroom was to the rear of the flat, and was not unique in any way except for the fact that there wasn't a bathtub, only a shower. I tried the water faucets. *Hmm, hot water, that's a nice touch.* There was also an armoire on the back wall near the bathroom filled with towels and linens, and a few extra empty drawers—for my clothes, I assumed.

Walking back to the living room, I stood staring at my casket, pondering whether or not I should open it. *What if I'm inside, my decaying body?* The thought of it un-nerved me even more than the snakes and rats. *Why would a few slimy, rabies-infested creatures milling about your feet worry you when you come home to spend time with your own decomposing corpse every night?* I tried to remember Jared's promise about Hell not engaging in torture; and clearly, I thought, spending time slowly watching my body turn to dust would qualify as torture. I tried to remember that lying, to Jared, would be a waste of time as I carefully, slowly, lifted the lid.

Like the first-time parachutist who is relieved to discover his chute deployed, I was equally elated to find that a decaying mass of flesh and bones that used to be me was not staring out at me from inside the box. Instead, I found a delicately wrapped red box with a package of English muffins, a canister of cocoa and a fairly decent sized wheel of Gouda cheese. The note read:

Raychel,
So glad to have you visiting Hell. We hope you will enjoy your stay with us. We believe that you will realize that you've been told many lies, and we look forward to dispelling them for you. The truth will set you free.
~Faythe

It was a little eerie to realize that someone whom I'd never met before knew my three favorite foods and left them for me in my coffin; but then I realized that like in Heaven, they had to have files on everyone down here. Otherwise, Jared's fears about being overrun would come true.

I took the care package to the refrigerator and began to look around for the bedroom. I couldn't find one. It seemed that the only place to sleep was indeed, my casket. *That's a little creepy, but I suppose if it was good enough to lay in after life, it's good enough to lay in after death, too.* Still a little creeped out, but incredibly exhausted, I climbed into the box, being careful to leave the lid open, and tried to sleep.

Faster than I thought possible, sleep consumed me urgently and forcefully. I don't recall any dreams, but that was probably a good thing. Being dead was taking a lot of getting used to, and the last thing I wanted was to have nightmares and be undead at the same time.

Chapter Fourteen
The Dog Park

    The next morning, after I crawled out of my casket, I was still trying to understand all the insanity of living in Hell. Things were so different than what I had been taught... and really different than life in Heaven. It was quite an adjustment, and I was becoming weary of adjustments.

    After a warm shower to drive the rain chill from my bones, a cup of cocoa and an English muffin drenched in melted Gouda cheese, I began flipping through the Guidebook. To my delight, I found the section about dead bodies. "You'll never find the decaying body of a deceased person in Hell. As in Heaven, Soul Energy is the only thing that remains with you after your life on Earth. The physical leftovers of what was once your body stays in the physical world. The truth of the matter is, it is impossible to move physical matter through the Gates, and even if we could do it—why would we want to? Dead bodies create an awful smell." I was relieved to find that Jared had been sincere, and that I wouldn't have to live through my afterlife being grossed out on a regular basis.

I was reading through a few more pages that expanded on the details of the brief tour I'd received from Eril on our trip from the Gate when I heard someone knocking at the door. The fact that there was some stranger knocking at my door didn't seem odd to me. After all, in the time since my death, with the exception of Thaddeus—and I'm told that was an anomaly—I still hadn't run into anyone that I knew from my time being alive; and I wasn't expecting to, either; at least, not in Hell. Most of the people I knew from Earth were still alive, and the ones that weren't would almost certainly have chosen Heaven over Hell. Not because they would actually think about their choice, but probably because of that nagging voice in the back of their ritual-filled head that told them they were supposed to choose Heaven; or because they had always chosen the "easy way out". And that's the textbook vision of Heaven; easy, simple, comfortable. After the week I spent up there, I wasn't so sure all that was true. But, if there were actually quotas to meet, my bet would be on Heaven reaching theirs before Hell.

The knocking at my door was becoming louder and more insistent in its repetitiveness. The thumping of first knuckles and then fist to wood brought me out of my contemplation. I wanted to say "brought me back to reality", but how, after everything I've seen since dying, could Heaven and Hell be perceived as anything even close to 'real'? *And don't even get me started on Purgatory!*

When I finally opened the door, before me stood a woman of about fifty-five years old, dressed all in black, with a style reminiscent of Rasputin. She had brown eyes, short black hair, and didn't wear glasses; although the way she was squinting at me hinted that she probably needed them. "Good day to you! I'm Faythe, your local Funeral Do-Over Director. I thought you might be interested in taking a walk and getting to know the neighborhoods of Hell a little better. I mean, how is it possible for you to make a decision if you haven't had a chance to mingle and get to know us a little bit, eh?"

"Oh, you're the one who left me the care package." I said, motioning toward the refrigerator. "Very nice of you, thank you."

"Well of course. And you're quite welcome, we're not all heathens here, you know. Come along now."

Faythe's invitation, I discovered, was not optional. She grabbed me by the hand, and led me into the streets, without giving me the chance to politely decline. In fact, I barely had the time to grab my rain slicker from the hook on the wall as we rushed down the stairs and out the door. Standing about five-foot-seven, and munching absentmindedly on a chocolate frosted brownie, I could see how she got her pudgy middle. Her clothes fit in a way that not so much accentuated or hid the extra inches, but rather, made me feel more comfortable that she had them, both the inches and the clothes. Visions of skeletons roaming the streets of Hell had been a part of my imagination since childhood. I was glad that myth had been debunked. The most striking thing about her appearance though, was the black leather fedora she wore at a slight angle over her left eye. A little Bogart, a little Dillinger... it was a little scary. It was only after we started out on our walk that I noticed the belt of prayer beads clinking with each step. The nagging voice inside me wanted to ask... but out of a sense of decorum, I decided to ignore it, for now.

"So, how'd you die; and which Purgatory Inn sent you?" Faythe's question, which came out in between bites of brownie, sounded a little like a teenage slumber partier from the beach blonde '60s.

"Um, Twain's Inn... but I thought we weren't supposed to talk about that other stuff until after we'd made a final choice?"

"Those control freaks in Heaven told you that, didn't they? Yeah, they're so damned politically correct up there, it's absurd. I mean, how are we supposed to be friends if we don't know a little bit about how we got here in the first place? The way someone dies can really tell a lot about a person, you know. Take me, for example, I was a disenfranchised Catholic nun. As a kid, I thought Catholicism was going to be the road to my salvation, but it turned out to be nothing but boredom and frustration. I mean, all that religious dogma, and so contradictory... how could you make a life like that? So I went on this amazing quest all over the world to find spiritual truth and, long story short, I had a heart attack while getting to know a really attractive Buddhist monk while we were searching for truth parked in his VW Bus outside a Jewish Temple in Queens."

"Wow. My death wasn't nearly that exciting. I just got squished at a stoplight in my SmartCar by a very large truck hauling grass seed and fertilizer just outside Detroit."

"Oh, I don't know, hari-kari by fertilizer truck sounds pretty interesting to me." There was a gentle smirk in her voice that I'm sure was supposed to put me at ease, but instead, it just creeped me out.

"You said you were the funeral director?" I said, gently trying to move the subject away from death. It's really not that pleasant a topic of conversation, you know; most especially when you haven't actually fully accepted yours yet. "It seems like that would be a pretty go-nowhere career choice down here. What exactly do you do?"

"Funeral Do-Over Director, actually. Well... if you were unhappy with your funeral, and I know you got to see yours, we all did, it's part of how that meddlesome crone, Liza gets her kicks..." There was more than a hint of contempt in Faythe's voice. Clearly, there was no love lost between the two. "Anyway, if you were unhappy with your send off, I can help you make it better than it was; better, funnier, more solemn, whatever you want. You see, we make all these choices in life, we write it all down; get lawyers to promise it'll be done our way. But the truth of the matter is, once you're dead my dear, everyone else takes over and does it the way they think is best. A lawyer will change the wording on most any document if it means a few extra bucks in his pocket; and they justify it by saying you're dead and you won't know the difference anyway. Most of the time, a person's funeral ends up being nothing even close to what you wanted. You should hear the list of complaints. By the way, as you might imagine, most of the lawyers are pretty shocked when they get here to learn that they screwed everything up—but even in their own deaths, it never turns out the way they wanted either. So I guess you'd call it 'fair play is turnabout'. Funny thing, lawyers are some of my best clients...

"Where was I... oh yeah, so, I can fix it for you; give you the funeral you really wanted instead of the one you got. I can get you a DJ, get you some really scrumptious food, extraordinary speakers, everything you could have ever wanted for your last day on Earth. My motto is: I put the "fun" back in funeral." Faythe laughed robustly. It was clear she enjoyed her afterlife.

The whole notion of having a second funeral when the people of your Earthly life couldn't experience it seemed like so much mental masturbation to me, or at best—an excuse to have a party—but Faythe believed that she was providing a vital service to the dead. And as we walked along the streets of Hell, I learned that Faythe had an even bigger, all-consuming obsession: the "Casket Upgrade Plan". As it turns out; Faythe is a true connoisseur of death boxes.

"How do you like your casket? I mean, is it comfortable enough for you? Or would you like something more, something different? Most people don't really take into consideration when they're planning their loved-one's funeral, that the casket they choose for the dearly departed is going to be with them forever. I mean, if more people understood the impact they were having on the comfort of eternity, they might buy better boxes."

Faythe was right. I'd never considered the thought that the casket you see someone in at their funeral, would be their "forever bed", if they ended up in Hell. Now in Heaven, the box is obsolete, but in Hell, it's a standard part of the decor. From what I read in the Guidebook, beds don't fly here, nobody has one. In fact, it didn't say specifically, but from the rhetoric I read in the Guidebook, they might actually be outlawed. Boxes are the only sleeping option available—I have yet to see even a picture of a couch or futon in Hell... and there don't seem to be any bathtubs, either—so unless you enjoy crashing on the floor, the box is it.

"You know, we have some really fantastic, top of the line caskets available, I'm sure we could find one to fit your style and comfort just perfectly. You can get them in standard or extra-wide depending on if you sleep on your back, stomach or curled up. We've got premium woods like cherry, rosewood and mahogany; and titanium is all the rage for long-lasting durability. We've got some with satin or silk interiors; or, if you're more of a simple-comfort kind of gal, which it seems to me that you just might be, we can get you one with soft, cozy flannel. Some even come with these nifty little drawers for you to keep special memorabilia in for all of eternity, kind of our answer to the nightstand." I started to ask a question, but never got the chance. Faythe was on a roll. The patter came out of her with practiced finesse, much like that carnival-like appliance salesman I'd seen on TV, but with a bit more... compassion.

"The cushions are tremendously diverse, too. We've got the regular mattress-type, we've got memory foam and even sleep-number jobs that will guarantee your sound sleeping pleasure forever; and when I say forever, I mean FOREVER! You should really consider an upgrade if you decide to stay. But remember, you've only got forty-eight hours after moving down here for good to make your selection; and after that, there are no upgrades. Sorry, it's the rules." And then half under her breath, as if someone might hear her, Faythe added, "We can talk price later."

Faythe was working very hard at convincing me to take an upgrade; which also sounded like trying very hard to convince me to stay in Hell. It made me wonder what she earned in commissions on both Souls and caskets. In her pitch ramblings, Faythe struck me somewhere between a compassionate wet nurse and a slimy used-car salesman. It was difficult to take her seriously—but something told me that probably I should. This was not an act, and it was a little intimidating. It was time to change the subject.

"So Faythe, I have to ask, what's with the prayer beads? Don't most nuns give that stuff up when they leave the convent?"

"Oh, I'm so glad you asked." Again, her reaction was giddy with excitement. It was hard telling if she was genuinely pleased that I asked; was simply being sarcastic; or never got the attention she craved. "These aren't your standard set of prayer beads. These are special. There's one bead for each of the lies that organized religion has told. The more I trounced around the world, trying to discover the truth about the stories and lessons that Earth's religions taught, the more I learned that although there seem to be a few universal truths, the whole thing isn't really about truth at all. It's about perspective and the prism that we choose to look through. So, I wear this belt to remind myself that a belief system is more about perspective than about truth. It was the big epiphany I had just before my untimely demise, and so when I got down here, I decided to make this belt as a reminder. I knew that if what I discovered about Truth on Earth was different than what the scholars, politicians, priests, and zealots wanted me to believe, then I had to expect that policy to follow in death, too. And as it turned out, I was right. In fact, I've added about fifteen new beads since my time on the visitor's pass."

There was a heavy silence that hung between us after that. I had shifted gears so quickly that it changed the happy, bubbly, funeral director back into the emotionally psychedelic pragmatist she had become just before death. That's the sort of thing that stays with you, I think. I don't know how long Faythe has been down here, but this stuff is still just as open-wound-fresh for her as is was the day before she died. I've never been very good at comforting despondent people. I didn't know how to fix the situation, so I just walked along, taking in the scenery and wondering when our little excursion would be over.

At last, I couldn't stand the heavy, strained silence any longer. "Faythe, thanks so much for the little walk this morning. It was really good to meet you, and thanks again for the care package, that was really very kind of you. But if you don't mind, I think I'll go exploring on my own for a while. This dying thing has been a little overwhelming, and I need a little time to adjust."

Faythe seemed a little hurt, but she responded well. "Oh, not a problem, Raychel. We all have to acclimate in our own way. I'm sure I'll see you around town in the next week, and certainly at the Festival on Friday."

"I'd like that, Faythe." And as I walked away, reaching for the Guidebook from the pocket of my slicker, I waved and smiled. As I turned and flipped the Guidebook to a new chapter, I discovered that Hell had a Dog Park.

****

Okay, let me say it again, just so you're clear. Nothing after death is what you expect it to be.

Between two streets, which the Guidebook listed as Sodom and Gomorrah... in a park, next to a butcher shop, where the rain didn't seem to fall, except to keep the grass green and the stream full of fresh drinking water, there was a tree of great height and girth. It was a white birch, with a wide trunk and many branches coming out from its center. The trunk was uniquely shaped. The base looked like a wrist coming up from the ground, and about three feet up, it mushroomed into what looked like the palm of a cupped human hand, complete with life lines. The branches flailed out from this center structure like the fingers of a hand... and after I looked a little closer, it appeared as if there were two hands, one cupped next to and a little behind the other, with many more than just ten fingers. The finger branches were very flexible, and somewhat rubbery. They would bend either forward or backward, depending on the direction a weight shifted their movement. No matter the weight, or the frequency of the bending, the branches never broke.

At the very top, nested in the finger branches in what kind of looked like a child making the letter 'W', was a large "Snoopy" style dog house. It was your standard dog house; arched doorway, peaked roof, long, rectangular shape. It too, was a strange eggshell white color with a wide dirt brown stripe running along the side. In fact, as the Guidebook pointed out, this tree and its house were the only white structures to be found in Hell. It was as conspicuous as a circus clown at a gothic convention.

As strange a sight as it was, a dog house perched in a tree like that, what I saw next was stranger still. I noticed several dogs playing in the tree. A golden retriever, a black Labrador, a brown toy poodle, a husky, a shih tzu, and some variety of medium-sized gray terrier that I couldn't identify. Each dog would take it's turn to jump into the palm of the tree, climb up a finger branch, and then slide down another nearby branch; bending it as it glided the dog down to the ground. I stood there for about five full minutes, watching the dogs until I realized, they were playing a game of "tag" meets "king of the mountain".

The scene was unbelievably comical. Each dog chased the others up the tree and into the branches only to slide their way down again; all the while, frantically nipping at their predecessor's tail. Every once in a while, a dog would make it to the dog house without getting his tail tugged. He would then perch himself in the doorway, and howl a gleeful howl. When this happened, the other dogs would stop the game, tuck their tail, and let out a cackle similar to a hyena laugh. And then the winning dog would climb down the tree. They'd huddle for a moment, gulp down some water, and then the game would start all over again.

When I looked to the Guidebook to explain more about this strange sight, and how it was that dogs were climbing trees, the answer it gave me was oddly sane.

The dogs found in Dog Park are special dogs. These are the Hell Dogs that have chosen to live down here most of the time, primarily because of their life-long jealousy and hatred of cats. They have harbored an unresolved anger about the injustices between cats and dogs; why cats got to climb trees, and dogs were relegated to stand on the ground below them, while the cats hissed and tormented them, just out of capture range. Dogs were never given a room with a view. The horizon was never something they could ever fully appreciate because their houses were all nailed to the ground. So, when they asked to be given a tree of their own to climb, and a view to enjoy, The Powers That Be decided that it was the least they could do, considering the eons of sacrifice dogs have made while upholding the moniker of "man's best friend". They had to give up a lot to be with humans, and so now, they get to have a little fun.

The dogs asked for this tree? How? I kept reading.

We have some language experts of our own, you know. Heaven doesn't hold the patent on understanding, although they'd like you to believe otherwise. We asked the dogs what they wanted, and they told us. Animals get to make choices, too. They have Free Will, but on different terms than humans. It's because they are who they are, and who they have been for so long, and the array of Humanity's

> limitations, that they are the only ones allowed to change their minds from time to time. That's why you and I are stuck with our choice of Heaven or Hell for eternity, and they get to travel back and forth on a whim. See Rainbow Bridge, page 65.

As I heard the gleeful howl of another winning dog, I quickly flipped to page 65.

> The Rainbow Bridge is a real bridge between Heaven and Hell; and it's not a one-way route, as most people are led to believe. However it is only available to the animals; and for the most part, domestic animals are the only ones who use it. The animals can choose how much time they spend in each realm, and when they come and go they use the Rainbow Bridge. Service and Entertainment animals, those whose dignity was ripped from them under the guise of giving them "jobs" on Earth, can even go back and visit Earth if they want to. It's an extra perk they get for all the suffrage we humans have put them through.

I thought it was a nice touch that, on at least this one issue, Heaven and Hell agreed about the proper usage of the Rainbow Bridge... and got it right. But the other element, I didn't understand completely. *Suffrage of animals? What does that mean?* I read on.

> The suffrage animals have had to endure at the hands of Humanity includes, but is not limited to, training wild animals against their nature to do things to entertain us or make us feel comfortable; locking them up in zoos; eating them; stealing their natural habitats; and scientific experiments. Because of Man's continually exploding ego, the animals have always been at a subservient disadvantage since the dawn of time. The Powers That Be deemed that it's only right that we return their dignity and grant them a little

more freedom in death.

I had to admit it, the Guidebook made a good point. Hell was beginning to seem a little more equitable than I thought it would be; at least for the animals. And as Gandhi said, that's a good sign that Humanity, or in this case, the afterlife, is doing alright.

****

As I continued to meander through the neighborhoods jutting off Main Street, I noticed something unexpected. The address markers of Hell's apartments, houses, shops... they were all tombstones, just as my grandmother had explained when I was barely seven years old.

"Yes my dear, a tombstone is the address marker for our loved ones. After they've passed, we need to be able to find them, to talk to them, to remember them. A tombstone is that marker—our loved one's entry in the eternal address book."

However, as I read one after another, I didn't find the traditional, respectful inscriptions. Instead the named tombstones had the ability to change their inscriptions like the marquee in front of a movie house; and their messages were as diverse as the Souls they addressed. One simply said "don't bother knockin', I've gone fishin' ". A second, that of a former rock star read, "played hard, died early, still playing hard, catch us Friday night on the banks of The Styx". A third, very ornate black marble stone with an animatronic talking gargoyle on top, bearing the name Geoffrey Hunter Harrison, Esq. in gold block lettering announced, "I'm dead. I'm out having fun. Sue me." My personal favorite was a seemingly classic looking gray tombstone which marked the final address of a former Benedictine monk. Defiantly, it declared, "No collars, No sandals, No celibacy".

Each tombstone held a slot or drawer, depending on the design, where messages could be left if the deceased wasn't at home. More than just an address marker, I realized my grandmother was right; these were actually the mailboxes of Hell. I looked it up in the Guidebook. I found the entry on page 103.

> "The mailboxes of Hell are an important communication tool. Since it's nearly impossible to pry the Power of Prayer away from those control freaks in Heaven, we had to come up with an alternative way for Hellions to hear from their loved ones back on Earth. We have a team of volunteers who meet weekly and dutifully transcribe the notes from Earthly loved ones and pen them to parchment. Then, we have an army of volunteer postal people who deliver those notes to the tombstones as required. It's extremely gratifying... but sadly, like most acts of love, unrequited. We have no way to return messages to those who send them. Heaven secured the patent on Dream Dispatches and even though we put up a good fight in court, we lost. Sometimes, we attempt a reverse connection through Nightmares and Night terrors—the two communication avenues those twits in Heaven **generously** allowed us to access—but few humans can remain calm long enough to understand the message. Emotionally driven creatures rarely look for the underlying communication in any situation, let alone in their Nightmares and Night terrors. It's hard for them to decipher our vivid presentations as deeply held messages. It's still a very valuable service; though... imagine never hearing from your loved ones ever again—it could mean a very depressing after life. Visit the Welcome Center if you are interested in donating a bit of your time to this noble cause; and perhaps brighten a Hellion's day."

I walked the streets captivated by this postal creativity, and the idea that compassion found its way into Hell. Soon, I ran into a former Earthly postal worker, looking a little like Elvis, and still wearing the traditional blue uniform; shirt with white stripe, shorts, and lifeguard-style hat with the red stripe along the rim. He introduced himself simply as Jack. When I asked why he chose Hell, he said, "Well, my life had always been run by the clock... tick-tock, tick-tock, tick-tock... every second another nail in my coffin of stress. But I truly enjoyed delivering the mail. So now, I still deliver the mail but, it's on my time now. No one seems to mind my delivery delays much. It's not like there are any life or death deliveries down here, no registered letters, no lottery winnings. And, have you noticed..." he said with a grin; "there are no clocks in Hell! I still get to have my fun delivering the mail, but without all the stress. It's really quite nice."

After meeting Faythe, Jared and now Jack, it was strangely comforting to know that there were people of service living in Hell. "Well, I've got to run, this bag is getting heavy and I've got a date with a picnic basket and a beguiling young lady later this afternoon." And so, with a little wink, Jack the mailman was off stuffing letters and packages into tombstones as he walked down the road, whistling Vivaldi.

Curiosity got the best of me, and so, after consulting my Guidebook, I headed off west. Sure enough, a couple of blocks down the road, I discovered the Tankoos Tombstone Shop. As I stepped inside, I noticed a sign hanging above the main counter that read, "Stones carved while you wait—No rush deliveries!"

Browsing the shop, I saw a few sample headstones placed strategically around the room, but most of the carver's work was showcased in beautiful leather-bound photo books on shelves lining the south wall. Some particularly ornate stones were displayed in sketch and photo pairings, hung on the north wall in dramatic frames. Flipping through a couple of the books, I snickered as page after page, the Soul for whom the stone was carved stood by, a jubilant smile on their face, as if they'd just adopted a new puppy or bought their first car. Although some of the tombstones were the standard dull gray or black stone you might expect, most were extremely colorful and tremendously charismatic.

On one wall, surrounded by an ornate bronze frame with a chocolate suede matte, there was a clipping from a newspaper article quoting Tanner Tankoos, Chief Headstone Carver:

> *I've been in this business for nearly a millennia, and I take great pride in the diversity of my work. I like to think of myself as an artist rather than a simple mailbox manufacturer. Oh, yes, there is much more to it than that. The comprehensive consultation work we do with the client before carving begins is an integral part of the process. After learning a client's specific artistic leanings, we will create a model, and once approved, craft for them the tombstone they've always wanted, one they can be proud of for centuries to come. Of course, this is their mailbox, but more than that, it's also an artistic representation of the Soul.*

I'd been thumbing through the pages of Photo Book Two when Hell's Chief Headstone Carver stepped out from the back room and said hello. "Welcome to Tankoos Tombstones. I'm Tanner, chief carver, what can I do for you today?" Tanner appeared to be about forty-five. He had a long, slender face; blonde wavy hair that hung to the nape of his neck; and a never-shrinking cigarette that dangled precariously from the corner of his mouth. Clad in Levi's and bare feet, he looked like a Bohemian rock star mixed with a Roman gladiator's blacksmith. His bare chest, muscles bulging just enough to add resume value, was emphasized by a black leather apron. A hammer and chisel rested peacefully in his stone-dusted hands. His voice was raspy, and periodic coughing punctuated his words as a thin line of smoke danced upon his eyelashes. He didn't seem to be a man I should be afraid of, but he did jolt a little lightning bolt of curiosity.

"I'm interested in the possibility of a new tombstone, but I've still got five days left on my visitor's pass. Can I see what mine might look like now, or do I need to wait?"

"No, no need to wait. Why don't you have a seat over here, and we can talk about what you're looking for." Tanner set his tools on the counter, brushed his dusty hands on his apron, and showed me to a small alcove on the east wall of the shop with a wrought iron table and chairs. The table held piles of brochures and photos in neatly aligned stacks. There was also a color swatch book and an ashtray. Tanner snuffed out his smoke and gave me a gentle smile. "Now, why don't you give me a simple description of what you like, and I can sketch something up for you real quick."

"Oh, that would be great! My favorite color is blue, and I really love horses, can you do anything with that, or do you need more?" I was strangely giddy at the thought of having a custom-made tombstone.

Tanner offered me his one raised eyebrow look of doubt and pushed his chair back from the table just a bit. Yes, I know I was channeling Hailee's perkiness in that moment, but I couldn't help it. The thought of finally getting something I wanted was exciting. I now understood why the Casket Upgrade Plan that Faythe offered might be appealing. Getting to choose without limitations—it was an enticing concept.

"Horses are not a popular theme down there, what with the fable of the Four Horsemen and all, it's not something that people like to dwell on. Those four guys really got a raw deal... and most other illustrations of horses I'm familiar with are usually depicted as 'majestic and Heavenly'. You can imagine why there's not a lot of call for that down here."

"You mean you don't have horses in Hell?" I was stunned.

"Oh no, we've got horses, wild Mustangs, mostly; but no one keeps them as pets. It's not like we've got a Dude Ranch or anything. We sort of have a policy outlawing slaves of any sort; animals included."

"Well that's nice." I said in my mother's sweet, condescending voice. *Now I'm channeling my mother? This being dead thing is very weird.* Tanner raised his other eyebrow. "Uh yeah..."

And then, with a distant stare, Tanner stood up and started pacing around the shop, murmuring to himself while considering materials and design elements. "I'd need to find some way to represent the horse as a neutral, natural creature. Not too cute, not too powerful, just simple elegance." It was as if he had decided that my simple request was now his greatest challenge. "Hmmm... it would be very unique. I don't think it's ever been done before. It would need to be classic yet contemporary. Bronze? No, that's so two centuries ago, and marble just wouldn't convey the right fluidity of movement..."

He stopped in his tracks, one hand palming a marble sphere and the other fingering the leaf of a potted plant. And in that moment I could have sworn I saw a cartoon light bulb appear over his head. Quickly, he scuttled back to the table, lit another cigarette, ripped open his sketch book, picked up a piece of chalk and began to sketch, flinging each rejected idea to the floor with artistic flourish.

"Hmmmm... glass... now there's an option... maybe something in a rich cobalt blue with pewter accents. We could have it rearing military style... no, that's just too cliché." Parchment fell to the floor. "Perhaps laying down, gently sleeping... no, they die that way." *Rip*, and parchment hit the ground yet again. "But maybe... yes, that's it... the masterful jumper but without a rider—no oppression—just Free Will. I could carve a stone wall and..."

He continued to sketch for a few minutes more, and when he was finished, he snuffed out his cigarette and presented me with the drawing. I was astounded at the result. A beautiful blue and pewter stallion captured in mid-jump over a stone wall that looked as though it had been ripped right out of the Scottish countryside. In the middle of the wall, under the steed's girth was a plain iron mail slot. There was a single stone that held my name and date of death, nothing more. It was simple, elegant, and perfect.

"Extraordinary! This is perfect! When can I have it?" I was so caught up in the artistic beauty of the drawing and the thought that it could really be mine; I'd completely forgotten that this was a Hellish purchase. I didn't even know how much it would cost me. And still, I wanted it. *That temptation thing is strong down here... it must be the incense Tanner is burning.*

"Well, first, you need to finish out your visitor's pass, and then, if you choose Hell, I can have it ready by the next Festival of Eve—about a month." With that, he shook my hand and apologized for needing to get back to work.

Walking out into the street, I dog-eared the Tankoos Tombstone Shop's page in my Guidebook. If I chose Hell, I'd need to find this place again in a hurry!

****

It was about two hours later when I ran into Faythe again. She was approaching a man in front of a vegetable stand. Faythe greeted him warmly, with a giant hug and kiss, like he'd been a friend for decades, which was quite possible, since time stands still after you die—a perk no one has thought much of until that day Edgar comes for them. It turns out that all those anti-aging creams and potions that were marketed to stop the aging process were simply wasted money. Death does a much better job of it than Cover Girl or Olay ever could. I approached the pair just as Faythe delivered her jaunty greeting.

"Zeb, old friend, how are you? What's it been, a dozen years or so since we talked last? You look a little haggard, where've you been?"

"Three weeks. It's been three weeks, Faythe," said Zeb in an irritated monotone. "I took a hermitage to the South Islands to hang with the Dinosaurs for a bit. It was nice, but not enough rain, if you ask me. Who's your friend?"

"Oh, silly me, this is Raychel; and Raychel, this is Zebulon who used to be Fred." Faythe loved getting people together.

"Um, nice to meet you." I said, taking his hand and delivering it back to him with a slight twinge of uncertainty.

"So, what did you do on your hermitage, Zeb? Anything exciting?" Faythe had clearly recuperated from our last conversation, and her "valley girl" vocal repose was back.

"Nope. Just a little camping on the islands. Bonfires at night on the volcanic ash are pretty; all that red and orange against black. It's soothing, really. Takes a few minutes to get used to the sulfur stench, though. I did read an interesting book, Michael Connelly's *The Poet*; quite a page turner. If you haven't read him, you really should. Very interesting stuff." Zeb talked about his book reading hermitage with tremendous enthusiasm in complete monotone. I could tell that he was excited about his latest literary discovery, but his stoic delivery made me wonder if he was truly excited, or if I just wanted him to be. His face was speckled with freckles and tied neatly with a reddish orange bow-tie moustache, which barely quivered.

"So, Zeb," insisted Faythe. "Don't be rude. Tell Raychel here, how you died."

"Oh, that. Well, it's really quite simple; you see, I was on a brief hiatus from Humanity, up in Alaska by myself, working on getting through Dante's Inferno translated in Inuit, when a couple of grizzlies figured me for their dinner. It didn't take long; and no, it didn't hurt much, either. By the second paw swipe I was pretty much out of it. So that's my story, from librarian on holiday to grizzly chow in five minutes. Not very exciting. How about you?"

"Oh, me, nothing special. Squished in my SmartCar while sitting in traffic." I responded patently.

"See now, isn't this nice," said Faythe, looking to me with a Cheshire cat grin. "Here we are, only your second day in Hell, and making friends already."

Zebulon excused himself politely and moved away. I got the impression that he'd met his quota for small talk for the day and was tapped out.

"Don't mind Zeb. He really is a nice guy. Just a little quiet, is all." said Faythe.

A few minutes later, and Faythe and I had circled around back to my flat. Faythe said her perky good-byes and reminded me again to think about the Funeral Do-Over and Casket Upgrade Plans. She promised to call on me again in a day or two. It was an interesting afternoon, I must admit, but I was exhausted and needed to decompress a little. I just wish I'd had a nice comfy bed to do it in. That flannel sleep number box was beginning to sound pretty good. But for now, I'd just have to settle for some peanut butter on toast, a glass of juice and a nap in the bargain basement casket my parents bought.

They really should consider teaching a class about this stuff in high school... Funerals 101. We should be more prepared for the afterlife.

Chapter Fifteen
A Harmless Haunting

    I was walking through Hell the next afternoon. It was drizzling, as usual, so I stopped by a cafe for a warm up of cocoa. It was a relatively quiet day. Not much really happening. I was reading through the tabloid, just checking the day's top stories... yet another Elvis sighting; reports about which local celebrity got Eve pregnant, again; and Joseph's repeat visit to rehab. It's not like this was actual news, it was doubtful what could be believed; but I must admit the headlines were certainly eye-catching... and the photos... *Oh, so that's what Eve really looks like.* Classic portraiture was always 'ify', so much left to imaginative interpretation; but photos, well, that's where the truth lies... or not. For all I know, Demons could have invented PhotoShop.

    Anyway, I was sitting there, milling through the tabloids, drinking my cocoa and eavesdropping on a conversation of a nearby Ghoul. I'm not quite sure how he got that way, but there he was, green skinned, deformed face, long fingers with an impeccable manicure. I didn't have the courage to ask him where he came from and how he acquired his unique look. In all honesty, I didn't want to know the answer; Hell was challenging enough to process without learning the origins of possible curses. I figured, what I didn't know, couldn't haunt me.

The Ghoul was talking to an Albino with pink eyes and button buck spikes on his head about their recent trip to the Nether Regions, and the fun they had there. I couldn't hear everything, but the phrases "Frisbee football with his brain"; "second verse, same as the first"; and "no harm, no foul—except that one—he was really foul!" reached my ears. As their conversation reached a crescendo, in unison they blurted out—"What happens in the Nether Regions stays in the Nether Regions" and they "high-fived" each other, cackling like two old witches from *McBeth*. I hadn't heard of a place called the Nether Regions, but it seemed something Jared would have mentioned; it was odd that he didn't. I flipped frantically through my Guidebook to look for the entry; but I couldn't find it. So, after about ten minutes of playing "should I—shouldn't I", I mustered up some courage to ask the Ghoul. This was far too interesting a tidbit to ignore.

"Hey," I said, walking to their table as nonchalantly as possible; "I don't mean to barge in on your conversation... but I overheard you talking about the "Nether Regions". I've looked in my Guidebook, but I can't find it. Can you help me out?" From the way they were looking at me, I wasn't sure if they were going to help me or eat me... but I figured it was worth a shot.

"What's your name, little lady?" asked the Albino in what I'm sure was his very best lounge lizard drawl.

"I'm Raychel." I said, tentatively; not really knowing if I was on the menu as entertainment or lunch.

"Oh, are you new here? We haven't seen you around before." The Ghoul chimed in. "And we know most everyone."

"Um, yeah, I'm on my visitor's pass... just trying to get the lay of the land, you know, so I can make a choice. So how about it, are you two willing to tell me about the Nether Regions?" I said, hand place strategically on my hip, school principal style. I didn't want to seem more invasive than I already had been, but at the same time, I wanted to make sure they knew that I wasn't interested in playing games. I'm not sure if there's such a thing as undead virginity, but if there is, I was pretty sure that I didn't want to lose mine to a Ghoul and an Albino.

"Aw, come on and have a seat, Raychel. We didn't mean anything by it... just being friendly, you know? I'm Gaspar," said the Ghoul, flashing a smile that showed off his perfect dental work. "And this is Adrien." He said, gesturing to the Albino; who silently waved and smiled; frustrated that his charm had gone unnoticed. "We were just on Holiday in the Nether Regions, scaring the crap out of some old friends. It was terrific fun!" The two laughed together, and sipped their flaming lattes.

"Yeah, about that," I inquired again. "I tried to look it up in the Guidebook, and I couldn't find it anywhere. Where is this place? I mean, if there's fun to be had in Hell, I'd like to know more about it."

"Well, Raychel," said Gaspar. "It's not so much a where..."

"... as a when." Adrien grinned.

"What do you mean, time travel of some kind?" I asked, perplexed.

"Sort of," said Gaspar. "It's a way that you can go back to bother the ones you've left behind. You know, play a few tricks, do a little harmless haunting..."

"... it's all in good fun, of course." Added Adrien, and again, the two giggled together.

"But, I thought that trying to go back was, first of all—forbidden; and also, a depletion of your Soul Energy, which I'm told can be downright dangerous. But you two don't seem to be under arrest or exhausted; so what gives?"

"Okay," said Gaspar, leaning in closer, speaking in a whisper. "We've found a small wrinkle that allows you to reach out and touch those you left behind, without ever really leaving Hell. It's a perk."

"Yup," giggled Adrien; "a definite perk. They don't know about this in Heaven, you know. And if they did, they'd probably create some Mass dogma to outlaw it and make you feel super guilty about using it." He grinned like an aardvark who just discovered vacuum suction. "But we go to the Nether Regions all the time, and we don't have any issues; do we, Gaspar?"

"Nope. Just good clean fun;" said Gaspar, looking particularly gargoyle-ish as he leaned back in his chair.

"It sounds like a great way to spend an afternoon. I'd love to try it out, but I've got limited time, I'm just on a seven-day pass, remember? Can you maybe take me today?" It truly did sound like Hell's fun house attraction, and I was excited to test it out. And... as long as there weren't any nasty side effects, what would be the harm? I had a 'friend' back home that I wanted to reconnect with, and so I pressed them again. "Come on, guys... what do you say? Show a girl a good time?" I threw in a coy little wink, just for good measure.

"Well... we're not supposed to show newbies." said Adrien hesitantly, looking to Gaspar for help with his backbone. "The rules say it's reserved for residents only."

"But since you're so nice and all... Aw, why not! Sure, let's do it!" whooped Gaspar. Adrien, having absolutely no functioning spine, either physical, spiritual or emotional, went along begrudgingly. He reminded me a lot of a girl I knew in elementary school who always ended games we weren't supposed to be playing early because she was sure she was going to get caught. I thought my mother instilled good guilt; but her mom was the champion!

We headed off down the street, away from Downtown Hell, and caught the train to Dragon's Lair. From there, we hopped a ferry to Volcano Island, and then chartered a rickshaw around to the back of Dinosaur Alley. Once there, the boys led me into a dank cave, just the other side of Pterodactyl Place. Inside, about thirty feet down, there was a large wooden door. Gaspar pushed it open and we entered an odd, two dimensional space. I immediately felt like a piece of paper that someone had forgotten to crumple up and throw away. "So," he asked; "who'd you like to reach out and touch?"

"Well, there's this guy..." I began.

"Yup, knew it had to be a guy," scoffed Adrien, throwing his hands in the air and turning to make his way back out the door.

"No, it's not like that," I protested. This guy, from my junior high school, he was a real jerk; his name is Joe; he treated me like crap, and got a bunch of other kids to pick on me too—and—and I wasn't the only one he tormented. I feel like a little payback is in order." I explained.

"Oh, that's perfect." rejoiced Gaspar. "We really hate bullies! Let's do this!" I gave them Joe's last name and the last address I had for him. Evidently, it was still good. He turned out to be as big a loser as an adult as he had been as a kid, and the last time I'd heard anything about him, he was still living in his parent's basement, on probation. He'd already done fifteen years in prison for dealing to kids. He really deserved a lot worse than just a good scare, but this was the best I could do, given my limitations.

I'm not sure how the boys made it happen, but a few minutes later, I was standing at the end of Joe's bed, Ghoul and Albino by my side. "Well," said Gaspar. Have at it!" I wasn't quite sure what to do next. I stood there, silent, not sure of my lines or blocking; so the boys helped me along.

Adrien went over and knelt down beside Joe's bed. He leaned in really close and then SCREAMED like a little girl, right into his ear. Gaspar picked up both of his legs and dragged Joe to the floor, where he landed with a loud THUMP. Joe never woke up through the whole thing, but I could tell that he was becoming more distressed with each prank the boys played; kicking, pinching, hair pulling. And now, it was my turn.

I walked over to Joe, who was now curled up in the fetal position on his bedroom rug, and got right down next to him. I've never been a physically violent person, but the tirade that came next, I must admit, wasn't anywhere near rated G, and I feel it would be uncouth to repeat it in all its colorful splendor, especially in mixed company. Suffice to say that I used every word I'd ever heard that my parents, Rabbi, teachers and even boot camp instructors would never approve of coming out of my mouth, let alone living in my head. I reminded Joe of the middle school atrocities he perpetrated against me and others, and how cruel a human being he is. I went on to extol his stupidity in getting kids hooked on drugs. I went on to succinctly explain why I thought it was that he should "off" himself and save the rest of us a great deal of grief and aggravation. I was pretty upset, and I allowed myself to channel that young pre-teen pain and adult disgust into my haunting of Joe.

The more I spoke, the more I screamed, the more I swore at him, the more I could see his body contorting as his mind flailed inside his Night terror. After fifteen minutes, he cried out... and then begged me to stop. Which of course, I did. After all, Hell is about misery, not torture, remember? The boys led me back outside the cave and helped me navigate my way back to my flat. On the way, I reveled in my accomplishment. "Wow, you guys! That felt great! Whoever said a little retribution wasn't good for the Soul, had it all wrong."

"We're glad you had a good time, Raychel." said Adrien.

"But how come I don't feel exhausted, in fact, just the opposite; I feel energized. Why is that? Is that whole energy depletion thing they fed me in Heaven just a ploy to get me to be nice?" I was excited and confused, simultaneously. It was an odd version of euphoria.

"We only occupied two dimensional space and time." explained Adrien. "So, technically, we weren't really there. That's why you didn't deplete your Soul Energy."

"Technically, two dimensional energy can't be tracked, so it can't be subtracted, either." offered Gaspar.

"Incredible!" I said with an exuberance that was impossible to contain. "When can we go back?"

"We, can go back anytime we like... you, on the other hand..." began Adrien;

"...must wait until you make a choice. If you choose Hell, well then, the world is your two dimensional oyster. But..." said Gaspar;

"...try to convince your friends in Heaven that this is real, if that's where you end up..." quipped Adrien;

"...and you'll be railroaded back to traipse around Purgatory forever, with no hope of parole." said Gaspar.

"Yeah, they're not fond of bending the rules up there." finished Adrien.

It was a little unnerving that these two completed each other's sentences—a lot. It gave me the impression that there was something much deeper going on between Ghoul and Albino, besides casual friendship. But, I wasn't going to ask—not my business.

I kissed them both on the cheek and skipped up the steps to my flat. I fell into my casket, content for the first time since getting off the boat. There was something to be said for this haunting thing. I'm not sure I would want to make a habit of it... but it was a good technique for making a point.

Chapter Sixteen
The Pound

Day four in Hell brought me an adventure I hadn't expected. I found it on page 666. The Guidebook listed it as a "curiosity": *Zatvor Island, the home for Stray Souls*. The six short sentences lent it a sense of creative avoidance. It was one of those places you should probably know about, but probably didn't want to visit. And so of course, that meant that I had to visit. I walked down to the docks and looked for Captain Eril. He had just arrived; Jared and two new visitors were stepping on shore.

"Hey, Raychel. How goes it?" said Jared, friendly as ever.

"Oh, fine... Just fine, thanks Jared." I was a little distracted and probably not as nice as I should have been. Fortunately, Jared didn't seem to care. He was focused on the fun of introducing poison ivy lays to his new friends.

"Ahoy, Captain Eril! I seek passage to Zatvor Island," I called. "Can you take me?"

Both men stared at me as if I'd just asked to be dropped in the mouth of a sputtering volcano.

"Oh, Raychel, I'm not so sure you'll be wanting to go there." Said Eril. "It's not the best of Hell, you know. Wouldn't you rather visit Sodom City? There's so much more to see and do, plenty of excitement for a young girl like you."

"Yeah;" said Jared, taking a few steps away from his new charges and speaking in a hushed tone. "You won't have a good time there... it's really not a nice place. How about you come back to The Tree with me and the newbies. You'll have more fun."

"Thanks, Jared. But I've already seen The Tree. It's nice and all, but I really want to go to Zatvor Island. It intrigues me." I said, trying to be as appreciative as I could be.

"Suit yourself." He said, leading his visitors away from the docks. He was working hard not to glance over his shoulder as I boarded the ferry.

"I don't like it... don't like it one bit." sputtered Eril. "But, if you're determined Miss Raychel; I suppose we'll be off, then."

"Thank you, Captain."

As the boat moved downstream, the weather began to change. The constant drizzling rain turned to steam rising in billows off the river. The air became hotter, and the clouds darker. The moon faded from orange to blood red with slow, chameleon-like transformation. Boiling swimming pool-sized craters of black tar popped and gurgled from the rocky riverbank in a sinister symphony of dread. Eril was clearly uneasy. His eyes darted from port to starboard, from stem to stern. The gentle hands that had steadied us from the Gate to shore were gone now. In their place, hands charred black from burns and exposure tossed us forward with palpable pain at every cast. A look of worry wrapped around Eril's face and his hands shook as he worked to steady the tiller.

"Must remain steady," he whispered. "Capsizing here would be beastly."

Twenty minutes down the river, I noticed a rickety dock jutting from the jagged shoreline. A few planks were missing and the stanchions were weak and moldy. Nailed firmly to a pylon nearby, a new sign painted in horror-film white lettering warned:

Zatvor Island; Enter With Caution

It was meant as a deterrent, but to me, it seemed more of an invitation. Even in my childhood I defied the warnings and took terrific leaps of faith, believing in my own immortality. And now that I no longer had mortality to worry about... well, I just had to see for myself what everyone else feared.

Eril laid a gentle hand on my shoulder as I began to step onto the quivering dock. His eyes held a terror I hadn't expected to see. "Be careful, Raychel. Horrible things live here. Don't let them steal your Soul." He thrust a small panic button into my palm. "Press this and I'll be back to get you cheetah quick."

"Thank you, Eril." I pocketed the button and walked into the wooded unknown. About fifty yards from the riverbank there stood what looked like a small DNR guard shack. As I got closer, a woman of about thirty, dressed in a camo-brown military-style fatigues, long-poll taser in hand, stepped outside.

"What brings you to Zatvor Island?" She called with a commanding voice.

"My name's Raychel, I'm on a visitor's pass... saw this place in the Guidebook... thought I'd check it out." I held up my Guidebook as a sort of proof of my intentions. "What is this place?"

"This is Zatvor Island... Hell's jail. Welcome, I'm Taryn", she said as we shook hands. "We don't get many visitors out here. What made you decide to make the trip?"

"Six simple sentences, actually. I think it's the shortest entry in the book. It says this island is the home to Hell's Stray Souls. It made me wonder what a Stray Soul was... so here I am. Jared and Eril seemed to be scared of the place; but I figured, I'm already dead, what more is there to be afraid of?"

"Plenty. Are you interested in the tour?" Taryn looked as though she was psychically willing me to turn back. I'm sure my answer was a complete disappointment.

"Absolutely; lead on!" I had the sensation of standing in line at the amusement park while waiting to board the scariest roller coaster on Earth. My stomach lurched and my heart rate quickened. I'm so glad The Powers That Be let me keep my adrenaline rush. Death would be pretty dull without it.

"Okay, but remember, you asked for it. Stay close." Taryn ducked into the guard shack, picked up a hand-held radio and pocketed another battery for the taser.

We walked up a winding path toward a complex of buildings. The compound looked like any prison you might see back on Earth. Low, two-story dormitories with a twenty-foot chain link fence and a large roll of barbed wire on the top. Hanging on the fence at ten-foot intervals were signs warning of high voltage. As we approached the first entry gate, Taryn pushed a button on her key fob. The gate swung open, and then closed and locked behind us with a metallic clank, after we entered the yard.

"So what's the deal?" I said. "I thought that the Law of Free Will meant that jail wouldn't exist—certainly not in Hell. Doesn't everyone just get to do what they want down here?" I knew it was pointless to be logical in a completely illogical place... but I really wanted to understand.

Taryn took a deep breath as she surveyed the perimeter, speaking softly and carrying her electric stick. "Here's the thing. Yes, you get Free Will, but even if you choose Hell, we still have rules. Maybe not as many as they have in Heaven, but we still have them. You know about the depletion of your Soul Energy, right?"

"Sure, trying to skip town and go back to visit Earth does that to you. Deplete your Soul Energy too much, and you wind up wandering in Limbo for all of eternity, right?"

"That's right. But it's a little different for those who have chosen Hell. The repercussions are a little more severe down here." Taryn took one last look behind us, her face contorted as if swallowing a foul tasting medicine, and then she opened the first dormitory door.

We entered a large, dark room. Strange red and gray shadows bounced in from skylights perched overhead. A strong stench of sulfur hung in the air, and the ambient heat was making me start to sweat. We walked slowly down a corridor lined with cages—like prison cells, only smaller. They were about 6' x 6' x 6', stacked two tall, a red and white high voltage warning sign hung from each door. There was a low rumble radiating from the place, it sounded like the collective growls of a thousand empty stomachs; and although the volume didn't change, the intensity was growing. In a fit of anger or perhaps a moment of poor choice management, a pewter-colored, spindly, three-fingered hand darted out toward me. It encountered the hot gate and withdrew in a howl of agony. If I'd still had skin, I would have jumped right out of it!

Taryn immediately had her taser at the ready, poised to deflect another attack. "You okay?"

"Um... yeah, I think so. What was that thing?" I said with a frightened stutter.

"That... was a Stray Soul. The opportunities for escape are rare, so they jump at it whenever they think they might have a chance. That one's fairly new. It hasn't figured out that the gates are not to be messed with. Poor thing." I could see why Taryn held this post. She clearly had sympathy for these things that few others would consider worthwhile.

Regaining my composure, I walked closer to the cage door and peered inside. There, in the back corner, holding its left arm close to its chest, crouched on a small cot, was what I could only describe as an alien. Its skin was ashen; it had no hair; it had a misshapen head and large oval eyes, just like all those lunatics described in every abduction story I'd ever read and every alien abduction movie I'd ever seen. There was no mistaking the resemblance. These were Rosewell Aliens!

I looked at Taryn, dumfounded. "What the... Aliens... really?" Taryn took me by the elbow, steering me toward the middle of the corridor as we kept up a brisk pace through the long building. I stared at the contents of the cages as we walked by. I heard the echo of gnashing, clawing and screaming as the captives from above and every side, tried to reach through the wires. It was a torturous scene. This was the picture of Hell that I had been taught... the one that I had imagined. And it was beyond frightening. Once we got out the door at the far end of the building, Taryn took a moment to explain.

"Some Souls, after making the Free Will choice to live their eternity in Hell, escape. They go back to Earth with a wicked plan to terrorize the people who still live there. Maybe it's out of jealousy, maybe they're emotionally and mentally unstable; or perhaps they're just plain cruel. But whatever the reason, they go back not just to visit, but to maliciously haunt those they left behind. It's dastardly, and after they do it, these warped Souls become just that ... warped. Most regret their choice and try to return to their afterlife in Hell, but they can never regain the previous energy of their Soul. Their Soul essence becomes distorted, transforming into that strange "alien" shape you see. They lose their ability to think reasonably or speak with any coherence; and it gets worse with each escape attempt. They become dangerous to the other Demons who are just trying to live out their afterlife in Hell, peacefully. Sometimes, the Stray Souls hurt the others... it's not pretty. Once we catch them, which is no easy task, mind you; they spend their eternities here, where we can keep an eye on them, on Zatvor Island, the stockade for Stray Souls."

"How awful. But why all the electric fences? Wouldn't simple cages be enough?" I was simultaneously mortified and curious.

"Not really. Remember, your Soul essence is pure energy. It's manipulative, and controllable, to an extent. If you wanted to manipulate your Soul Energy to take on another form, you could do it... it would take practice and it would be exhausting over time, but you could do it. That's one of the advantages of no longer having a physical body to deal with; you don't have any of the limitations with form and function. That's why the electric fences. High voltage energy is the only way to control Soul Energy with any reliability, and sometimes, even that doesn't do the job."

In the next moment, we were charged by two Stray Souls. They came at us like the dinosaurs from the film, Jurassic Park. Working together, they pounced on us from opposite directions, dividing the attack so that Taryn couldn't fend them both off simultaneously. While she was working to subdue one, the other kicked me to the ground and began to tear at me with its three-fingered hands. Although it had no claws, the force of the blows were surprisingly sharp. This was not an encounter with the gentle

ET. It sat on my chest, pounding on my head. I tried to use my arms to brace against the impact, but being new at having only energy to work with, it was incredibly difficult. Just when I thought I might lose the battle, the thing screamed out in anguish as short, blue lightning bolts connected with its face and neck. I rolled away to escape a reactionary blow, and watched as its eyes reflected yet another taser shock.

Another guard came from around the corner, brandishing his taser. "You two alright?"

"Barely," shouted Taryn. "Help me get these two into holding. Raychel, just stay here a minute until we can get these two contained."

"That won't be a problem," I said, wheezing from the shock of nearly losing my life... again.

It was about fifteen minutes before Taryn and her comrade came back to find me. "Hey, you okay?" Taryn said, as she looked down at me, still laying inert, where she'd left me.

"Yeah, I'm exhausted, but okay, I guess. At least I'm not bleeding, and nothing feels broken."

"That's good news. It means this was just a superficial attack, and it didn't get to the core of your essence yet. If that had happened..." Taryn didn't finish, and honestly, I was okay with that.

"Why did they attack us... and how did they get out? That place looked like a high voltage Fort Knox. I couldn't imagine anything getting through those gates." I pulled myself to stand, and the two of us walked back toward the yard's gate.

"These were a couple Stray Souls we hadn't caught yet. They try to regain their energy by feeding off newer Souls, that's why they were attracted to you. They sniffed you out. That's why we don't get many visitors out here. Most everyone knows to avoid this place. Actually, it's kinda a good thing you don't play by the rules; otherwise, we might never have caught these two. So... um... thanks." she said, clapping me gently on the back.

"You're welcome, I guess." Once back at the docks, I pressed the panic button and hoped for Eril's speedy return. Taryn stayed with me until he got there, and made sure I was safely stowed on board.

I learned the truth of Hell that day. The forfeiture of your Soul only happens when you make the choice not to leave evil at the Gate, either Gate. These Stray Souls had been reduced to their very base form of existence, their Soul Energy had been completely depleted, and there was no chance to repent and recharge. Once it was over, it was over. This was the difference between Angels who try to go back with positive intentions, and end up wandering through Limbo, simply lost; and Demons who try to go back with evil plans, and end up demented and locked in cages to suffer endlessly.

These Stray Souls were given every privilege and every opportunity to exercise Free Will on a whim and live comfortably in Hell without a lot of responsibility. Those who thought that wasn't good enough; those who felt they had to step outside the boundaries and torment people left on Earth, were punished with this final, suffering fate. Yes, I thought that it was cruel and unusual... but I knew it was appropriate.

Chapter Seventeen
A Date with Jared

After five days in Hell, there was another knock at my door just after I'd finished breakfast. Expecting Faythe again, I was surprised when I opened the door and found Jared. He wore a sheepish grin and dug his fists into his pockets as he teetered back on forth, toe to heel. Teenage angst, it seemed, was surviving well even after being here for so long.

"Um, hello Raychel; I thought maybe... if you weren't busy... we could go hang out for a little while. You see, I have to babysit the Gate during the Festival—Marco is going to be sick—so I thought maybe we could... you know... hang out today, instead." Jared's shy stammer was endearing.

"Sure," I said. Let me grab my slicker." Jared's smile could not be contained. It's amusing to watch young people get what they want, especially when they think they won't. We headed off down the road and past The Tree in an awkward first-date silence for some time, when finally, I broke the nervousness. "You said Marco was going to be sick? How does he know that?"

"Oh, it's not really that he's going to be sick, he's taking a vacation day—but that's what we call it down here... not sure why."

I understood very clearly. An internal smile of remembrance tickled my brain of that one weekend, calling in sick; just to spend an extra twelve hours with Thaddeus. "So, where are you taking me?"

"Well, I thought that maybe you'd like to go to the range. Newbies usually don't get there, the guys at the Welcome Center don't think it's safe for the newly dead... but I think you're different... you're smarter, I think. Want to give it a try?" Jared was hopeful and working hard to impress me.

"Sure, sounds like fun. What kind of range is it—like guns and archery?" I asked.

"Sort of... it's difficult to describe... you'll have to wait 'til we get there." Jared apologized.

We hopped the next tram toward the southern part of town, around the cove where we saw Marco escorting a group of new Souls from the docks, and got off near Zoloft Springs. We walked through the forest for another quarter mile or so until we reached the range. The guy in the little hut waved at Jared as we walked by, never questioning our intent. "It looks like you're pretty well-known around here." I said, trying again to start conversation. I'd forgotten how insecure teenagers can be—and it seemed it was true even for those who have been dead for some time.

"Yeah," he replied. I've been here so long, they pretty much figure I'm safe wherever I want to go."

"How long have you been here?" I asked—it seemed like the right time.

"Since 1783... just after that cannon took out a battalion of us during the War Against the States. Boy, that was a time, I'll tell you. Scared kids blowing up all over the place. You know, I would've thought the adults could have figured it out by now—but from what people tell me—they're not even close yet. You know, I've heard there have been dozens of wars—or what everyone besides the generals would agree was war—since then. It's stupid."

Jared was deeply moved by the subject of war—and who could blame him? After what he'd seen and experienced... I wanted to ask him what side he was on and what that time was like for him, but thought that perhaps I didn't have that right—*who was I to question his motives in an action that was so filled with emotion?* I also thought it best not to mention my years of Navy service. They didn't even have a Navy when he was alive... I figured it to be a subject for another day... or perhaps never. *Why pour salt peter on old wounds?*

As we rounded the corner, and trudged up a small hill, we saw the range—much like a rifle range back on Earth. Benches, meter markings downrange, and targets with bull's-eyes on them at various points. Nothing special. Then I heard the crackle from the station three benches to our left. A guy, black hair, medium build, about my height, normal looking enough—burst flames from the palms of his hands toward his target. He hit it, dead on. A few seconds later, another woman, looking like someone's kindergarten teacher, a few benches off to my right, sent lightning bolts toward her target and decimated it. "Clear the range!" she hollered, and the two walked confidently down to the two hundred meter mark to replace new targets.

"Oh my gosh!" I blurted. "How'd they he do that?!" Adrenaline rushed through me in what I'm sure would have been a lethal dose, were I still alive. I looked at Jared who was smiling broadly. "HOW DID THEY DO THAT?!" I stammered, again.

"Practice." Jared snickered. I gave him an incredulous look, expecting more. He delivered. "It's not really all that hard. All you have to do is focus your energy. Imagine the form you want your energy to take, and then set it on course. Imagine pushing the energy... whichever you want... you know, fire, wind, lightning... whatever, in a pulse toward the target. Here, let me show you." Jared took a poised stance and calmed his breathing. He lifted his right hand, palm toward the target; and a bright blue spark ran from his hand to the target, hitting it in the third ring, on the right. "I'm a little rusty," he said. "But you get the idea."

"So, I can choose any energy form I want, and it'll come out of my hands?" I was staring at my palms, dumfounded with what I had just learned. "And this doesn't take away from my Soul Energy?"

"Pretty much... oh, but not water. We don't do much with water down here," offered Jared. "And, it's not a restriction of your Soul Energy, you're just using the energy you already have, in a new way. In fact, practicing like this recharges your Soul Energy. Think of it like... um... calisthenics. It's all about focus."

"Yeah, I suppose I get that." I answered, still in a stunned fog of exuberance.

"Go ahead and try it," invited Jared.

"Okay, here goes." I stood at parade rest—the most controlled, yet calming posture I could think of; I breathed slowly for about five seconds. Then, I raised my left hand, palm facing the target, imagined a lightning bolt and... nothing happened. "Rats!" I mumbled, looking at my hand in frustration.

"Don't worry about it; this is just your first time. As I said, it takes practice. Go ahead, try again." Jared was full of encouragement.

So I tried it again, this time with better results. I was actually able to get a pastel blue lightning bolt of about six feet to erupt from my hand. Not nearly long enough to reach the first target twenty-five meters off... but exciting, nonetheless. "Try another form of energy," suggested Jared. So I did.

My next attempt was far more effective. When I imagined the fire bolt pushing from my hand toward the target, I actually hit the thing. "I can't believe it! That was so cool!!!" I screamed, jumping up and down like I was fourteen again. "Can I do it again?"

"Sure, go ahead," laughed Jared. "We can stay as long as you like." He was pleased that I was having a good time on our date.

Over the next several hours, I got fire bolts, lightning, sound waves, wind and what I imagined to be anti-matter to erupt from my hands. I got pretty good at hitting the target, too. Most of my shots... after several test runs, of course... hit within the three smallest rings. I even got a few to hit dead on in the center circle. Jared and I challenged each other on speed and accuracy. It turned out that he was faster than I was... but I had a better aim. He wasn't disappointed, though. We laughed through the whole afternoon—kids playing games. "You've got great Soul Energy control," he said. "Most Souls don't learn that kind of control for several years after they've died. I knew you were different."

"Thank you." I said with complete sincerity, but meaning much more; still dumbstruck that I even had the ability, let alone the control to spew anti-matter from my hand toward a target.

On the walk back to my flat, Jared's hand tucked gently in mine, I was in awe at the irony of fun in Hell... just as I had been with the restrictions in Heaven. I didn't dwell on it though. It was a nice day, Jared was a nice guy, and I was going to my casket happy—again. *Who would have thought that a possibility?!* I would deal with the philosophical discussion later.

"Well, here we are," said Jared as we reached the door to my flat. "I hope you had a nice day, Raychel."

"I had a great time, Jared. You've shown me a side of Hell, and myself, that I didn't know was possible. And you made it a ton of fun, too! Thank you for thinking of me." I kissed him gently, showing my sincerity.

"Thanks, Raychel." He said; his face crimson with delight. "Have fun at the Festival. I'll see you again on your way back to the Gate." Jared turned and waved as he made his way down the alley, back toward The Tree; a small skip in his step.

Jared was a sweet kid, but after hearing Hailee's reasons for choosing Heaven, and her experience with nurturing war orphans... I knew I could never see Jared as a man to date, despite his chronological age. In my eyes, he would always be a young boy, hurt and alone. To me, what he needed was the mothering he'd lost so early in his life – not a New Soul to share his casket. I wished I could give that to him... but I knew it would never be possible.

Chapter Eighteen
The Festival Of Eve

It was the Festival of Eve, the last Friday of the month after my first week in Hell, and a full moon. To say it was a party would be an understatement. It appeared as if all of Hell was there, and still, there seemed room for more. Downtown Hell was filled with "regular" looking folk, people who you wouldn't suspect were Demons if you'd met them anyplace else. And then there were the others, too. Those characters from mythology, song and story that I'd always imagined were... well, imaginary.

Not far from where I stood, two teams of Centaurs were playing badminton and another two played volleyball. To my right, a gaggle of Dragons huddled around a half dozen or so poker tables; to my left, a quartet of Satyr loitered near The Tree playing their pipes in perfect harmony; and even the big guy himself, Mephistopheles was there. I didn't expect to see him. God and Jesus were absolute no-shows in Heaven; I kind of figured that the precedent had been set. But as I saw him mingling about, chatting it up with the undead, I was reminded, again, that nothing was ever going to be as I expected, ever again. I didn't see Satan, but there was a small troll-looking person always just within pitch-fork poking range of Mephistopheles. He was diligent about keeping

Mephistopheles' goblet full.

Aside from all that, it pretty much looked like a frat party had landed square in the middle of an apple festival in Oklahoma. Lots of bushels of apples; jugs of apple cider—spiked and normal; flaming Sangria for the really brave; dozens of donuts; a petting farm with reptiles and goats; camelback races, and large bonfires with drum circles scattered throughout. Undulating around each bonfire, jungle women danced their heathen steps while scantily clad—as my grandfather would say—in loin cloths and grass bikini tops, enticing those who seemed willing to join in the night's debauchery. I helped myself to a cup of the spiked cider and a cinnamon donut, and stood back taking in the show of card playing Dragons. A few moments later, Zebulon sidled up alongside me, gnawing on the hoof portion of a buffalo leg.

"So, are you having fun at our little Festival?" Zebulon mumbled in between mouthfuls.

"It reminds me of college. What's not to like?" My words were a little sarcastic, but I was genuinely having a good time. Most of my inhibitions had fallen asleep, maybe it was the cider, and maybe it was Hell. "So Zebulon, I have to ask you, I'm fascinated by the fact that you used to be a librarian and yet, chose Hell as your eternal address. It certainly wasn't what the alive me would have expected. I mean, isn't the peaceful quiet of Heaven what book nerds crave?"

"You've heard of the concept that humans have wrestled with for decades, right... 'don't ask, don't tell'... well, I've always been a big supporter, and I discovered that the concept is alive and kicking right here in Hell."

"Well, sure, I could see how being gay might be an affront to those in Heaven..." I tried to avert my eyes, hiding my politically incorrect statement.

"No, that's not what I was getting at. I mean, yes, I'm gay, but that's not the point. The point is that in Heaven everyone wants to know your business. If you want to disappear for a couple weeks, they really get all over your case about it... *where are you going, did you get clearance to go there, what will you be doing while you're gone, when will you be back...* but that doesn't happen here. I can pretty much come and go as I please, no 'checking in'. I move at my own pace, keep company with who I want, when I want, and no one bothers me. I was in Heaven for seven days, like everyone else, and they must have asked me a thousand questions. Here, they just showed me around a little, handed me the Guidebook, and let me go. For a solitary Soul like me, it's perfect. In fact, the only reason I come to the Festival is because where else can you see poker playing Dragons set the cards on fire when they lose? And no rain to put it out."

It was then that I realized that ol' Zeb was right. The rain had subsided and given way to swaying pines and a less gray sky with a hint of light blue. But the fair weather pattern only prevailed over the Festival grounds. The alley back to my flat, and the one back to Faythe's were both gloomy and wet, as usual.

The Satyr quartet stopped for a break. That's when we heard Faythe's perky rooster call from across the square. "Hoo, Yoo Hoo; Raychel, Zeb... over here!"

Her arms were flailing wildly in the air, prayer beads clinking in the wind as she came prancing toward us. She was faster than I had expected, faster than Zeb had expected too, as she caught his arm just before he could take his third step of escape.

"I'm so glad I found you!" she said with exuberance. Then she drew nearer and lowered her voice. "Langston was reciting his latest edition of Hellish Haiku, and I just don't think I could have stood hearing even one more. Don't get me wrong, he's a very talented guy, but how many of those things can you hear in a day and not lose your mind? I wanted to slap his silly notebook out of his hand, but that would have been rude, wouldn't it? Finding you two was just the excuse I needed to get him to release me." She took a breath, albeit a short one. "So, Raychel, how are you enjoying our little frolic?"

"Actually, I'm finding it rather enjoyable. I am surprised to see Mephistopheles here, though. I thought he'd be pretty scarce. You know, I've only seen that poster of him hanging over by The Tree." Mephistopheles was pretty easy to spot, even from a distance. He was the only one who looked completely inhuman, and yet not dangerous enough to be Satan.

"Oh, M being here isn't that unusual, is it Zeb? He comes pretty much every month. And Satan, well..."

"Satan... doesn't exist." Zebulon's stark statement in between gulps of Sangria caught me off guard. I nearly coughed up my partially digested donut.

"What do you mean Satan doesn't exist? Dogma from almost every religion for centuries has been pretty definite about him living in Hell." I braced myself for yet another blow to the Truth that had been patterned into my daily life since I could understand language.

"He doesn't exist." Zeb spoke the words as Faythe shook her head wearily, gazing at her shoes and fingering her beads. "M runs the show in Hell, always has. I did the research. The pointy-tailed horn-headed, pitch fork wielding sadomasochist you've heard about in stories and seen in pictures is an aberration from M's little imagination. He loves to influence through fear, it's a power thing, and what better way to do that than with a scary looking Soul-stealing Demon? Who would believe that an easy-going, near-sighted, lacrosse-playing alcoholic could be King of The Underworld? No one, that's who. So, he created an alter ego, wrote a couple short stories about him, leaked the pages to some guy in Heaven who was curious enough to ask the question, invested a few underworld drachma in some rouge Dream Dispatches in a few gullible humans—all extremely illegal, by the way—and viola, the Devil was born."

"Yeah, M really is a pretty nice guy, once you get to know him; not at all the tyrant people think." And in that moment, Faythe was almost as wistful about Mephistopheles as Hailee had been about Tuan. *Being dead certainly is weird.*

"So what you're saying is that Mephistopheles had a marketing plan?"

"Bingo." said Zebulon.

"Well, he did a good job; it's still working." I said.

"Yes, we're pretty proud of him." said Faythe.

"But no more than he is of himself." There was a loud grumble of disgust in Zebulon's voice, and his face squirreled up tragically, as he yanked another bite of bison from its bone.

Faythe, on the other hand, looked as though she had two special all-access passes to a Rolling Stones concert. "Would you like to meet him?"

"I can meet him... he'll actually talk to me?" I was astounded at the opportunity to meet a real-live undead legend. The closest I'd ever gotten to social royalty was when I met Gordon Lightfoot after a benefit concert for the Merchant Marines in Detroit when I was a teenager.

"Sure," Faythe assured me. "He talks with everyone who's interested in hearing his story."

"He really loves telling it." Although Zebulon enjoyed living in Hell, it was clear that he was less than impressed with Mephistopheles. He skulked back to the rainy part of town as Faythe and I squeezed through the crowd toward the Demon In Charge, holding court near the Dog Tree.

"Excuse me, M; this is Raychel. She's on a visitor's pass and would like a few moments of your time." The tone of Faythe's voice sounded like a concubine in-training; soft, lilting, and slightly hypnotic.

"Of course, I've got nothing but time. What can I do for you, Raychel?" Mephistopheles had a radio announcer's voice, crisp, clear and completely memorable. I mentioned earlier that he was easy to spot because he looked undead. The truth of the matter is, he looked pretty human, except for the red skin and wings. I know what you're thinking, *no wings in Heaven—but wings in Hell?* It's nuts, I know. Mephistopheles appeared to be about thirty-five, had jet black eyes, a perfectly sculpted weight lifter's body and a spiked haircut. He was shirtless—which I have to admit I was okay with—wore black leather pants and exceptionally stylish red leather calf boots that showed off his muscular legs. A black leather cape hung over the back of his chair, and his wings were tucked around him giving the impression that he sat in a throne, rather than a common lawn chair. Clearly, this guy carried rock star status in Hell, and his appearance did not disappoint.

"Well, not to put too fine a point on it, but I've just learned that Satan doesn't really exist, and that you wrote the original marketing plan from Hell. I'd like to know a little more about that." My voice quivered just a little bit. He was unusually attractive in an "bad-boy" sort of way. It was difficult to keep my composure. I mean, after all, this guy was a legend. Faust came from him, or was written about him... at this point I wasn't sure which. But the point was, he's a pretty well-known guy; and I was a little intimidated.

"You know those 'Seven Deadly Sins' you've heard so much about?" Mephistopheles began; "Well, the word SIN is an acronym I made up... it actually stands for Simple Indulgences of Nature. I just added the 'deadly' part to make them seem more interesting. It was common knowledge that God created an imperfect human. I mean, really, after only spending seven days on the whole project and then leaving Humanity to the last day or so, there were bound to be some flaws in his plan. Not very thorough, that guy. He just doesn't have that 'seven generation vision'. So I took a closer look and identified the stuff that came most easily to Man, the stuff that didn't require a lot of thought or conviction, and called shotgun. God gets bored easily, and hates to put a lot of work into anything. At the time, he was happy that I was helping out. You know, the whole Creation story was just the beta version, right?"

I was wide-eyed with disbelief. "No, I didn't realize that Earth and Humanity were just a test run..."

"Well, that's a story for another day; maybe after you choose Hell... Anyway, God wrote the first half of The Book hoping that he could teach Humanity the rules of his game, but that didn't work so well. Too many people got confused with all the parables and poetry, it just wasn't sinking in. He's not a great writer. So then he sent his holier-than-thou lackey, Christ down for thirty-three years to try to fix the situation. With the exception of creating a few zealots who still scream his manufactured 'wisdom' from their pulpits, that really didn't do the job either. You know as well as anyone, always being a good little kid is hard work, and most humans, given the option, will take the easy road nearly every time. That's why he had to publish The Sequel. He was grasping at straws, trying to find some way to control his pets."

Mephistopheles took a long drink from his goblet, draining it, and signaled for a refill. "I did my part by offering to write the ending. I was creative enough to offer an alternative to Humanity. He didn't notice until it was too late. He doesn't like rules much; I don't know why He thought that you would. That's when He had to create a universal axiom. He called it Free Will. In his head, it was the only answer, the only easy answer for him, anyway. But it backfired. Humanity was already confused enough, and this just made it worse. And while watching you all run around trying to follow some obscure code of conduct with no confirmation if you were doing it right has its entertaining moments; it's really not fair to Humanity."

"So you're saying that basically, God gave up on Humanity and let us run amok, calling it Destiny?" I sputtered.

"Yup, that's pretty much it. Deity abdication. It's pretty pathetic when you think about it. No responsibility. The ultimate in Deadbeat Dads. He's always been a spoiled brat, my brother. Mom and Dad's favorite... no accountability. He made this really cool toy, and then decided He didn't want to play with it anymore. So He convinced you that you were in charge, with some grand reward in the end if you got it right. But, as you've figured out, it was all a sham. He gave up, plain and simple, and now you're all stuck with the fallout."

His brother? I was stunned. This was a new one on me. No one even considered that God had collaborators; certainly we never dared to think He had family. *After what Galileo got, people with this kind of thinking would have met with a flaming end, I'm sure.* "So where is He now?" The concept of God playing hooky when there were countless Humans suffering every day through this pack of lies back on Earth made me crazy. Not to mention the unnecessary stress Souls were handed when they found out they had died and had to choose. It was nuts!

"Who knows, he's always off someplace creating some new toy to play with." M was clearly unimpressed with his brother, and agitated that he had to babysit the leftovers.

"So why did you stick around? I'm guessing you've got the same ability to roam as your brother, right? What's keeping you here? It can't be just pure entertainment." I hoped I would get a straight answer, but I wasn't counting on it. So much after you're dead is left up to personal interpretation—I figured this would be no different.

"Look, I'm just trying to save a few of you a little humiliation, is all. I figure, if I wrote the marketing plan correctly, enough of you won't play his game and you'd get to death a little more prepared for the outcome. And, if I give you a soft landing place to deal with all the misinformation, well then, maybe it'll teach Him that He's not all that and a bag of chips; you know what I mean? Someone's got to keep things balanced; it might as well be me. Besides, these enlightened Souls, he said, "gesturing around him, "who have chosen to hang out in Hell are pretty nice to have around. Friendship is a good thing; at least my screwed-up twin brother got that part right."

Chapter Nineteen
Raychel's Last Soiree

It was my last day in Hell. It had been, oddly enough a fun and interesting week. It's really amazing what you discover when you spend time in a place. Religious dogma goes right out the window when you actually get to visit the places of fairy tales. Nothing is ever as it seems, remember that. The Powers That Be will periodically throw things out there that will confound you and frustrate you; but you can work through it.

I learned a lot about Hell, but was still no closer to making a decision. There were so many conflicting ideas and stories. It was hard to remember what I was told on Earth and weigh that against what I had actually learned after death.

On my last day in Hell, Faythe threw a small going away party for me. She led me to the center of town, to a little bistro in full view of The Tree. Everyone came, and they all wished me well. Jared, Eril, Zeb, and Taryn even made the trip from Zatvor for the big send-off. We had flaming steak Diane, sangria, cream brulee and absolutely no vegetables. This was a party, after all, and not intended to be good for me.

"So," began Faythe. "This is your last hurrah, so to speak. We wanted to tell you how much fun we had meeting you and remind you of the fun you had while hanging out with us these past seven days."

"Yeah, I would have brought you a gift," remarked Jared. "But we're not allowed. The Guidebook says we're not allowed to give you anything to take back to Purgatory. They don't want you to have anything that might make you change your mind at the last second. I don't see how a little handful of kitsch could do that... but them's the rules." Jared's mocking drawl was meant to be heard by the Powers That Be; and he didn't care... much... although he and the others did glance briefly over their shoulders, just in case.

"That's okay," I said in a reassuring tone. "I don't need any gifts. You have all shown me such a good time here. I never would have guessed that Hell could be such fun. I must say, though; I'm a little disappointed that M couldn't be here. I would have enjoyed just one more conversation with him. I didn't really get all my questions answered."

I spoke the words. Faythe cleared her throat. I turned around. M walked through the door. It's really amazing when you think about it... the speed at which things can happen after you're dead.

"I hear you had more questions?" He was wearing a deep purple cape this time, lined with what looked like zebra skin... although I'm sure it wasn't real zebra. The stripes were too perfect for it not to be synthetic. His calf boots were matching purple leather with little black tassels. He wore no shirt, as usual. His wings rustled from an imperceptible gentle breeze as he glided past me and helped himself to a cup of sangria. There was no throne for him. He was clearly disgruntled.

"Here, M;" Faythe said in that lilting tone only reserved for him; "I found you a higher chair; it'll help keep your wings from getting crushed." She slid a tall bar stool over to him, and invited him to sit down. He accepted her gesture, but ignored her, as was his custom. She didn't seem to mind.

"So, you said you had questions?" M repeated, now with a graveled distain in his voice. I chalked it up to not enough alcohol.

"Okay, since you're so willing... What's with that whole Mayan calendar thing? They said the world would end on December 21, 2012; yet the ol' thing just kept on a' spinnin'. What gives?" The sangria had kind of hit my head and I was beginning to get silly and not really concerned about what I was saying or how it was heard. *I'm dead, what more is there to worry about?... Oh, except for those Stray Souls... they were pretty creepy—but back on the island, safely away from me—I hope.*

"And while I'm at it... what's the deal with the Seven Horses? Why seven of them... and why horses? Why not giraffes or hippos; hippos can be pretty apocalyptic—have you ever seen hippos in the Nile—it's quite surprising." M was looking at me now through eyes of a Demon. Finally, something dogmatic was taking place. It's just too bad I was too soused to remember all the details in the morning. To this day, it's still pretty sketchy.

M continued to stare at me, sipping on his drink, formulating his answer. It was almost like he was sizing me up to decide if I was supposed to hear the truth or the propaganda machine's version of the truth. At last, he spoke. His voice was like a low rumble of thunder, hanging somewhere just above the C2 string of a cello.

"First off, the horses are a personal issue. My brother had many Pegasus when we were growing up, and his fascination with those things was pretty nauseating. White, wings, always perfect... ugh! How can anyone stand that much nice?! So the Seven Horses were a personal dig back at him. Black, flaming feet, strong as all get out—the blueprint for what would become the Clydesdales later on—and snorting mean. We used to have races between the two teams... and mine always won; that is, until He decided to make His team cheat by flying. He's never really played by the rules, you know. Very rude, if you ask me." He took a generous sip of sangria and continued to tell his story. All eyes were riveted on the rhythmic heaving of his wings as he breathed, and our ears were perked to complete attention as his low, single bass line voice began to transform into a cacophony of strings.

Anyway, there's seven of them because in His arrogance, He named His after the stupid seven day gods... Thor and his rabble. I'm not sure why He had to go and personify the darkness and the light, but He did. He has this thing about always talking with things that don't really exist... probably comes from His inability to play well with others. Anyway, I created seven horses simply to make it an even match. At one point, we were racing through Earth... it was early in the time of the Humans... and I guess the story just took on a life of its own. You can't blame us, we were just kids..."

The next thing I knew, I found myself back outside the Gate of Hell. I don't remember how I got there, what time of day it was—as if that really mattered... and unfortunately, I don't remember M's explanation for the Mayan calendar... all I remember is Jared's lilting teenager voice as he passed me off to Liza, and my screaming sangria headache. "Be careful with her, she's had a rough few days."

The irritation of Hell, I can testify, is deeply pervasive.

Chapter Twenty
Raychel's Choice

Fourteen days in Heaven and Hell can really take it out of a girl! When I got back to Twain's Inn, I was astounded at how much my brain and body ached. This transition from the physical to the energetic was a tough one to grasp. I felt like I'd been in a triathlon. Everything was sore, again. Weary from the sacred work in Heaven and the demonic indulgence of Hell, I was having problems thinking clearly about all I had seen and done, let alone consider the concept of making an eternal address choice.

"You know what I could really go for?" I asked Liza while absently nudging the porch swing with my toe, staring into the nothing.

"What's that?" said Liza, taking sip of her coffee.

"A cup of cocoa and a massage."

"I can make the cocoa happen," she said; and it did. Right there, from out of nowhere, on the little table next to me, with dark chocolate sprinkles floating on top and steam rising from around the rim of the cup.

"Now that's a great trick." I said, picking up the cup and relishing the first, glorious sip of liquid relaxation. Instant gratification on this level was still difficult to understand.

"The massage, that's not really a possibility here. We try not to encourage any physical Soul contact until you've had some real time to adjust. I've seen that first physical encounter set Souls back weeks on the acclimation time-table. It's sad to watch. I'd hate that for you. But I can arrange the next best thing. Grab your cocoa and come with me."

Liza led me up the stairs, past my bedroom and all the way to the end of the hall. That's when it occurred to me that I hadn't really seen much of the Inn since arriving. *Strange that there wasn't a tour.* Liza opened the door marked Soul Baths, and I discovered a true miracle. A glorious Roman-style bathhouse. The temperature was cozy and humid, there was a warm, gentle breeze floating about, soothing the humidity into what before would have been my skin—I can't tell you what it was soothing into at that moment, but it felt fantastic. Tapestries of body transforming into energy hung on the walls. There were a dozen tubs speckled about the beautiful mosaic tile floors, just the right size for one person to soak comfortably. The air smelled of jasmine and the large windows on the far wall revealed a spectacular horizon of a crystal blue lake with sunshine twinkling on its ripples, with an Autumn tapestry of color upon the mountains surrounding the lake's boarders. I was stunned.

"Yup, best view in the house." said Liza, her eyes gazing at the lake in exactly the same way mine were.

I was near speechless. This was not a view you could see from the main floor, or from anywhere along the journey to and from the Inn. "How is it that there is such beauty in the middle of nothing? And how is it that I've never seen it before now?"

"Well, some things need to wait until you are ready to receive them. In my opinion, this one room is the best object lesson from The Powers That Be. There's serenity everywhere, even in the nothing. I'll leave you to your soak. The changing rooms are over there." Liza said, pointing to the wall of doors to my left. "And there are towels there, too. Take as much time as you like. Dinner will be ready for you when you're done. It's lasagna night tonight." Liza left and continued doing whatever it is that she does when there isn't much to be done.

I went to the changing room, slipped out of my clothes and wrapped myself in a towel. I selected a tub right in front of the window. After all the fog and nothing of Purgatory, it was an intoxicating vision—so much beauty. I slipped into the warm, almost too hot, water and immediately felt a new sensation. Instant relaxation. Zero stress. There was no pressure. On Earth, water has a sensation of being heavy and difficult to move in. Everything is weighted and moves in slow motion—although scientists call it weightlessness, which I think is backward—you can feel the pressure of the water on your muscles and chest. The water on Earth alters how you breathe when your chest is under water and your head and neck are above it.

But here, that was all gone. I felt truly weightless. No heaviness, no sound. It was perfectly soothing, perfectly peaceful. My memories of my time in the womb came back to me with such clarity that I let go a few tears of wonderment. The recollection of the emotional buoyancy was so deeply connected to my Soul, that I was comforted by it in a way I find difficult to describe. I closed my eyes and sank further into the tub, letting go of my need to breathe. Letting go of my need to think. Letting go of my need to need. And then, a new thought. *Could Purgatory be the Nirvana that Buddha described? Not Heaven. Not Hell. Just someplace in between with no judgment and no expectation?*

I can't tell you how long I was held in that space. But I can tell you that when I came out, my perspective on life and death had been altered. And I knew my choice.

****

After an incredible dinner of salad, five-cheese and venison sausage lasagna, broccoli and garlic bread, I excused myself from the other Souls and headed out to the veranda. I was hoping to catch a little glimpse of the blue skies and sunshine I'd seen from the window of the Baths, but not today. Instead, I discovered Liza sitting alone, seemingly contemplating the the depth of the purple fog just beyond the fence line. I took a seat nearby and after a moment of silence, struck up the conversation I'd wanted to have since our walk back from Heaven on that first day.

"So, Liza, why are you here? Shouldn't you be in one place or the other; Heaven or Hell? Or are you being punished? How long have you been here, anyway?" After seven days in Heaven, seven days in Hell, and the weird episode with Roger my first day in Purgatory, I was feeling like a different Soul. I was done hiding my questions. I'd been so overwhelmed since my arrival that I didn't take the time to really get to know Liza as anything but an agent of my confusion. Now, I was starting to relax into and tolerate my demise. It also helped that my body, or whatever this thing was, wasn't screaming anymore.

Liza stood up from her porch chair and walked to the railing, gazing longingly into the nothing. Her voice was soft and slow. "It's been a long time. I've forgotten how many years now; except that I know I was here before Samuel, if that gives you any idea. The Powers That Be gave me the same options they're giving you now. Choose; Up or Down. Oy! Who can choose? How can a person choose something definitively black or white in a world of nothing but gray... or purple? Life is not made up of straight lines, you know. There are surprises around every curve... hills and valleys alternating with the bends and straightaways. Mortal existence isn't about absolutes; it's a beautiful canvas of unpredictability. I just couldn't give that up." There was a strange combination of exuberance and reticence in Liza's voice. Indeed, this woman was a walking dichotomy. "I knew my place was here, sheltering those who need to choose until they are ready. It's what I was called to do."

I found myself admiring the little woman. For all her strength, devotion to the rule book, and passive-aggressive tenancies, Liza still finds beauty in the unknown and comfort in the fragility of the bridge we all walk upon; in life as well as in death. It was a soothing thought, to have a protector.

Liza abruptly pirouetted back to face me; a half-full brandy snifter cradled in her left hand. "Ha! Got ya, didn't I?! You really don't think I believe all that crap, do you?" Liza took a drag from a cigarette that also seemed to have appeared out of thin air.

"You mean you..."

"Are you kidding! That's just the party line—it forces people to think that eternity only has two options. It's all part of their little control game, their race for quotas." Liza took another long drag, letting the smoke billow from her nostrils like a contented Dragon who'd just won his hand. I was again overwhelmed with confusion, and even more so when another snifter appeared on the table to my right.

"Shhh!" I said. "They'll HEAR you!"

"This is Purgatory, baby. No one can hear you here. Have a drink, you look like you might need it." Knowing she was right, I lifted it gently, shocked and awed at the control Liza seemed to weild.

"Look, I really like you, so I'm going to let you in on a little secret. I told The Powers That Be that the whole thing was a crock. It's a sham. Your little tantrum when you first got here was absolutely on track. They create you, expect you to live out your days doing nice things because of some implied reward, when really, it's all nonsense. The reward of Heaven is an eternity of comfortable monotony, constant community service, no retirement, lots of political games; and the monotony of Hell is no better. Our lifetimes have always been filled with a generous mixture of excitement, boredom and something in between. It's been unpredictable, stimulating and, if nothing else, different every day. Given the option, why would anyone surrender that in death? I mean really!"

I coughed a little after a quick sip of the brandy. I'd forgotten... *you shouldn't rush the brandy.* "So, how did you end up here?"

Liza stubbed out her cigarette on the porch railing and flicked the butt into the fog. "Well, quite simply, I refused to choose."

"Refused? You can do that?" Liza sat lazily on the wicker settee next to my brandy gulping confusion and flung up her legs to their full two-foot stretch, easing her head back on a comfy pillow.

"Why sure, you've got Free Will, don't you?" It took me a minute or two to process this thought.

"Look," said Liza, shifting her gaze to meet mine; "Once they explained to me about the whole Free Will thing, I knew that I didn't want to be locked into one dull existence or another for the rest of eternity. I didn't want to give up the spontaneity that my life had always enjoyed. And this became even more clear to me after my initial visits to Heaven and Hell. They're both so predictable. Same routine, day in and day out. Some people need that kind of structure; they take comfort in it—but not me. Ick! I also had an encounter like you did with Roger, only the person I met who tried to crossover too soon wasn't anyone I knew. Being here seemed much more unpredictable and much more fun. So I refused to choose."

I set my empty glass down on the table, and waited a moment for the Inn to stop spinning. I regained my balance—sort of—and I stood, a little wobbly, making my way to the railing, looking into the vast nothingness. After a moment of foggy contemplation, I turned back to Liza, bracing myself against vertigo as I grasped the porch railing and blinked hard. "So, what did they say?"

"What could they say? There wasn't really a precedent for this sort of thing. Before I got here, there was a "floater" from Heaven and another from Hell that would take turns managing the Inn, each Inn, in fact—you know, there are thirteen of them scattered around Purgatory. But it didn't work very well; still doesn't at the other Inns, actually. Each Angel or Demon tried to convince Souls to choose their Gate. Each realm has quotas to meet, but there are rules for this process of choosing. The biggest one is no outside influence. Everyone is supposed to have the same opportunity to decide, the same option of Free Will; and Purgatory was supposed to be the neutral decision-making place. I was the first who actually wanted to stay here without foisting my views or preferences on anyone else. The truth is, I really don't care which side they choose; it really doesn't matter to me. I have no vested interest. Really, I don't care. So, I was the perfect caretaker for the Inn. I guess it took them a couple of days to see the pragmatism of it, and they finally gave in. It might have been months or years—though I can't be sure, time is a little wacky up here. In any event; I solved a problem for them, so they let me stay."

"And you don't regret your choice—not choosing? You don't wish you were in Heaven or Hell—living in the nothing is okay with you?" I asked.

"What's not to like? I get to live in this fabulous Victorian mansion; I get to hang out with Mark Twain occasionally; enjoy all of my virtues and vices whenever I want with no guilt and no oversight: and I get to meet really interesting people. I never get bored with the people I meet, because none of them stays past the point of becoming dull. They move on, and I get a new batch of dead people to play with. And... Edgar isn't a bad perk, either. It's everything a girl could want."

Liza toasted the air with the last quarter-inch of her brandy and dispatched it with a contented smile as a small golden retriever puppy appeared from around the corner, jumping up to settle sleepily on her lap.

And so, it had been confirmed. Not choosing was still a choice. Now, I had to figure out how to do it for myself.

****

When I had finally made my choice, and knew with every energy synapse in my Soul that it was the right choice for me, I found Liza in her office, and gave her my decision.

"Okay, so how does this work? What happens next? Do I get an engraved invitation or a ticket to eternity?" I knew it was a silly statement, but at this point, I figured anything was possible. And, I was still holding on to some thought that at least something—anything—of Biblical proportion might happen. *If there wasn't a giant Book of Life, maybe it would be an engraved invitation?*

"No, no engraved invitation and no tickets." said Liza. "The way it works is, I send an email to The Powers That Be with your choice; and within twenty-four hours, they have to either grant their approval or deny your request."

"Twenty-four hours, really? I would think something like this would happen instantly. You know, speak it, and it happens? And besides, Free Will is Free Will, can it really be denied?" I was getting tired of the politics of being dead.

"Instantaneous? No. After I hit the send button, you get a day back here while they think about it. They take that time to tally up the numbers and pat each other on the back. And, if your choice is one that they like, off you go. And if it's not, they try to convince you to change your mind. It's all a numbers game, really; and this one will be extra confusing for them. They won't know how to add up the numbers. It'll take them at least a day, maybe longer, to figure out the math." Liza, I could tell, was happy with my creativity. A smile crossed her face as she shuffled the tablet from one side of her desk to the other... almost like moving the cover of the old shell game, waiting for the nut to appear.

"And if they try to convince me to change my mind; then what?" I was worried that maybe I wouldn't get Free Will after all.

Liza sat back in her chair, folded her hands atop her head, and looked up at the rafters. A low snicker emitted from her throat and her eyes got really big. "Then I'll come to your defense. I'm sure they don't want to lock horns with me again." Her smile was devilish, Jared would have been proud, and envious. In fact, it was a look I don't think that Mephistopheles himself, could have mastered with such finesse. It reminded me that Liza was not someone you wanted to cross; and I was glad that she was on my side.

Now all that was left was to hit send and wait.

Chapter Twenty-One
Eternity

The day I truly began my after life in eternity, I wasn't sure quite what to expect, and that's part of why I chose it.

It took three days for The Powers That Be to grant my request, and I had to put up quite a fight to get it. Liza had been extremely helpful in that process. I explained to them in my rebuttal email—no one ever gets to speak to The Powers That Be directly—that I made this choice because I so was disenfranchised with my time spent in both Heaven and Hell. Neither one turned out to be what I had expected... what I had been taught, told, promised... and because I felt they owed it to me based purely on poor planning and outright deceitful communication, and a huge dose of false advertising, I chose to live out my eternity in the one place that hadn't been misrepresented to me—Purgatory. In all my years of religious indoctrination, I'd never really heard much about Purgatory, so it was easier for me to take it at face value.

Chaperoning New Souls wasn't a good fit for me. No offence toward Liza and Edgar, their positions are essential, but I would feel incredibly hypocritical shuttling people in and out, never really giving them the complete truth about what was going on, or what they should expect. I understand the reasons for giving people choices... and the need for visitors' pass participation... but I just couldn't endorse it. I needed something else, something... more... meaningful. It made me crazy to engage in the idea of supporting a quota system rather than The Book we'd all been brought up believing.

I was, however, exceedingly astonished to find Thaddeus had made the same choice. We met on the front steps, in almost the same moment. I'd like to believe that The Powers That Be had some small hand in our destiny... but that goes against everything I'd learned since the moment of my death. Still, though, it was a comforting thought—so I kept it.

"What are you doing here?" he asked, nearly bursting with glee.

"I was just about to ask you the very same thing." I said. "Is this your final answer? Are you going to do this, too?"

"Yes. I think it's the right choice; and I think it's best that we do it together." He took my hand and squeezed it, just as Edgar mounted the steps behind us.

"Well, well. It looks like a choice has been made. Congratulations. Not many couples are granted the ability to buck the system and live out their eternity in rebellion... together... let alone here. I know you'll be perfect for the post." Edgar was beaming with the pride of a father, walking his daughter down the aisle to her forever love. And he would be right. We were meant to be eternally together—albeit unverifiably so.

Edgar ushered us into the vast foyer of Purgatory's Nursery once again; and we were silently elated. We walked with him to a small waiting room with cozy, comfortable love seats and he invited us to take a seat. "Someone will be with you shortly, to walk you through next steps. I'm so glad you'll be taking this assignment. You're by far, the best fit I've seen for the job since the Cherubim were created. Good Luck to you both. And know that you have our love, Liza and me."

"Thank you, Edgar." I said. "I can't tell you how much I appreciate your guidance. This is the right choice for us both," I said, looking at Thaddeus and knowing, deep in my Soul, that this was the best use of my Energy. "Thank you." I hugged him before he left; Thaddeus shook his hand and offered a smile that I knew would stay with Edgar for all of eternity.

When Edgar left the room, Thaddeus and I sat down to share a moment before the next phase of our existence began. "Why did you choose this? Why was the Nursery so important to you?" he asked with genuine interest.

"I thought that it was imperative to do my best to prepare the young Souls for their time on Earth, and most importantly, their return to the afterlife." I said, almost in a whisper.

"I know exactly what you mean. I hope that the little bit I might be able to convey to them before they are assigned to Earth might help them to better understand their purpose and the transition at the end of their life. The idea of them doing is all blind really settled uneasy with me." he responded.

"I don't know how much they will remember, or how much influence we'll have," I said with a hopeful breath; "but after talking with Edgar and Liza, I truly believe that at least a little bit of what we can give to them in the way of stories and songs, might imprint and stay with the children. "Perhaps in that way, we can make their Earthly time a little bit easier for them."

I took a deep breath and looked around the room, taking in the perfect silence and effervescent warmth of The Nursery. "I'm not out to change the way the Universe operates, Thaddeus. I just want to ease the young ones through the rough spots with a little more love and a gentler hand than they've received in the past. It's a big, scary world out there... I think it's our duty to ease them into it in the best way possible."

"I agree. And, I must admit, when I saw you here that first trip, watching the young Souls with such intent, and following the movement of each Cerebrum that took care of them—I knew exactly where your heart would lead you." Thaddeus took both my hands in his and kissed them gently. "I'd already done my stay in Hell, I knew what you'd find, and I knew it wouldn't be enough for you. You have a service heart—and neither Heaven nor Hell could ever meet your expectations. My choice is here, not only because I believe in what we'll be doing," he said wrapping his arms around me and bringing me close; "but because you'll be here—and we'll be doing it together. I love you."

"I love you, too, Thaddeus—forever." I nearly cried. Tears don't exist in The Nursery—and it's a good thing. So much emotion would be difficult to explain to those who haven't yet experienced Earthly Love.

If there has ever been one, perfect, passionate kiss that is earmarked just for two Souls to share throughout an eternity—we shared it that day. I can't even begin to describe the ecstasy that pierces perfection when Soul Mate Energy is shared at the ethereal level. It defies emulation and it defies description. It is the embodiment of all I believe God expected us to enjoy when first we were created.

In the next moment, the lights dimmed slightly and a fifty-four-inch flat screen plasma HDTV appeared before us. We giggled and settled back to watch the Orientation video together, holding each other... knowing Love would forever be changed.

Diana Kathryn Plopa

Throughout the years of raising her son, Zachary, Diana has found many creative ways to support her family. She has spent time in the theatre as a technical director and lighting designer, worked as a nanny, a pre-school computer teacher, and a medical transcriptionist. During Zachary's teenage years, she opened a website design company called Wolfe Technologies, Inc.

Today, she is associate publisher and editor for Grey Wolfe Publishing. Diana's focus is on mentoring other writers and supporting their dreams of publication... and in her free-time, she writes with enthusiastic abandon. Diana has previously published a book of poetry, *Ideate Avail* and a memoir, *Wolfe Cub*. Her second novel, *Tryst of Fate* will be released in early 2015. And, she has six other books waiting in the wings.

When she's not writing or working at Grey Wolfe, Diana enjoys volunteering as a mentor for new authors, horses, rock climbing, hiking, kayaking, canoeing and spending time in nature with her husband, Dave; their Golden Retriever, Bear and their Rescue Mutt, Alex.